BIRD OF DEATH

The stewardess entered the social hall and beckoned to Dr. Waite. "It's the lady in 49," she informed him when he had followed her into the hall. "You know, the old maid schoolteacher who's a bad sailor."

"Can't cure that," said the doctor. But all the same he tapped on the door.

"Doctor," said Miss Hildegarde Withers, cutting through his bedside manner like a knife through cheese, "is it possible for seasickness to produce hallucinations? Am I delirious?"

"Pulse normal," he told her. "Half a degree of temperature. No, you couldn't be delirious. What you need is—"

"A piece of salt pork on a string," she finished. "I've heard that one. Well, if I'm not delirious, then will you explain to me just how something with wings could come in my porthole and waken me by walking up and down on my face?"

"Uh?" said the doctor. He backed away a little, but Miss Withers was holding out for his inspection a copy of *Alice in Wonderland*. Across its open pages were a double line of faint, damp bird tracks, marked in blood.

Bantam Books offers the finest in classic and modern American murder mysteries. Ask your bookseller for the books you have missed.

Stuart Palmer
The Puzzle of the Silver Persian
The Puzzle of the Happy Hooligan

Craig Rice
My Kingdom for a Hearse
The Lucky Stiff

Rex Stout
And Four to Go
Bad for Business
The Broken Vase
Death of a Dude
Death Times Three
Double for Death
A Family Affair
The Father Hunt
Fer-de-Lance
The Final Deduction
Gambit
The League of Frightened Men
Murder by the Book
Not Quite Dead Enough
Plot It Yourself
The Red Box
The Rubber Band
Some Buried Caesar
The Sound of Murder
Three Doors to Death
Three for the Chair
Too Many Clients

Victoria Silver
Death of a Harvard Freshman
Death of a Radcliffe Roommate

Max Byrd
California Thriller
Finders Weepers
Fly Away, Jill

R. D. Brown
Hazzard

Sue Grafton
"B" Is for Burglar

Robert Goldsborough
Murder in E Minor

Ross MacDonald
Blue City
The Blue Hammer
The Moving Target

A. E. Maxwell
Just Another Day
   in Paradise

Rob Kantner
The Back-Door Man

Joseph Telushkin
The Unorthodox Murder
   of Rabbi Wahl

Ted Wood
Live Bait

Barbara Paul
Kill Fee
The Renewable Virgin

The Puzzle of the
Silver Persian

Stuart Palmer

BANTAM BOOKS
TORONTO · NEW YORK · LONDON · SYDNEY · AUCKLAND

*This low-priced Bantam Book
has been completely reset in a type face
designed for easy reading, and was printed
from new plates. It contains the complete
text of the original hard-cover edition.*
NOT ONE WORD HAS BEEN OMITTED.

THE PUZZLE OF THE SILVER PERSIAN

*A Bantam Book / published by arrangement with
the author's estate*

PRINTING HISTORY
First published in 1934
Bantam edition / November 1986

*Bantam Books are published by Bantam Books, Inc. Its trade-
mark, consisting of the words "Bantam Books" and the por-
trayal of a rooster, is Registered in U.S. Patent and Trademark
Office and in other countries. Marca Registrada. Bantam
Books, Inc., 666 Fifth Avenue, New York, New York 10103.*

PRINTED IN THE UNITED STATES OF AMERICA

KR   0 9 8 7 6 5 4 3 2 1

DEDICATION

To a detective inspector at New Scotland Yard,
to a sergeant who is about to face his exams,
to a commander in the United States Naval Reserve,
and to all others whose tall stories made this
book possible, in the hope that they will find it—
even remotely—probable . . . .
Also to all authors anywhere who have tried to
find a new way of pointing out to their readers that
"All characters in this book are fictitious."

S. P.

Mousehole near Penzance, Cornwall

CONTENTS

CHAPTER I

Surprise! Surprise!

It all began with Tobermory, who was trying with tooth and nail to tear his way through the traveling case of imitation leather in which he had remained prisoner for an eternity or so. Tobermory was a cat who walked by himself, but all places were not alike to him. From time to time he thrust a wicked gray paw through his tiny window and uttered a soft and eerie wail.

Tobermory's unhappiness was increasing in direct ratio to the growing swing of the vessel. The broad-beamed little passenger freighter *American Diplomat* had long since shown her stern to the verdigris'd fat lady who stands for Liberty in New York Bay, and now was beginning to wallow in the high Atlantic swells which came rolling in past Ambrose Lightship.

The door of stateroom 50 finally opened, and someone began to bustle among the luggage. Tobermory knew that it was not his mistress, the Honorable Emily, for she smelled less of starch and more of lavender and heather. He yowled in appeal, and heard the latch of his case snap open.

"Nice pussy!" offered Mrs. Snoaks dubiously. Tobermory came striding from prison, lashing his magnificent tail and looking like the diminutive ghost of a long-haired Siberian tiger. The silver hairs of his ruff and back stood out warningly, and Mrs. Snoaks called on her Maker to witness that she had never seen so much cat at any one time in her life.

Tobermory surveyed his surroundings without enthusiasm, and then instantly made up his mind. Only one exit offered itself—a round and inviting window above the divan. Tobermory sprang for it. As his saber claws caught the porthole, a capful of salt spray slapped him full across the whiskers. His amber eyes widened as he saw that there was

1

nothing beneath him but ocean—an infinity of restless, alien ocean. Tobermory changed his mind.

He was already halfway out of the porthole, and it was rather late to change his course. Only at the loss of his dignity and by dint of much scrambling did Tobermory save all nine of his precious lives. Otherwise this tale might have had a very different ending, or perhaps none at all.

Ruffled but unabashed, the big cat lingered long enough to regain his self-respect by spitting silently and nastily at the whole Atlantic Ocean, and then cast his long silver-gray body downwards in an effortless leap to the pillow of the opposite berth. There he at once began to lick the dust of Manhattan from his padded paws, staring balefully at Mrs. Snoaks the while.

That personage hastily completed her unpacking of the Honorable Emily Pendavid's clothes, uneasy in the unwavering stare of those implacable amber eyes. She hung the last tweed suit on its hanger, tucked the last suit of woollen underwear in a drawer, and went out shaking her head.

Halfway down the passage she met the immaculate blue-clad figure of Peter Noel, the handsome bar steward. He seemed to have more uniforms than the Old Man himself, did this gentleman of parts, though naturally he wore somewhat less of gold braid than Captain Everett.

Mrs. Snoaks plucked at the crisp blue sleeve. "Mark my words!" she began. " Do you happen to know what day this is?"

"Thirteenth of September," Noel told her. "So what?"

"Exactly! *And* a Friday. That gray hairy ghost of a cat in Number 50, he knows. Tried to jump ashore, first off I let him out. And when cats leave a sinking ship——"

"Rats," Noel corrected her calmly. "Rats, not cats." He disengaged his arm and continued aft. Peter Noel was completely free from the superstitious beliefs which even in this enlightened day hold sway over the minds of those who go down to the sea in ships.

Still smiling a little at the stewardess, he came to the end of the passage, which opened directly into the small social hall of the cabin-class ship. Ahead and to the left hung a worn brown curtain bearing the legend "Smoking Room." Behind that curtain had gathered a few passengers, for he could hear their impatient voices.

Directly on his left was a narrow door bearing an imposing red seal stamped with the eagle of the U.S. Customs. Peter Noel leisurely broke the seal and stepped into his pantry. He did not hurry himself, although the *American Diplomat* had dropped her pilot and was now officially on the high seas.

Only a single rolltop partition above the counter separated him from the people in the smoking room. Noel sat casually down on his stool, drinking in the stale odors of the windowless pantry perfumed with orange peel and drops of spilled cordial and the rich aroma which rises from a loosely corked bottle of Bacardi. Noel liked the heaviness—he was seaman enough to distrust fresh air in any form.

He helped himself to a fat corona from the showcase and lit it. Then he puffed contentedly, polishing his finger nails on his palm. Here he was king—until he opened the barrier and became a flunkey again. The tall black bottles in the rack behind him jingled with the roll of the ship, as if readying themselves for action, but Peter Noel still took his time.

Someone was tapping impatiently upon the outside of the partition, and he heard a loud tenor voice intoning: ". . . those who stood before the Tavern shouted, 'Open then the door . . . !'"

"Bloody fool!" said Peter Noel. But all the same he moved to unhook the partition and raised it. He knew as soon as he looked across the counter that this was going to be a dull trip. There was a sailing list of fifty-odd, not bad for the beginning of the winter season. Yet only seven of them were thirsty enough to hurry through their dinners and join in the sacred rite of opening the bar!

"Well!" said the young man who had been tapping. "After all these years! Make mine a double rye." He was a wide and high young man, with brown curly hair, a big mouth and jaw, and a red necktie. There was a twinkle in his eye. "What'll you have, everybody? The first round's on me."

"No rye," Noel told him.

The tenor was busily urging the various little groups to come forward and join him in Rotarian jollity. The easiest persuaded were a young couple who—Noel instantly decided—were New Yorkers by their dress, and married by their attitude. They looked smart and a bit tired and fever-

3

ish and anxious to be amused. "Well, Mr. and Mrs. Hammond?"

The girl's blue eyes were older than her young, smooth face. "Cointreau," she said pleasantly. Tom Hammond took a brown pipe from the wide mouth beneath his little mustache and said he could do with a cognac.

In the farthest corner two girls were giggling and striking matches for each other's cigarettes. "What's yours, Miss Fraser? And what'll your friend have?" The young man with the tenor voice was one of those passengers who spend their first few hours on board learning the names of everyone else, and the last few hours writing down addresses.

"Thank you so much," drawled Rosemary Fraser in a too cultured voice. "Nothing for either of us."

Everyone stared. Tom Hammond nudged his wife. "Loulu, they're smoking cigars!"

Loulu Hammond shook her head. "They're showing off," she informed him. "Puerto Rican brown-paper cigarettes." She turned her casual glance back toward the bar again, but not before she had noticed every detail worth noticing about Rosemary Fraser.

She had seen a girl of twenty or thereabouts, dark-haired and pale, wearing a softly lovely coat of squirrel that reached to her slim ankles. Around her throat was a scarf of midnight blue. The face was oval, with big gray eyes and a high-bridged nose, and escaped beauty only because of the babyish, overripe mouth.

"Not a beauty," Loulu decided, "though Tom will think so. But she's got something. . . ."

The other girl was just that—another girl. Her face was tanned almost as dark as her brown-paper cigarette, and she was perhaps five years older than her companion, whom she resembled in a colorless way. She wore a dark blue worsted suit and looked dependable. Like Rosemary, she seemed to have a secret amusement of her own.

The tenor was undiscouraged. He approached a couple who were sitting on the lounge, engrossed in old copies of *Punch*. The woman was monocled, fortyish, and very tweedy. Her companion was young, palely masculine, and he wore a pink shirt and brown plus-fours with tassels on them.

4

"Don't mind," accepted the Honorable Emily, a bit stiffly. "I'd like——" She was about to order a whisky and soda until she remembered that all Americans are rotten with money. "A champagne cocktail," she finished. Then she nudged the young man beside her. "Nephew!"

"Oh—quite," said Leslie Reverson. "MindifIdo." He smiled a very pleasant smile. "Gin-and-it." It was his largest contribution to the conversation that evening.

The drinks were placed on the counter by Noel. "Where's my double rye?" complained the tenor.

"No rye," said Noel clearly. "I've got Scotch, and I've got Irish, and I've got Bourbon. But no rye."

The tenor ordered a gin fizz in a tone which proclaimed that his faith was gone and wrote "Andy Todd" across the bill in staggering script. Then they all drank, in a silence broken by small talk from the Hammonds. Even that died away when the tanned girl put down her dark cigarette and approached the bar.

"Two crême de menthes," she ordered. She wrote "Candida Noring" on the bill, and carried the drinks carefully back to her corner.

Peter Noel strangled a cough behind his counter. "Well!" gasped Andy Todd loudly.

Loulu Hammond was pointing at his glass. "You're spilling gin fizz on your trousers," she said softly. So he was.

Tom Hammond saved the situation by buying another drink for Todd and a fresh cognac for himself. Then he sat down and let the larger young man tell him the story of his life. Boiled down, it amounted to this—working his way through the University of Washington at Seattle, with time enough for crew and track and Phi Beta Kappa. Now he was going for a higher degree via a Rhodes scholarship. "And I'm going to have some fun out of this trip, too," Todd was insisting. "I've had my nose to the grindstone long enough."

Rosemary Fraser, across the room, whispered something to her companion, and both girls laughed. Loulu Hammond guessed that the Fraser girl had suggested that Todd's nose could stand a bit more grinding from an artistic point of view.

Rosemary and Miss Noring were standing up, the former pulling the collar of her squirrel coat around her ears. "How frightfully chilly it is in here," she said as she went out.

5

"She'd be warm enough if she were wearing something underneath that coat besides a suit of lounging pajamas," Loulu Hammond said to herself. She had caught a glimpse of crimson silk trousers beneath the squirrel coat.

"High hat, eh?" said Andy Todd indignantly to the bar steward. But Peter Noel did not answer. He was staring after the two who had gone and straightening his tie.

The two girls came out into the main social hall. It was a wide, low room well aft in the ship, and furnished with a bad piano, a good gramophone, ten bridge tables, and two easy chairs. Along one wall were five old ladies at five writing desks, scratching away with pens that were no doubt honorably retired from the post offices of America. Each rose from time to time to drop a fresh sheaf of stamped fat envelopes in the near-by letter box, though it would not be opened until the ship reached London.

A few bridge tables were in use, and half a dozen children were chasing each other and screaming merrily. One fat-faced youth of seven or eight was quietly whittling at the leg of the piano, his tongue protruding in the intensity of his labor.

"How horribly dull," said Rosemary Fraser. "Candy, why didn't we wait for the *Bremen*?"

Candida Noring agreed. "Not a man on the boat, my dear. That cute English boy is under age, and Hammond is married. . . ."

"Not too married, if I know the look in his eye," said Rosemary. She looked back toward the smoking room. "No, I wouldn't go so far as to say that there isn't a single solitary man on the boat worth developing. . . ."

"You surely don't mean Cecil Rhodes' gift to Oxford?"

"Him!" said Rosemary. "Too, *too* sick-making." She headed for the door. "Let's take a turn or two of the deck and then go down and fight over who has to take the upper berth."

Two hours later Rosemary thumped her pillow. "He has the strangest eyes!" she decided aloud.

Candida Noring put down her book and leaned over the edge of the top berth. "Who, in heaven's name?"

"You wouldn't have noticed," said Rosemary comfortably, and opened her fountain pen. From beneath her pillow she took a leather-bound book, unlocked it with a tiny golden

6

key, and pressed her cheek against the smooth creamy pages with their faint blue rule.

At the head of the first page she wrote *"Friday, September Thirteenth,"* then was thoughtful for a long while and finally began: *"There's a man on board, diary, and when he looks at me. . ."*

At the moment when Rosemary was filling the creamy pages with her round script, back in the tiny smoking room Tom Hammond was having his fifth cognac. The others had gone, and the bar steward was leaning on his counter and talking swiftly and agreeably.

"You said just now that you are with a manufacturing chemist," Noel began after lighting himself a cigar. "You know, I had a bit of that thrown at me when I was with the Chilean navy—in '27 and '28. There was only one cruiser, with three-inch guns that were falling to pieces and full of bird's nests besides. It was up to me and four greaser rear admirals to concoct a powder weak enough to fire salutes with and still not blow the guns to bits. We were just getting there when the government overturned and some new rear admirals took charge. I got the sack and some of the new greasers got blown sky-high. . . ." He looked happy when Hammond asked a question.

"Me? I was a rear admiral too. We were all rear admirals on board except for two captains and a cook. Gold epaulettes and a hundred Mex dollars a month. Great fun while it lasted."

Hammond looked a little envious. "You've been around."

"Sure!" Noel grinned. "This is just marking time for me, this job. I'm pulling strings to get into the Chinese flying corps in Manchuria——"

There was a knock on the pantry door. The stewardess, Mrs. Snoaks, stood outside.

"Two more gin and bitters for the fussy couple in 44," she ordered. "Colonel Wright says please will you use Booth's instead of Gordon's like you did last time?"

"The Colonel will drink what I mix," said Peter Noel viciously. He rattled with his rack of bottles. "Now, when I was with the White Russians, in their Secret Service——"

But Tom Hammond was departing. "See you tomorrow," he called back. The social hall was empty now. He took a turn or two of the boat deck, found the wind so high that his pipe became overheated in a moment, and he knocked it out. Then he went back below and followed the corridor to C cabin. It was the best on the ship, with a real bath, four portholes, and a genuine double bed. Two berth settees lined the wall, and on one of them was a tumble of bedclothes from which protruded a small fist, threatening even in relaxation. Tom Hammond walked softly, so as not to call down on himself the Vesuvius of trouble which was condensed in his eight-year-old son.

Loulu Hammond, propped against pillows in the big bed, smiled at him. "If you wake Gerald you may have the joy of beating him. He did twenty dollars' worth of damage to the ship's piano tonight."

"It was your idea, bringing him," Tom said. He slipped into a silk dressing gown. "For myself, I'd rather travel with a goat. The twenty can come out of your allowance, for you should have been watching him."

"I was too busy watching you with your eyes glued on the little snip in the squirrel coat," said Loulu. "Spend a pleasant evening?"

"She didn't come back to the bar," Tom said quickly. "But I saw her just now, stretched out in the *gayest* pair of red pajamas. . . ."

"What?" Loulu sat up straight in bed.

"Through the porthole, when I took a turn around the promenade deck," he went on. "The curtain was blowing."

Tom Hammond was ready for bed. Loulu put down the *New Yorker* she had been reading—it was her Bible whenever she was out of the city—and her husband reached for the light switch.

Tom drew back his hand as if something had snapped at him. Gerald Hammond raised his rumpled, triumphant head from the blankets and shouted in a soprano voice that penetrated half the ship: "Daddy saw red pajamas! Daddy saw red pajamas!" He took a fresh breath. "Daddy saw——"

Tom Hammond got his hand across the mouth of his son and heir, but not before an impatient maiden lady in the next cabin had been awakened and had rapped sharply on the wall for silence. She had just managed to doze off, after eight hours of *mal de mer*, and now she was unwillingly awake again, conscious of the endless and persistent rocking of the billows.

"And this was a trip for pleasure!" moaned Hildegarde Withers. Which was hardly the exact truth. She had been left in such a nervous state as an aftermath of her participation in the unraveling of the murder mystery at Catalina Island in the late summer, that her physician had refused to allow her to go back to her desk at Jefferson School that fall. Luckily, the unexpected payment of a comfortable reward by the millionaire owner of the island permitted her to indulge a long-standing desire to see Europe.

She took up a worn linoleum-bound copy of *Alice* and tried to forget that eight more days of the unfriendly Atlantic lay between the ship and the muddy mouth of the Thames. The book opened at the Hatter's tea party. "'*I didn't know it was your table,*' *said Alice.* '*It's laid for a great many more than three.*'"

Miss Hildegarde Withers smiled grimly, and wondered if she would ever sit in her chair at the ship's table this trip.

At any rate, her place was vacant at dinner the next evening. The rest of the arbitrarily arranged group at the doctor's table was there intact, however.

Dr. Waite, bald and sniggering, was a good master of ceremonies, for all that. The head steward always put the "young crowd" at the doctor's table, plus one or two steadier women for balance. This evening saw them properly arranged—on the doctor's left was the Honorable Emily Pendavid, then her nephew Leslie, then haughty Rosemary, then Tom Hammond and Loulu—minus Gerald, who gulped his food at a wall table with the rest of the children, under the eye of the stewardess—next Andy Todd, with Miss Withers' vacant chair on his left, and beyond that the tanned face of Candida Noring, and the doctor again.

Dr. Waite was talking, and he could out-talk Andy Todd. "What a crowd and what a voyage *that* one was!" he finished. "Dancing until eleven or twelve every night."

Loulu Hammond said something about the pace that kills. But Andy Todd wanted to know where there was any room for dancing.

"Pull up the rug at one end of the social hall," advised Dr. Waite wickedly. "Turn on the Victrola and leap to it. If the bridge players object, let them go complain to the Old

Man. He's on the side of youth and beauty, and he may come down off the bridge and trip a few fantastics himself."

Candida Noring had been on the bridge and met Captain Everett, who stood eighteen stone. "God forbid!" she said fervently.

There was dancing in the social hall that night, in spite of the slow, shuddering roll of the vessel. The bridge players, instead of raising objections, paired off in sedate couples and got onto the floor. From time to time they overruled Leslie Reverson, who was self-appointed selector of the records, and played a waltz or one-step.

The five old ladies at the five writing desks glared disapprovingly, but after a little while they finished their letters and went off to bed. The doctor appeared on the scene, danced with the Honorable Emily, with Loulu Hammond, and finally with Candida. He sought for Rosemary, who had watched coolly as a spectator up to this point, but found her dancing in the corridor with Tom Hammond. Their cheeks were very close together, and the bar steward had closed up his bar for lack of patronage and was watching them

Loulu Hammond was in the arms of Leslie Reverson, who danced beautifully and impersonally. She swung, when the music began again, into the strong and somewhat smothering arms of Andy Todd.

Andy didn't bother to be diplomatic. "Shall we go on deck and look at the moon?" he leered. "You needn't mind your husband, he's having a good time."

"What good taste he has," said Loulu sweetly. But she didn't go to look at the moon with Andy Todd. There was an easy chair beside the doctor.

He lit her cigarette, nearly burning off her eyelashes in the process. "You know," he observed generally, "it's funny what people will do when they get on shipboard. They just seem to cut loose, sort of."

"They run hog-wild and dance until eleven or twelve, don't they?" agreed Loulu. She was thinking of something else.

"And romance! Say, there's nothing like a shipboard love affair," continued the medico.

Andy Todd and young Reverson both approached to ask Loulu for the next one, and Leslie was vaguely surprised and pleased to find that he had won. Andy wheeled uncertainly and saw that Rosemary Fraser was approaching—alone. She looked like a princess in a wine-colored dinner dress, and carried her squirrel coat over her arm.

"Miss Fraser!" he shrilled, in the high tenor which he could never control. "Can I have this dance?"

"Sorry," said Rosemary. "But I never dance." She passed lightly out onto the deck, as if to an appointment there. Slowly a red flush rose along the neck of Andy Todd, mounting to his ears. Loulu felt so sorry for him that she was very nice to him all the rest of the evening—and regretted it whole-heartedly for the rest of her life.

One by one the dancers began to leave the floor, yawning. The doctor and the Honorable Emily withdrew into a corner and began to have a heart-to-heart talk about fits. She herself complained of fainting spells, and she had always had her doubts, she confessed, about Leslie—him being so quiet and all. Even Tobermory, she complained, had thrown a fit last summer.

"Worms," diagnosed Dr. Waite sagely. The Honorable Emily brightened. She wondered if Leslie had worms too.

The ship's bell struck eight tinny times for midnight. Loulu fell to playing rummy with Candida Noring. Once she looked up startled, to hear light running footsteps on the boat deck above her head. She relaxed again. It couldn't be Gerald. He was asleep, and for good measure locked in the stateroom.

Andy Todd heard the footsteps, too. He was prowling around the long boat deck, throwing away cigarette after cigarette. Once he heard the beating of wings above his head, and a slow, fat bird fluttered into his face and then swooped away into the night. Even the gulls were crazy tonight, muttered Andy.

He rounded a corner and was nearly tripped by the darting figure of a small boy. Gerald, it appeared, had broken loose again. He neatly nabbed the urchin.

"What do you think you're doing?" he demanded. "Kids like you should be in bed."

"This is more fun," gasped Gerald, wriggling. "We're playing a new game." Another youth appeared, with flashlight clutched in his fist. "It's Virgil," said Gerald. "I gotta go with him. Lemme go, we're playing Trap the Neckers."

Andy Todd found a quarter and displayed it. "What sort of game is that?"

Gerald took the quarter. "Tell you for a dollar," he bargained. He got a cuff on the ear. "Well," he temporized, "we try to find a couple necking. Virgil says there's lots of them do it. Then we sneak up real close and flash the light on 'em and run."

"Oh," said Andy Todd. He was still a little red behind the ears. Finally he bent down and gave Gerald Hammond definite instructions, instructions which would have displeased that lad's young mother exceedingly. "A dollar, remember. I'll be in the social hall for an hour or so."

He saw the merry lads run back along the dimly lit boat deck and heard the faint slick of their rubber-soled shoes. Then, well satisfied with himself, Andy Todd went below, where the charming Mrs. Hammond was more charming to him than ever. He made a willing third at the rummy game.

The stewardess entered the social hall a few minutes later, and beckoned to Dr. Waite. "It's the lady in 49," she informed him when he had followed her into the hall. "You know, the old maid school teacher who's a bad sailor."

"Can't cure that," said the doctor. But all the same he tapped on the door.

"Doctor," said Miss Hildegarde Withers, cutting through his bedside manner like a knife through cheese, "is it possible for seasickness to produce hallucinations? Am I delirious?"

"Pulse normal," he told her. "Half a degree of temperature. No, you couldn't be delirious. What you need is——"

"A piece of salt pork on a string," she finished. "I've heard that one. Well, if I'm not delirious, then will you explain to me just how something with wings could come in my porthole and waken me by walking up and down on my face?"

"Uh?" said the doctor. He backed away a little, but Miss Withers was holding out for his inspection a copy of *Alice in Wonderland*. Across its open pages were a double line of faint, damp bird tracks, marked in blood.

"Of course, it's a nightmare," said Miss Withers reasonably. "But if it is, it's lasting a long time!"

The nightmare, although the school teacher did not suspect it, had already begun. It was to encompass every passenger aboard the little vessel, and to cling to them as they sailed over the curve of the earth, hover darkly above their heads as they went down the gangplank, and redouble its terrors as they set foot upon terra firma in London Town. Thus began the Nightmare of nightmares.

Back in the social hall Loulu Hammond was still playing rummy with Andy, Candida Noring, and young Reverson, who had just joined them as an alternative to going to bed. A tapping came on the porthole behind her, and she turned to look. No one was there. Todd, who faced her, rose suddenly, spilling his cards.

"Got to see a fellow," he apologized. In a moment he came back in off the deck, replacing his billfold.

"On deck, everybody!" he called. The Honorable Emily, who was reading *Punch* again, put it down.

"Whales?" she inquired eagerly.

"Just come along—quietly," he ordered, and led the way. There was that in his manner which induced the others to follow, puzzled and intrigued. Candida Noring was first, then Loulu, Reverson, and the Honorable Emily. A chill wind struck them as they came up on the deserted boat deck.

"What a laugh!" said Andy Todd mysteriously. There was something hateful in his tone, Loulu felt. Yet she followed. . . .

He led the way forward, past the long lines of folded deck chairs, and pointed to a large and boxlike affair which was set between two engine-room ventilators.

Loulu was holding onto Candida Noring's arm in the semi-darkness. She felt the girl shudder. "It looks like nothing so much an oversize coffin," whispered Candida.

"Nonsense," Loulu told her. "It's the locker where they keep the steamer blankets."

Andy Todd was chuckling. "Watch this, now," he whispered. Even his whisper was loud. He felt on the deck until he found one of the big wooden disks used as counters in the shuffleboard games. "Somebody found the padlock open, and crawled in," he confided. "But *somehow* it got fastened tight. Now watch the circus. . . ."

"I say," began the Honorable Emily, adjusting her eyeglass, "is it quite sporting?"

13

But Andy Todd had sent the wooden disk flying across the deck. It hit the lightly built locker with a resounding smash.

"Surprise! Surprise!" shouted Andy Todd. But *he* was the one surprised. Nothing happened. There was no sign of the frantic double Jack-in-the-box he had hoped to show. He had planned on hearing the cracking of light wood. . . .

He cast his borrowed flashlight forward and saw that the padlock hung from a broken hasp.

"How silly!" said Loulu Hammond. She had a horrible feeling that this was the first chapter of a seven-and-sixpenny thriller, and that the Body was about to be discovered. "Let's go back."

But nobody wanted to go back. Todd led the way, whipped open the locker, and looked down upon an anticlimax of disarranged blankets. "They got out!" he said sadly.

The Honorable Emily had expected whales. "*Who* got out?" she wanted to know. But Andy Todd did not answer. As far as Loulu Hammond was concerned, he did not need to answer. The flashlight showed clearly enough that caught in a crack on the inside of the locker lid was a wisp of soft gray fur.

CHAPTER II

*

Sex Rears Its Ugly Head

"But darling, no one *knows* that it was you," Candida Noring was saying. "There are dozens of other girls on the ship, and for all that anybody can prove, it might have been almost any of them. There's a lot of difference between guessing and knowing."

Rosemary Fraser lay sullenly in her lower berth, not even making a pretense of reading. "Oh, if people would only mind their own business!" she cried out. "If they——"

"You're on shipboard," Candida reminded her. "You should have remembered that before you let some man put you in such a ridiculous position. There's nothing else for people to do aboard ship but gossip and guess. What they don't know they imagine. But it's all a tempest in a teapot. Forget it, and just remember that in three days less than three days more—we'll be in London and booking passage around the world!"

"I don't care what you say, I'm not coming down to dinner," Rosemary retorted. "Why, I'd die of shame when I came to sit down at the table."

Candida pulled a tam over her straight brown hair. "But it's not just dinner. Tonight's the captain's dinner with wine on the table and balloons and horns blowing and gifts . . ."

"The gift I'd like," Rosemary told her dully, "would be that Todd person's head on a silver charger."

Candida was patient. "But, my dear, you can't spend the entire voyage in your stateroom. Why, even the funny old-maid school teacher with the horsy face tottered out on deck today! The sea's calm as a millpond."

Rosemary still shook her dark curls. Candida's brown eyes narrowed. "Tell me—is it that you're afraid to meet the man in the case, whoever he was? Afraid of something he might say?"

"*Him?*" Rosemary laughed unpleasantly. "No, heavens, no! He wouldn't *dare* say anything!"

Candida nodded. "Because of his wife?"

And then Rosemary was furious. "You promised, Candy! You swore you'd stop trying to find out who it was!"

Candida Noring said that she was sorry, and softly closed the stateroom door behind her. She was the last person in the world, she told herself, to throw stones.

She walked slowly aft, toward the social hall. Today was Friday—a week since sailing day. And Rosemary had spent most of it in the cloistered seclusion of their cabin. If only she had cloistered herself a little earlier! Candida thought to herself. When Rosemary failed to show up at the *captain's dinner*, now that the sea had calmed down to a rippled mirror, the last shred of doubt on the part of the gossiping passengers would be dispelled. That would be an admission of guilt—if it *was* so terribly wrong to have crawled into that warm and blanketed locker with a man that she fancied. Candida wasn't sure.

For lack of any other objective, Candida Noring wandered into the bar. As she came through the curtain she heard Andy Todd's high tenor: "You don't suppose they crawled into the blanket locker to play checkers, do you?"

He was still harping on his own pet scandal, this time for a group consisting of Loulu Hammond, the Honorable Emily, and Leslie Reverson. Peter Noel was rattling things behind the bar.

"I must confess that I hadn't thought much about it," Loulu Hammond told him.

But Andy Todd couldn't be squelched. He leered at her wickedly. "Oh, haven't you!" said he. Loulu's teeth clicked against her glass, and the Honorable Emily tried to think of something to say.

"I saw some porpoise this morning——" she began. Then they noticed Candida. Andy Todd muttered something about fresh air and left.

"Don't let me interrupt," said Candida Noring. "I just wanted a pack of cigarettes."

Peter Noel opened the case and offered her a meager choice. "No black ones," he grinned. Noel was in good humor this afternoon.

"We were thinking of some bridge," suggested Loulu. "Care to join us, Miss Noring?"

Candida Noring said that she only played poker. Noel cleared his throat and leaned on the counter. He saw a chance to act Munchausen again.

"Poker—that reminds me of the tightest spot I ever was in," he began. The five drew a little closer, for they were bored with seafaring, and listening was easier than talking.

"It was when I was with the Goldfields outfit in Alaska," said Peter Noel. "Little poker game one night at the Frenchman's Place in Nome, about five years ago. I'd spent a season up-creek and had come back to Nome to pay off my crew of dredgers and wait around for the old *Victoria* to steam in and take us back to Seattle and civilization. Even today Nome is a fast town in the fall of the year, and the card games are steep. That night at the Frenchman's a Russian vodka-runner dealt me a pat hand—an ace-high straight flush in hearts!

"Yes," said Peter Noel. "There she was, the highest hand in poker. I kept a straight face, and the betting started off brisk. The others dropped out after a while—the Frenchman brought back a plate of ham sandwiches and stood gaping at the money piling up in the middle of the table—and finally I came to the end of my roll. I knew I had the Russky beat, even if he did have quick, clever fingers. He dug up all the money he had, two thousand, and put it into the middle of the table. I had to *see* him, or drop out. In my pocket I had payroll money for my firm, and I risked it. A man'll do anything when he gets a royal flush.

"Well, he threw down a measly full house. When I showed him my hand there was a long silence. As I raked in the money, another Russky behind the dealer yelled: 'It's an illegal hand! Christmas has got six cards in his hand.' (They called me Christmas because of my name bein' Noel.) I was waiting for that.

"'Six cards my eye,' I said. And I showed 'em the cards. Then they accused me of pocketing one. Get the idea? I'd been dealt two cards stuck together, so I'd bet big and then lose everything according to the rules because of the extra card. Well, the Frenchman is a straight guy. He helped 'em search under the table and through my pockets and everywhere else. But they couldn't find the sixth card the Russky

17

card-sharp had dealt me. Finally they had to give up, and I took the dough, just as I finished my ham sandwich."

Peter Noel smiled reminiscently. "That was my narrowest escape," he said.

"But what *happened* to the other card?" Leslie Reverson insisted.

"I ate it in the ham sandwich," Peter Noel told them. Loulu Hammond let go her breath in a long sigh, and forgot to feel of the smooth place on her finger where for nearly ten years she had worn a rather fine diamond—until today.

"We ought to have a drink on that one," suggested the Honorable Emily. She had a dislike of signing bills. "Leslie, run and get my handbag off the berth in my room. Careful, now, and don't let Tobermory slip out of the door."

Young Reverson was back in a moment, bearing the handbag. With him was Tom Hammond.

"Any of you people care to get in on the pool this afternoon?" Hammond wanted to know.

The Honorable Emily shook her head, and Candida Noring said, "I've never guessed the ship's run yet within fifty miles."

"This isn't the ship's run," Hammond told her. "The Major won that hours ago. This is a private pool that Andy Todd is doing. The stewards, the sailors, everybody is in it. You see, there's a land bird of some kind fluttering around the deck, and the ship's cat is stalking it. Person who guesses the time within fifteen minutes of the kill gets the pool."

Loulu Hammond stood up and faced her husband. "Are you in on this?"

"Yes, for a dollar. Why not?"

"I rather think I hate you," she told him. She started out of the smoking room, but the Honorable Emily was before her.

They came out to the rail and forced their way through a small crowd of passengers who were staring down at the well deck, where a lean black tomcat was pretending not to notice a plump, bewildered bird which fluttered aimlessly above his head. Again and again it came to rest on a winch bar or a bit of rigging, and ever and again the black tom sidled closer.

"Rotters!" The Honorable Emily gave tongue. "Catch that bird, somebody! Oh, cruel, cruel!" She was startled entirely out of her usual phlegm. "Poor little sea gull!"

Loulu Hammond stared at the fluttering creature. "Why—why, it's a robin!" she cried, much as she might have said, "It's Uncle John!"

Dr. Waite was at the rail, and he turned toward the women. "Not much use to try and save it," he said. "Happens every trip. Lots of land birds are driven out to sea by storms, and they fly until they're exhausted or they see a ship. They come and roost around the deck until the tomcat gets 'em, as he always does. We used to take 'em in sometimes and try to save 'em, but they always die. They're too tired to care about living when they once get on the ship."

"Well, I'm going to save this one!" announced the Honorable Emily. Amid the protests of the bettors and the high tenor objections of Andy Todd, she set off down the steep iron ladder intent upon upsetting the law of the survival of the fittest. Loulu Hammond started to go with her and then thought better of it.

For half an hour the intrepid lady pursued the tired robin without once getting within reach. The black tomcat withdrew and watched from a discreet distance.

Finally the Honorable Emily saw the robin flutter forward into the foremast rigging and had to give it up. Darkness was approaching—and, anyhow, the "pool" had been effectively stopped.

Andy Todd had to return their dollars to the twenty or so men who had signed up for it. "Damn the S.P.C.A., anyhow," said Andy Todd.

Tom Hammond took his refunded dollar and went forward to dress for dinner. He was forced to give it up to his scapegrace son in order to have peace in which to don his dinner clothes. Tonight, for the first time in their married life, Loulu had not put the studs in his shirt.

She came into the stateroom, already dressed in a soft black velvet gown that made her look, Tom thought, like a Medici virgin. If there were any such. The silence which had marked most of their moments alone together during the past five days still stood, like a pane of plate glass, between them.

Tom threw away a collar and whirled on her. "Loulu!" he said.

"Yes?"

"Loulu, I don't know what's got into you."

"Don't you?" asked Loulu Hammond. She chose a string of Técla pearls.

"Loulu, if you think that I and that round-heeled Fraser girl—I mean, if you want to know where I was the night that you all played peekaboo on deck, why don't you ask me?"

"I'm not interested," she said softly.

"Well," he plunged on, "I was shooting dice in the doctor's office, with Waite and the Purser and the mate!"

"I saw Gerald headed for the bar with a dollar bill a moment ago," she interrupted. "Perhaps I'd better go and prevent him from killing himself on candy." She closed the stateroom door behind her, leaving her young husband to mangle his collar in sulphurous silence.

In the next stateroom Miss Hildegarde Withers was sadly surveying the wrinkles in her one evening gown of plum-colored crêpe de Chine. Someone beat a furious tattoo on her door, and the school teacher, still weak from her days in the grip of the sea, started violently.

"Wha-what is it?"

The door opened, and the Honorable Emily poked her head in. Her face was a mask of worry.

"Have you seen him?" she demanded. "I've looked everywhere. I thought he might have slipped through your door and gone to sleep under the berth. . . ."

The two women had a nodding acquaintance due to the fact that their staterooms opened off the same short corridor. Miss Withers regained her composure. She had not seen much of her fellow passengers, but she was quick to understand.

"Why," she inquired, "do you imagine that your nephew would slip through my door and go to sleep under my berth?"

"Not my nephew!" said the Honorable Emily impatiently. "Tobermory, my Persian cat. Is he here?"

Both women looked under the berth. There was no Tobermory. "When I came back to my stateroom just now I found the door ajar and Toby gone," went on the worried woman. "There are many nephews, but only one Tobermory. He's traveled all the way to the World's Fair with me, and now that we're almost back home . . ." She bustled out of the place, deaf to Miss Withers' sympathy.

The school teacher shook her head and resumed dressing. Except for her short stay on deck in the noon sunshine today, this evening was her first appearance on board. She looked forward to the dinner, having had nothing but sketchy and unappreciated lunches on the voyage, which resulted usually in increased qualms and in crumbs on her bedclothes. But she wished it were not a gala dinner. Such things bored Hildegarde Withers, bored her to tears.

However, no one was to be bored at the captain's dinner that Friday night. The passengers entered the dining saloon to a welcoming din which rose from the table next the wall where the unlucky Mrs. Snoaks attempted to cope with the younger generation. Gerald Hammond, his fattish face alight with joy, blew interminably upon a particularly horrible tin horn, while with one hand he spun a discordant clacker, and with the other wielded a pin against the balloons in the hands of his milder companions. Yet there was nothing importunate about the demon Gerald. He let one chubby girl of four blow her balloon until it reached the proportions of a watermelon before he stabbed it and sent her into convulsions of tears.

At the doctor's table the group gathered slowly. Dr. Waite, in his best dress uniform, was the first, as always. The Honorable Emily, in a ludicrous pink taffeta gown, came next, adjusting her eyeglass and loudly bewailing the passing of Tobermory.

"He'll turn up!" the doctor assured her.

But the Honorable Emily was not so sure. "Toby has been trying to get off the ship ever since we sailed," she announced. "If I were superstitious, as of course I'm not, though I did have a Scotch grandmother . . . "

Loulu Hammond, still the Medici virgin, sank into the chair which was held for her by two eager table stewards. She surveyed the brilliant table, laden with flowers, confetti, and favors. "How *nice*," she remarked.

A moment later—hardly long enough to show that they had not come down together—Tom Hammond arrived, in splendid dinner clothes but with a tie which drooped sadly. He glared at the heap of balloons which lay in front of his plate.

Leslie Reverson sauntered in, supremely unconscious of the fact that he wore the best-cut trousers in the place. He

21

sank into his chair and his face brightened as he saw the balloons. "How frightfully gay!" said young Reverson. He blew one to moderate proportions and sent it sailing.

Loulu Hammond caught his mood of mild amusement, and joined him in balloonatics. They hardly noticed the advent of Miss Hildegarde Withers, who stared curiously around the table as she was shown to her chair. Dr. Waite had the usual congratulations to impart. "*Knew* you'd live!" he boomed.

Then came Andy Todd, in a dinner jacket which it would seem that he had inherited from a great-uncle. It was shiny in the lapels, narrow in the badly pressed trousers, and Loulu Hammond knew at one glance that the black butterfly bow which graced his high collar had come readymade, with a rubber band to hold it in place.

"Well!" said Andy Todd. He seemed extremely well satisfied with himself, for some reason or other. All his chagrin at the collapse of his pool on the hunted robin was gone, and he was internally bubbling.

Miss Withers looked at him curiously. "There's a young man who is up to something!" she instantly decided.

At the other tables soup was being served, and the constant pop of bursting balloons was heard. "Shall we wait for Miss Noring, or start?" inquired the doctor. "All here but her."

"How about her friend Miss Fraser?" inquired Loulu calmly. "Surely she will be with us tonight?"

Everyone looked at everyone else. Miss Withers realized that there was a secret here, or at least something which was a secret from her.

"Will the poor girl come, do you think?" asked the Honorable Emily. No one answered her, for all were wondering. People at other tables were craning their necks to see. Candida Noring had been right. There was nothing for people on shipboard to do but gossip—and guess. Andy Todd's peekaboo party on deck the second night of the trip had got around.

Tom Hammond looked extremely casual as he placed a paper helmet on his sleek blond head. "Why shouldn't she come?" he inquired. "The sea is calm as dishwater."

A woman pushed her way between the tables, almost brushing the wide shoulders of Captain Everett as she came. The captain was holding forth among his group of elderly somebodies on the dullness of seafaring and the joys, which he anticipated, of a duck farm on Long Island.

The woman was Candida Noring, her tanned face strangely pale. Perhaps that was because for the first time tonight she wore lipstick, and a sleeveless dress of characterless beige.

"You haven't been waiting for *me?*" she said, as she sat down next the doctor. That told them what they wanted to know. Rosemary Fraser was not coming down to dinner, not even to the captain's dinner.

The soup was served, and a dry white wine was poured into the tall goblets in front of each place. Andy Todd was strangely restless. . . .

"We may as well open our gifts," said the doctor. He took up the tissue-wrapped package which lay across his bread-and-butter plate. Swiftly he tore off the string—it was the "prop" cigarette box which he received as a gift every trip, and Dr. Waite had little interest in it. "Come on, everybody . . . see what the Shipping Board has brought you for Christmas!"

Andy Todd was second in opening his present. It was another cigarette case, of japanned metal with a painted bridge on it. Miss Withers and the other women found powder boxes similarly decorated.

"How perfectly perfect," said the Honorable Emily. She was still worrying about Tobermory. Then she saw the slim figure of a girl approaching and forgot Tobermory completely.

Rosemary Fraser, in shimmering white silk, came like a wraith to join them. She smiled in answer to the doctor's greeting, and then stared at Candida, her eyes wide and hunted, as if to say, "You told me to!"

There was a long pause, punctuated by the sharp collapse of a balloon which Leslie Reverson had blown too full.

"Well!" said Andy Todd uncertainly. He drained his wine and coughed. There was the soft splashing of soup, and then Rosemary Fraser followed his example and downed her glass. She did not cough. A table steward filled it again, and again she drained it.

Rosemary, avoiding her soup, stared at the package in front of her. "Favors," sang out Candida cheerily. "Open it, Rosemary!"

23

Rosemary fumbled with the string, and Andy Todd leaned to offer his pocket knife. But she did not accept the offer. She untied the strings—more strings and knots than any other package had—and came at last to the round powder box.

She smiled, vaguely, and lifted the lid. Inside was a further package, and everyone leaned forward to see.

Rosemary, all unknowing, opened this—and found a single Yale key. Attached to the key was a card. . . . Rosemary was dizzy from the wine, dizzy and afraid.

She picked up the card and read it aloud, though she did not know that her lips moved. "Use this and save repair bills," she recited. "With our compliments the key to—to the blanket locker——"

They were all watching her. Eyes, pairs upon pairs of eyes, were watching Rosemary. She knew that she must say something, anything, so that the eyes would turn away, so that she could faint without being noticed.

She spoke, and her words were stark, horrible—"How—how convenient!" said Rosemary Fraser. She had meant it to be flippant, casual. And yet . . .

Andy Todd laughed first, his tenor guffaws ringing through the room. Dr. Waite was next, a shrill cackle. And then, from sheer nervousness, the table roared.

Leslie Reverson actually neighed into his napkin, coughing and gasping until his aunt, herself convulsed with paroxysms of hysterical laughter, had to thump on his narrow shoulders. Tom Hammond snorted, and then shook silently, Loulu Hammond told herself that she must not, would not, laugh, and heard her own clear soprano ringing out above the laughter of the others.

Only two at the doctor's table did not laugh—for Rosemary Fraser herself was laughing. There was madness in her laughter, but no one sensed that. Candida Noring bit her lips until the blood ran salty under her tongue. Miss Hildegarde Withers, who was perhaps the one adult on board who did not know of the ship's pet scandal, merely looked puzzled. But there was enough laughter without Miss Withers' and Candida's.

Loulu Hammond, who had been seething with repressed emotions for five days, fairly shrieked now. All the time her mind was saying, "I shall not laugh. I shall not!" Her long finger nails cut into her palms. . . .

Captain Everett stopped talking about his duck farm and smiled toward the further table. "The young people certainly do have high times together," he observed paternally. "That's the best thing about traveling on a small boat, the passengers get to know each other so well. . . ."

He stopped short as a young woman brushed past his wide shoulders again, clutching in her hand a cheap japanned powder box and a key.

"These young folks!" he smiled. "They have all the fun!"

Through the open portholes of the *American Diplomat* came a yowling cacophony which rose shudderingly in a horrible crescendo and then died away. "The tomcat must be having trouble with his robin," observed Captain Everett genially.

Somehow, the laughter cut itself short. Leslie Reverson sent vari-colored balloons flying in every direction, and Tom Hammond began to talk very loudly about the collapse of the American dollar in the foreign exchange, about London hotels, about anything. . . .

The others joined him, chiming in too quickly but with good intentions. Only Miss Withers and Candida Noring were silent. Before the dessert was served, both had left the table, Miss Withers to seek the deck and the fresh air which she had lacked for so many days, and Candida to go to her cabin mate.

She found the door locked, and her insistent knocks brought no reply. Finally Candida went out on the promenade deck, and came where she could see in through the porthole. She pushed aside the drawn curtain and saw that the light was on.

Rosemary Fraser, instead of sobbing brokenly on her berth, was sitting on the settee and calmly writing in a leather-bound book

"Rosemary! Let me in!"

But Rosemary kept on writing.

"Rosemary!"

The girl in white finally looked up. She stared full into the frightened, tanned face of Candida Noring. Her red lips opened and unbelievable sounds came forth.

25

"Damn you to hell—oh, damn you, go away!" Her voice was low and soft, but it rang through Candida's ears for long afterward. She tiptoed softly away.

The Honorable Emily passed Candida in the passage, but they did not speak. She came on toward her own stateroom, shaking her head. "These Americans!" said the Honorable Emily. Then—"Poor girl!"

She closed the stateroom door and rapidly changed her uncomfortable taffeta for a flannel robe. "I loathe practical jokes," said the Honorable Emily finally.

There was a faint scratching at the door, and she sprang, with a sudden access of joy, to open it. There stood Tobermory, his silky silver fur torn and bedraggled, and with the lust of battle still shining in his amber eyes. He entered quietly, carrying in his mouth a bundle of feathers.

"Toby!" cried the Honorable Emily.

Tobermory, startled, let go the feathers, which immediately resolved themselves into a fat robin. The robin swung to his feet, and spread his wings. Tobermory struck him down with a swift paw and looked up at his mistress.

"Mine!" he said, in unmistakable cat language. But Tobermory was manifestly uncertain what to do with his prize.

His mind was swiftly made up for him. Tobermory was grasped firmly by the slack of his neck and tossed into the berth. The Honorable Emily picked up the frightened, hunted robin, and held it against her cheek.

"Poor, poor Dickie-bird," she crooned. The robin, completely a pessimist by this time, did not even dare to flutter. He would as soon be eaten by a large creature as a small one.

Sadly the Honorable Emily noted the pounding of the bird's heart, its torn plumage, and the poor wounded claws which spoke for its futile clutching at rusty gear and swinging wires. "Poor, poor Dickie-bird!"

Then she rang the bell furiously. When the steward approached, she demanded that he produce a bird cage.

"I shall save him," she promised the robin. "I shall save his poor little life willy-nilly!"

The steward didn't know of a bird cage. But, upon extreme pressure, he admitted that perhaps the ship's carpenter could rig one up, out of wire and bits of rope, in the morning. "Chips is very handy with tools, ma'am," he told her.

The Honorable Emily cast her eyes around the little stateroom. "In the morning," she agreed. "Tell him to rush it."

She saw Tobermory, proud in wounded dignity, watching from the berth. Tobermory had taken this robin, by sheer right of conquest, from the ship's tomcat, who had made the mistake of underestimating his silky and effeminate-looking opponent, and who was now licking his wounds and wondering what struck him.

The Honorable Emily had a bright thought. Under the berth was Tobermory's traveling case. She pulled it out and inserted the robin, who hopped about inside and thought it as good as any other place. Any minute now he expected the worst.

Tobermory's eyes blazed. It wouldn't have been so bad if this woman had *eaten* his prey, but to put it aside in that manner amounted to sheer insult! It was not as if it had been a thin or scrawny bird, Tobermory felt. He sulked on the berth and would not purr.

Up on the boat deck, Miss Hildegarde Withers relaxed in a deck chair. The wind was warm and brisk, and it came sweeping across the ship's bow, almost from the direction of England. London would have to be awfully interesting, Miss Withers felt, to make up for this voyage. She felt vaguely annoyed by the little mystery, the tempest in a teapot, which had spoiled the dinner party. There had been something in the attitude of the girl in white which worried Miss Withers. She had been afraid of something, that slim proud Fraser girl.

Looking up, Miss Withers saw the girl of whom she had been thinking. Rosemary Fraser was coming along the dimly lit, windswept deck, wearing nothing but her white evening dress and an incongruous scarf, a long, trailing banner of a scarf, of midnight blue.

"Child alive!" said Miss Withers to herself. "You'll catch your death of cold!"

Her chair was set in the shadow of a lifeboat, and evidently the oncoming girl did not see her. Rosemary leaned far over the starboard rail, amidships of the vessel, and stared out at the misty darkness of the night. She was smoking a dark cigarette, and its sparks trailed gayly into the blackness.

"I ought to tell her to go back to her cabin and get a warm coat," said Miss Withers again. But she did not rise. After all, these young people of today had a physical resistance which was unknown in those distant days when Hildegarde Withers was a girl. They could drink innumerable cocktails, dance all night, and go out into the winter winds with only the sheerest of silk stockings, the lightest of underwear and dresses. . . .

"Perhaps we are developing a race that has a wonderful physical stamina," mused Miss Withers. "Ten years or more of prohibition beverages must kill off the weak ones, at least." She leaned back in her chair and closed her eyes. "I wonder if they have the mental stamina that we had to develop," she asked herself. "I wonder if they could—if they can——"

Her drowsy musings were interrupted by a worried feminine voice. "Excuse me," said Candida Noring, leaning over Miss Withers' deck chair. "I'm looking for Miss Fraser. I know she came up here—have you seen her?"

"Why," gasped Miss Withers, "she's at the rail, right there. . . ."

Her voice trailed off, for Rosemary Fraser was not standing by the rail. She was not on the deck, not anywhere.

"I came up the forward ladder," said Candida, in a puzzled tone. "She didn't pass me. If she isn't here, she must have come past you."

But Miss Withers hadn't heard the click of high heels on the wooden deck. "She didn't pass me," declared the school teacher. "She must be here somewhere!"

Bewildered, the school teacher rose to her feet. Candida Noring drew closer to her and shivered.

"Rosemary!" she cried once, into the wind.

Only the wind answered, in a language that they could not understand. But Rosemary Fraser was gone.

CHAPTER III

*

Confetti Blown Away

"She's tried to kill herself!" cried Candida Noring. Miss Withers rose from her deck chair and automatically consulted the tiny watch which was pinned to her bosom. It was three minutes past eleven.

They were both at the rail, staring down at the phosphorescent flurry of foam which slipped by the iron side of the ship. On either side the huge lifeboats towered, lashed down beneath their heavy canvas.

"They can lower a boat!" Candida thought aloud. "They can stop the ship and—" She ran forward along the deck, but Miss Withers caught her arm.

"Wait," said the school teacher. "Child, hadn't you better make sure? I heard no splash. She might have slipped past you in the darkness, or hidden here behind a lifeboat until you passed. I can't believe—did she have any real reason to take her life?"

Candida Noring shook her head. "No real reason—no. Of course not."

"You'll find her in your stateroom when you go below," counseled the school teacher. "Go and see, at any rate. I'll look around up here on the deck."

Candida nodded, and color began to return to her tanned face. She called over her shoulder as she went, "I'll meet you here. . . ."

Miss Withers made a brisk and thorough survey of the boat deck, from the ladders that led to the bridge past lifeboats, deck houses, shuffleboard courts, to the after rail. She peered into the window of the wireless room, where plump, genial Sparks was admiring his collection of French postcards in a fog of blue tobacco smoke. Sometimes passengers dropped in for a chat with Sparks, but tonight he was alone. She tried the lid of the blanket locker, and found it repaired and securely padlocked.

Finally Miss Withers returned to the rail, where she had seen Rosemary leaning with her blue scarf whipping in the wind. She stared into the night, but the night kept its secret. There was a chillness in the wind which she had not noticed before.

She waited ten minutes—fifteen, perhaps. Still Candida did not return. Did that mean that she had found her roommate or not? Miss Withers was thoroughly chilled by this time. She went forward along the deck, wondering. Had there been a splash? Had she by any chance dropped off for a moment's doze and not heard it?

She looked up toward the bridge and saw the broad shoulders of Captain Everett moving against the sky. This sort of thing was his responsibility, not hers. Why, no matter where she wandered, did the real or fancied troubles of those around her inevitably come to rest upon her shoulders? She felt weak and tired. . . .

Her tiredness was swept away when she saw Candida Noring belatedly appearing up the forward ladder. The girl came toward her, almost running. But she pushed past and clambered wildly up the bridge ladder. Miss Withers clutched the rail and listened. . . .

"She's gone!" Candida cried. "Stop the ship, I tell you. Go back, oh, for God's sake, go back!" Somebody barked a hoarse order.

The engine room signal tinkled mysteriously, and Miss Withers felt the slackening of the mighty engines far in the bowels of the ship.

Eight bells rang out for midnight at that moment. "Good heavens, woman," barked the voice of the captain, "what are you asking? Your friend is probably in somebody's cabin. I can't put my ship about and lose time because you fancy——"

Candida was clutching at his uniform. "I tell you I *know*!" she cried. "Just because nobody heard her fall . . ."

Captain Everett hesitated, and then gave the order, his wide shoulders limp. "Put her about," he told the officer. They made hurried calculations. He swung toward Candida. "When did you miss her?"

30

"Oh—I don't know. I've been searching everywhere for a long time." The captain shrugged hopelessly. First Officer Jenkins cut off "Metal Mike" and took the stubborn wheel.

Then he was startled by the apparition of a long New England face that rose unsteadily level with his ankles. Miss Hildegarde Withers peered onto the bridge. "The girl was last seen a few minutes before eleven, at the rail," she announced.

"An hour ago? Good God, we've come eighteen knots!" The captain seemed perceptibly to lose weight. He turned to Jenkins. "You can put back on the course, mister." Bells tinkled again, and the sky began to swing. . . .

"But you *must* turn back!" protested Candida. Captain Everett shook his head. "We couldn't get to that approximate spot on the chart inside of another hour. No swimmer in God's world could keep afloat in these waters for so long a time." He drew a deep breath. "Anyway, perhaps you're wrong. We—I'll have the ship searched."

He swung down the ladder as Miss Withers backed out of his way. Candida followed woodenly. "That girl wouldn't commit suicide," Captain Everett said, as if to reassure himself. "Why, she was so gay at the dinner tonight—you were all laughing and having high jinks."

Candida said softly that she hadn't mentioned suicide, but he did not hear her. "Mark my words, the Fraser girl is safe and sound somewhere. According to what I hear, she has a habit of hiding away in strange places. . . ."

He led the way down to the promenade deck, the two women following close behind. "We'll just have a bit of a look-see," said Captain Everett. "No need to alarm the passengers. We'll find her, never you fear."

The captain had a look-see until the sun was well above the horizon, with picked detachments of his officers scouring the ship, but Rosemary Fraser was not to be found. This time she had not crept away for a love tryst in any secret place aboard the *American Diplomat*.

"*Rosemary Fraser, aged nineteen*," Captain Everett wrote painstakingly in his log, beneath the date "*September 21st*." He added the fateful words, "*Unaccountably Missing*," and laid aside his pen.

Miss Hildegarde Withers sat up for a long time with Candida. "I can understand that her shame over a real or fancied sin of that kind could have driven her to suicide," the school teacher finally agreed. She was holding in her lap the leather-bound diary which had been Rosemary Fraser's. "But I don't understand why she should have gone without leaving a suicide note behind—or why she should tear half the pages out of this little book."

Candida Noring knew. "Rosemary took with her everything she had written," she said calmly. "Of course she would. She didn't want anyone to know what she had put down, to search out the secrets of her silly girlish heart. She didn't want anybody to know who was the man over whom she had lost what people would call 'her good name.'"

Miss Withers turned her keen blue eyes on the girl with the tanned face. "Do you know who *he* was?"

But Candida only shook her head. "I could guess," she said. "But I won't."

At that moment Tom Hammond raised his rumpled head from the pillow and saw his wife Loulu standing, fully dressed, in the doorway.

"I didn't hear the breakfast gong," he said cheerily. He stopped short as he saw the look on Loulu's face.

"You may as well know," she said, in a voice that was not her own, "that Rosemary Fraser went overboard last night."

Tom didn't say anything for a moment. "I thought you might be interested," his wife finished, and closed the door forcibly on his torrent of questions. Hammond slid out of bed, doused his head in cold water. He dressed quickly, without his bath. This morning, through some beneficent miracle, the Vesuvius of bedclothing on the settee did not erupt. It was a lucky thing for the demon Gerald that he still slept, for his father was in a mood to answer no questions.

The news came to the Honorable Emily via her steward, who rapped at the door at nine o'clock bearing a fearful and wonderful bird cage which the carpenter, true to form, had contrived out of light wire and a rusty oil tin. The Honorable Emily was so busy moving her new pet into its improvised cage that she did not at first grasp the meaning of what she heard.

Tobermory stared sulkily from the pillow, his eyes never leaving the bird, which was, by every right, his. The robin waited patiently for his certain doom.

The Honorable Emily then gave her attention to thoughts of Rosemary Fraser. Unconsciously she repeated her remarks of the previous evening. "Poor girl!" she said aloud. Then, "These Americans!"

She repeated them again as she went down to breakfast with her nephew Leslie Reverson. "I'm glad you weren't mixed up with a girl like that," she added.

Young Reverson told her that if he hadn't been mixed up with Rosemary that was Rosemary's fault and not his own. Neither one of them was able to eat much breakfast.

Dr. Waite was entirely unable to eat breakfast. He rubbed his bald head constantly and forgot to snigger. "Why," he kept saying, "she didn't look like that kind at all!"

Miss Hildegarde Withers was warming herself with a cup of tea. She turned and stared at him across Candida's empty chair.

"What kind?" she inquired suddenly.

"Why—the kind that would take her own life!"

"Suppose she didn't!" said the school teacher abruptly, and left the table. She went out on deck, wandering aimlessly in the bright sunshine. First she went to the place at the boat-deck rail where she had last seen Rosemary leaning far—almost too far—out. She stood there for a little while and then went below again. She came out on the promenade deck, striding up and down along the curtained portholes. "I'm getting what the French call an *idée fixe*," she told herself. "Why couldn't a suicide be just that—an ordinary suicide?" She watched a big wave leap up and then flatten again. "Particularly since Miss Noring says that the girl was terrified lest the Colonel and his wife, who knew her father back in Buffalo, would take it upon themselves to spread the scandal, and that she would thus be called home from her world tour in disgrace?"

That was motive enough for suicide, certainly—given a sensitive, emotional type such as Rosemary, for the first time in her life away from parental overseeing. Yet——

Miss Withers came back around the deck, talking to herself, and then she suddenly stopped short. A man in a natty blue uniform was leaning over the rail near the door of the social hall, and from his fingers bits of something white were snatched by the wind, which whipped them back toward the ship's wake.

She approached and saw that it was Peter Noel. He bade her a good morning. "Cleaning house?" she asked casually.

Noel nodded. "That's one advantage of a ship," he informed her. "Anything you don't want you can throw over the side. I just got rid of some playing cards . . . they should have gone weeks ago. They were like shuffling pancakes."

He ventured a polite grin and stepped back inside. Miss Withers still stood at the rail, staring back at the oily, tumbled trails of uneasy water churned up by the powerful screws. Back there to the westward lay America—somewhere nearer the curve of the horizon a proud, slim girl in white had found a chilly grave. . . .

Miss Withers was very thoughtful. Then her keen eyes noticed that a scrap of paper, smaller than a postage stamp, was staring at her from a looming iron stanchion, held firmly by the wind against the damp metal. She took it idly in her fingers, and then turned and walked forward again.

Locked in her stateroom, she began to study it, for lack of anything better to do. It was worth studying. Never before in her life had Miss Withers seen a fragment of a playing card made of cream paper with a blue rule lined across it. Never before had she seen a bit of playing card bearing the scribbled letters "—osem—."

For half an hour she tried to think of a word in English or any other common language into which that fragment would fit. Finally she put the scrap of paper safely into her handbag and rang for Mrs. Snoaks.

The stewardess became instantly voluble about the disappearance of Rosemary Fraser, but Miss Withers cut her short. "Please draw me a hot bath at once," she requested. Then, as the woman turned to go, "Just a moment." Miss Withers took a crisp five-dollar bill from her bag and crinkled it. "I want you to do something for me."

Mrs. Snoaks would have done anything, including arson, for a five-dollar bill. Her eyes widened when she heard her instructions, but there was that in the manner of Hildegarde Withers which prevented questions. "No matter where I am or what I'm doing," the school teacher insisted, "come and tell me." Mrs. Snoaks swore, and departed.

Half an hour later, refreshed in spite of her sleepless night, Miss Hildegarde Withers climbed out of the tub, dried her angular body, and donned a serge suit. Then she went to the top deck and knocked at the door which bore a brass plate—"Captain."

The master of every vessel, no matter what his age, is known on board as "the Old Man." Today Captain Everett looked the part. He sat at his desk, his eyes circled with dark rings, and stared at those fateful words—"Unaccountably Missing."

His face did not light up at the sight of Hildegarde Withers in the doorway. "Well?" he rasped. In his hand was a wireless form which Sparks had just handed him, from the line's moguls in New York.

MAKE EVERY EFFORT CLEAR MYSTERY OF FRASER GIRL STOP PARENTS DISSATISFIED AND VERY INFLUENTIAL STOP UNFORTUNATE YOU DID NOT TURN BACK AND LOWER BOAT STOP MAKE FULL REPORT HERE AND TO LONDON.

"I'd like to make a suggestion," said Miss Withers hurriedly. "Wouldn't it be a good idea to find out where various members of the passenger list were at the time Rosemary Fraser is supposed to have gone overboard?"

"What?" Captain Everett had an unpleasant feeling that this meddlesome woman was implying something frightening and unthinkable. "You mean to tell me that you suspect—that you think somebody had a hand in——"

"I'm not suspecting anything, yet," Miss Withers told him. "But if we knew where the passengers were, we might learn something from someone's hearing the splash—or not hearing it."

But Captain Everett shook his head. "It will only alarm the passengers," he decided. "They'll think they're being asked for an alibi, and I've done enough asking questions for one day. Besides, if any of them had heard anything, they'd have come forward." He turned back to his desk as a sign that the interview was over.

"There's more ways to kill a cat than by choking it with butter," Miss Withers told him somewhat cryptically, and withdrew in injured pride.

As she stood thoughtfully on the deck outside the captain's door she heard the clanging signal of the luncheon gong. That gave her an idea. She hastened below, and such was her promptness that she very nearly, but not quite, got into the dining saloon ahead of Dr. Waite, who had just emerged from his combined office and sick bay at the foot of the stairs.

Instead of avoiding discussion of the tragedy of the previous night, Miss Withers welcomed it. As the others straggled in, each contributed his own theory. Most of them agreed that it must have been a shame suicide, though Leslie Reverson surprised everyone, including himself, by venturing to suggest that perhaps Rosemary had fallen overboard.

"I've got an idea," said Miss Withers innocently. She was in a hurry to get this over before Candida Noring, the only absent member of the table group, should join them. "Suppose each of us tries to remember whereabouts on the ship he or she was between quarter of eleven and five after—which must have been the time the girl went overboard? Perhaps the estimated hour is wrong—if one or more of us was near the right-hand rail——"

"Starboard," said Tom Hammond.

"The starboard rail, thank you . . . and if that one did not hear a splash, as I did not, it will prove either that the girl went overboard at another time or from the other side of the ship!"

The various individuals at the doctor's table looked at each other. Loulu Hammond broke the silence. "I heard nothing," she admitted. "Because I had gone to bed and was sound asleep." She smiled. "And so was the pride and joy of the Hammond household, our darling Gerald."

Leslie Reverson tried to account for himself, but was very vague about it. He had wandered into the bar about that time, looking for a nightcap, but had found it unaccountably closed. He had taken a book from the ship's library in the social hall and read himself to sleep in his stateroom. The Honorable Emily stated that at approximately eleven o'clock she had been down below decks importuning the night pantryman for some crumbs to give her new pet.

"I myself was drowsing on the boat deck, as you all know," Miss Withers said. "Miss Noring was looking for her roommate, and came up the forward ladder at approximately eleven. She heard nothing, she says."

Only Tom Hammond had not spoken. He looked at the doctor. "I was three dollars ahead of the crap game," he said dryly, "at approximately eleven. Isn't that so, Doctor?"

Dr. Waite nodded, "Yes—I guess so—there were five or six of us in my diggings," he explained. "The purser, the third officer, Mr. Hammond, and the Colonel. Later in the evening Noel, the bar steward, wandered in and lost a couple of dollars." He turned to Leslie Reverson. "That was after you left, I guess."

"Oh, yes," said Reverson. "I forgot to mention that I went down there." He reddened a little.

Dr. Waite was conscious of Miss Withers' disapproval. "Just a little game for dimes and quarters," he hastened on. "It passes the time away. The boys were in and out of my place until one o'clock or so, but I couldn't set any exact hour. Anyway, we were too busy wooing the goddess of luck to hear anything."

He had finished his lunch, and Miss Withers rose and walked out of the saloon with him. "I'd like to see your office," she suggested. He held the door open and ushered her into a spick-and-span suite, surprisingly well equipped with hospital and medical apparatus. Along one wall was a medicine cabinet holding hundreds of neatly labeled bottles.

Miss Withers tried the handle and found the door unlocked. "You have quite a stock of drugs," she observed.

"Have to keep 'em," said Waite. "Can't send out to get a prescription filled here, you know."

There were two portholes on either side of the cabinet, above the thick soft rug upon which male members of the party had hazarded their dimes and quarters. This was the starboard side of the ship, and very nearly at the point amidships where Miss Withers had last seen Rosemary Fraser two decks above.

Upon pressure, the doctor admitted that in the course of the dice game several of the players had stepped out from time to time to get sandwiches and coffee at the near-by pantry. He was thus very inexact as to hours, except that he remembered that young Reverson had wandered in and out again shortly after ten. "The kid seemed nervous about something," recollected Dr. Waite.

37

Miss Withers nodded and pointed to the tightly fastened portholes. "Were these open last night?"

"Fresh air is bad for gambling," explained Waite. "They were just as you see them now. We couldn't have heard a foghorn through that thick glass."

"I don't suppose—" began Miss Withers. Then she stopped as a rap came on the door. It was Mrs. Snoaks, afire with tidings.

"Miss Noring is taking a bath!" she shouted, as soon as she saw that her search for Miss Withers was over. Then she departed, and after an uneasy moment the school teacher followed her, concealing a certain eagerness.

Dr. Waite sat down at his desk and prescribed three fingers of brandy for himself. His brow was wrinkled with perplexity. "Why in blazes *shouldn't* Miss Noring take a bath?" he asked himself aloud.

Something was going on that he did not understand. He walked out of his office and saw Loulu Hammond going up the stair. On a wild impulse he tried the news on her. "Miss Noring is taking a bath," he hazarded.

"Amazing!" said Loulu Hammond, and passed on out of sight.

At that moment Miss Hildegarde Withers, the most eminently respectable passenger on board, was on her knees before the keyhole of Candida Noring's stateroom. She had brought a twisted hairpin with her, but her own key turned with only slight difficulty in the lock. Miss Withers entered, locked the door behind her, and drew the curtain across the portholes. Then she looked at her watch. It was two o'clock in the afternoon, and she had fifteen minutes, perhaps, to do what she had come to do. Swiftly and methodically she set to work.

She went through baggage, both Candida's and that of the missing girl, with the speed of a customs official and with considerably more neatness. The result—apart from showing her that Rosemary had liked frilly things and that Candida went in for more sensible apparel—was exactly nothing.

In the rack above Candida's berth were three books: *Swann's Way*, Philip Macdonald's *Escape*, and the collected sonnets of Edna St. Vincent Millay. In the rack above Rosemary's berth were Colette's *Young Woman of Paris* and a copy of *True Story*. A pressed bunch of violets marked a place halfway through the Proust book.

Miss Withers thumbed through them all. She lifted mattresses, poked behind pictures, and even scrutinized the carpet very thoroughly. Last of all she went through Candida's pocketbook, finding only a packet of brown cigarettes, some silver and bills, and a pocket lighter.

Nowhere within that stateroom, she could have sworn, were the pages torn from Rosemary Fraser's diary. Feeling considerable prickings of conscience, Miss Withers replaced everything exactly as she had found it, stepped out, and locked the door behind her. She looked at her watch. It was sixteen minutes past two.

As she came down the corridor, hurrying a little, she saw a door open. Steam floated out, and then Candida Noring, in a brown bathrobe, came toward the school teacher.

Her dark hair hung stringily on her tanned forehead, and she looked both tired and ill.

"Heavens, child," Miss Withers accosted her. "You'd better let the doctor give you a sleeping potion. You look worn to nothing."

Candida stopped. "Do I? I haven't been to bed, for I know I shan't sleep."

"Nonsense!" Miss Withers patted her shoulder. "Don't feel that you have all the responsibility. Tomorrow night or Monday morning we'll be in the Thames, and Scotland Yard will soon straighten out the mystery. They'll know how to——"

"Scotland Yard?" Candida's eyes widened. "I didn't know——"

"The purser says that they always handle the formalities in case of a death at sea," Miss Withers told her.

"Thank heavens for that," said Candida, with real relief in her voice. "Now all I have to worry about is just what I shall have to cable to Rosemary's people. I believe I *will* go down and let the doctor give me something. . . ."

She hurried on, and Miss Withers sought her own stateroom. She lay down, intending to rest while she let her mind occupy itself with the intriguing puzzle of the missing pages of the diary. In a few moments she slept, so soundly that she heard nothing of the bitter family quarrel in the next stateroom—nothing of Loulu Hammond's soprano monosyllables and Tom Hammond's gruff bewildered phrases. Not even the shrill, joyful participation of the fat-faced Gerald could waken the weary school teacher this afternoon. She slept through dinner, wakened late in the evening, when the steward brought her soup and toast, and wandered for a short while through the oddly deserted ship. No one felt like dancing or bridge that night. The bar closed for lack of trade at ten o'clock, and there was no light beneath the doctor's door.

On deck she saw Tom Hammond sucking on an empty brown pipe and thinking his own thoughts as he strode endlessly up and down. A light fog drifted wetly against her face, and on the bridge she could dimly make out that Captain Everett had no less than two officers beside him as his hushed and saddened ship rolled smoothly on toward Land's End and the Lizard.

It was a hush which somehow lingered through the next day, in spite of vague efforts on the part of some of the older passengers to hold hymn-singing services on the Sabbath morning. The sound of the distant voices came faintly to Miss Withers in her cabin. They finished, as always on shipboard, with "Rocked in the Cradle of the Deep." It was a feeble, belated funeral service for Rosemary Fraser, Miss Withers fancied. Had the girl laid her down in peace to sleep, then?

No one went to bed on that Sunday evening, for the little *American Diplomat* was slipping in the fog past clusters of shore lights to port, past the white chalk cliffs of Dover, and then, miraculously, pushing on up a narrowing river that smelled as Miss Withers had always known the Thames would smell. The lights to port and starboard closed in steadily, and then, shortly before midnight, the throb of the engines stopped. The anchor went down with a roar of chain, and through portholes misted with rain Miss Withers could see a mammoth electric sign announcing the virtues of "OXO."

"Passengers in the social hall, please!" a steward was shouting. His gong rang endlessly up and down the corridors. Miss Withers opened her porthole and saw that a slim black launch, with one staring eye, was coming down the river from where the glow of the city shone brightest.

She tidied her hair and joined the excited, nervous gathering.

Everyone wanted to know if there was a chance of getting ashore tonight, and everyone was assured several times over that the British Customs close at 6 P.M. "Not until morning," the purser was saying, in his thin and worried voice.

"Then what are we here for?" the Honorable Emily demanded. Nobody told her, but through the half-open door that led to the deck Miss Withers heard the muffled beating of a powerful motor. There were voices on the deck, the motor rose to a roar and died away, and then Captain Everett entered the social hall. He seemed to have regained the weight he had lost the night that Rosemary Fraser disappeared. Behind him was Jenkins, the first officer, and last of all came a tall, bulky man wearing a bowler hat and a dingy yellow trench-coat.

In spite of his bland, innocent face, in spite of his slick blond hair and the brown spats he affected, Miss Hildegarde Withers was instantly aware of the fact that she was staring at an operative of the C.I.D. She knew it by the pale hazel eyes that looked once—and saw everything. She knew it by the neatly blacked shoes, bump-toed as are the shoes of any man who has ever walked a beat, in any city of the world.

The three men disappeared through the curtain of the smoking room—the bar had been locked since the ship entered British waters—and there was a long silence. "I'm a British subject," the Honorable Emily once began, and failed to finish her protest. The passengers were restless, but nobody felt like talking. Even the terrible Gerald was silent, staring intently at his unsmiling parents. Andy Todd pretended to read, and smoked cigarettes chain fashion.

At last the curtains opened, and Captain Everett showed his face. He beckoned to Peter Noel, who stood near by in his best uniform, and whispered something to him.

Noel nodded. "Miss Hildegarde Withers," he called. He held open the curtain, and Miss Withers entered to see the two ship's officers on the settee, and the Yard man facing her across a bridge table. She was not asked to sit down.

"This is Chief Inspector Cannon of New Scotland Yard," said Captain Everett gently. "He'd like to ask you a few questions. . . ."

Miss Withers started to say something, but the Yard man leaned forward. "You were the last person to see Rosemary Fraser?" he asked. He began writing in his notebook before she had worded her answer. Whatever ideas the good lady might have held regarding the telling of her story in her own way were instantly dispelled. She answered question after question, and in less than five minutes had told everything that she knew and nothing that she suspected about the passing of Rosemary Fraser. "Thank you," said Cannon, without obvious interest. She went back into the social hall.

"Miss Candida Noring," announced Peter Noel, after another prompting from Captain Everett.

Candida rose, ground out her cigarette, and walked to the curtains like Joan of Arc to the pyre. Her hands were buried in the deep pockets of a camel's-hair coat, and her knees did not seem as steady as usual. When Noel held the curtain aside for her, she swayed suddenly against him, and he smiled reassuringly. The smile was wiped from his face as if with a sponge.

Miss Withers saw him look quickly toward the three exits of the room. In each of them a ship's officer was standing. Noel frowned thoughtfully as he took up his former position a short distance from the curtains of the smoking room. She wondered if the fixed terror of Candida's face had spoiled his innocent pleasure in holding the office of master of ceremonies. His hand went to his coat pocket and was suddenly withdrawn. He straightened his necktie and waited. . . .

They all waited, waited interminably. Loulu Hammond looked at her husband, and when she caught his eyes looked suddenly away. The minutes dragged on forever—and then the curtains parted and Candida came forth. Every eye was upon her, searching for signs of hysteria, but Candida Noring was smiling. In her fingers a dark cigarette glowed.

Another pause ensued, and then Captain Everett showed himself again. He beckoned to Peter Noel, but this time he did not speak a name. And suddenly, Noel knew!

He drew a long, deep breath and straightened his shoulders. Then he went through the curtain. The thick draperies closed behind him, while little surprised murmurs rose among the passengers. Miss Withers strolled part way across the room, but she could hear nothing.

Inside the smoking room Chief Inspector Cannon was standing quietly, his notebook put away. The captain and the first officer were also standing.

"Well?" said Noel.

The Yard man spoke in a rapid singsong. "Peter Noel, in the light of information which has been laid before me, it is my duty to arrest you for the murder of Rosemary Fraser, and it is my further duty to warn you that if found guilty of this charge you may be sentenced to death."

Noel's handsome face was a mask of blank surprise. His mouth opened foolishly and closed again. But his brain was working swiftly.

"Do you wish to make a statement? It is my duty to warn you that you do not need to make a statement, and that if you do it may be used against you."

Peter Noel laughed suddenly, the fear soaking out of his heart. His hand was in the pocket of his blue uniform jacket, and as his laughter changed to a fit of coughing, he covered his mouth.

"None o' that!" cried Cannon, stumbling against the table. His methodical mind framed an entry for his notebook. "Prisoner upon arrest attempted to dispose of evidence by swallowing."

Noel was smiling. He held out his hands for nonexistent handcuffs.

"I have nothing to say except that this is a lot of bloody nonsense," he told them quickly. "Take me on shore if you've got to, but somebody has filled you full of poppycock. If Rosemary Fraser was murdered, this is the first I knew of it. . . ."

Chief Inspector Cannon had a sudden misgiving. This confident, calm voice was not that of a guilty man, not even that of a worried man. "I shall have a jolly good chance of making a charge of false arrest," went on Noel.

"Come along, then," he was told. The Law laid its hands upon him, and he was very briskly searched. Captain Everett fidgeted, and Jenkins protested in a loud whisper: "I tell you he was shooting dice with the doctor!"

Noel was coughing again, more realistically this time. He held back against the large brown hands of the detective. "Wait a minute," cried Peter Noel. "Wait a minute. . . ."

"None of tha' tricks, now!" boomed Cannon. He realized that he was holding the prisoner's entire weight. In his excitement the Yard man reverted to his native Lancashire. "None of tha' tricks, lad!"

But this trick of Peter Noel's was beyond the power of Scotland Yard. He clutched at the curtain, and staggered forward.

Women screamed in the room outside as a dead man, with his face twisted in an expression of complete and horrified surprise, plunged headlong among them.

CHAPTER IV

*

All the Devils of Hell

Black Thames water lapped softly against the stout iron sides of the *American Diplomat*, its ripples now faintly touched with dawning light from the east. In the ship's tiny smoking room Chief Inspector Cannon fluttered the closely scrawled pages of his notebook and sighed.

Facing him stood a smaller, grayer man, who chewed savagely upon a walrus-like mustache. Superintendent Harrington was in no pleasant mood. "It's a bloody disgrace," he told Cannon unpleasantly.

"Yes, sir," said the chief inspector, who actually thought so.

"You permitted a prisoner in your custody to take his own life."

"Yes, sir."

"If one of your men pulled such a trick, you'd call him a bloody fool."

"Yes, sir."

The two men were alone behind the curtains of the smoking room, but Cannon had a suspicion that his superior's words could be heard by the little group of uniformed men and detectives who lingered outside in the social hall of the ship. Long since, the passengers had been questioned and sent to their staterooms—if not to sleep, at least to ponder over Cannon's promise that they could jolly well stop aboard until they were told to go.

Harrington pulled his green cloth hat over his eyes and began to put on his gloves.

The chief inspector imperceptibly brightened. "Then you're not going to take over yourself, sir?"

"Take over? Of course not. The gov'nor will want a full report on this business when he gets down to the Yard at

45

nine o'clock. See that you ring me up before then. But it's your case, Cannon."

The superintendent was halfway through the curtains when Cannon spoke. "Which case?"

"Meaning?" Harrington stopped short.

"The disappearance or the suicide?"

"They're one and the same," cried Harrington testily. "Can't you see? You were assigned to the disappearance of Rosemary Fraser—but the suicide of this Noel fellow was a confession of guilt. He threw her overboard and had poison all ready in his pocket in case he was arrested for it. All you've got to do is to tie the loose strings together."

Cannon said something under his breath. But his superior went on. "If you like, take young Secker as your associate and turn the disappearance end of the case over to him. It's time he had something to do beyond haunting police courts. And he can't be much duller as a detective than you've shown yourself tonight, Cannon."

Superintendent Harrington disappeared in the direction of the waiting launch, which bore the "TI" insignia of the River Police. When he was well out of earshot, Cannon took a deep breath, let it go, and then stepped out into the social hall.

Across the room a tall, thin young man, dressed negligently in brown tweed coat and dark flannels, was watching the removal of the body of Peter Noel, now neatly covered with a blanket.

"Sergeant!" boomed the chief inspector. Young John Secker looked up and smiled. "What are you mooning at? As if you'd never seen a dead body before. . . ."

"As a matter of fact, I haven't," said the young man placatingly. "You forget, sir, that I've been a sleuth for just eight weeks come Tuesday. I was only wondering, sir, do all suicides have such a surprised look on their faces, as if they hadn't expected it was going to be exactly what it was?"

"Eh?" said Cannon. "Well, you may come along with me, anyhow. You're to have a chance at helping me with this affair, the superintendent says. Now we'll see whether passing examinations will make a Yard man or not."

There was a faintly concealed bitterness in the older man's voice, for John Secker, along with a dozen other very young and well-bred men, had come into the Yard under

46

the new policy of Lord Duggat, the recently appointed commissioner. He had served his six months' uniform service as a Bobby, passed detective examinations with flying colors, and now rated the sergeant's stripes that Cannon himself had earned only after six years of intense struggle. Cannon secretly considered the introduction of "kid-glove 'tecs" as an effort on the part of the government to find a place for the younger sons to whom the colonies, the army, and the merchant marine were no longer open. He was doubly suspicious of Secker because the young man had admittedly been to Cambridge. He had been sent down, but still he had been there.

"Right-ho," said John Secker. His voice was extremely casual, but he moved with alacrity.

"We may as well make an attempt to find out where the johnny got his poison," Cannon volunteered as he led the way down the corridor.

"You don't think he brought it with him from the States, then?"

Cannon mellowed a bit. It pleased him to have such an excellent opportunity of demonstrating his flair for sarcasm. "Not," he said, "unless Peter Noel knew beforehand that on this voyage he would meet a girl who would move heaven and earth, as her roommate says she did, to make him marry her just because he compromised her in the blanket locker."

Sergeant Secker said nothing. Cannon went on. "We can bank on it that Noel provided himself with the cyanide—which is what the police surgeon is sure was used, from the smell—in order to be able to cheat the hangman in case he was nabbed. It struck me that just possibly the ship's doctor——"

They were descending the main staircase, near the open door of the pantry whence issued delectable smells of coffee. The chief inspector stopped before a door marked "Doctor's Office" and hammered with his fist.

There was no answer. He knocked again, and finally tried the knob and found that the door swung inward.

"Anyone here?"

There was a sleepy answer from the cabin beyond, and finally an inner door opened, and Dr. Waite's bald head appeared, his eyes red-rimmed. He was clutching a flannel robe around his mauve pajamas.

"We'll have a look at your medicine cabinet," he was told. The chief inspector walked over to the cabinet which loomed between the two portholes and opened the glass door. A triple rack of neatly labelled bottles faced him.

The cryptic symbols meant nothing to Cannon. "Make a note to discover if Noel had any knowledge of pharmacy or chemistry," he ordered. The sergeant was already writing busily.

Dr. Waite's teeth chattered audibly behind them. "Where's your cyanide?" Cannon demanded.

Dr. Waite wanted to know which cyanide. "Cyanide of potassium, I suppose," Cannon told him testily. The doctor pointed to a slender bottle near the end of the second shelf. The chief inspector took it gently in his thick pink fingers. It was full to the brim.

Waite was apologizing. "You don't think that I—that this was—naturally, we keep a complete pharmacopœia on board, but——"

The chief inspector took the bottle, removed the glass stopper, and sniffed gingerly. "You are prepared to swear this stuff is potassium cyanide?"

Dr. Waite pointed to the neat symbols, "KCN," and grinned feebly. "If you're in doubt, you might taste it."

His mouth dropped when he saw Cannon wet his finger and touch a bit of the dull white powder to his lips. "Look out, man!" The sergeant kept his look of mild interest.

Cannon smiled and handed back the bottle. "Epsom salts," he decided.

Waite, horror-struck, sniffed. Then, very amazed, he tasted. It was all too true.

He reached for a lower shelf and brought up a much larger bottle bearing a characteristic label. It was about half full. "You mean, somebody stole the cyanide and filled up the bottle with this?"

The chief inspector was busily writing in his own note-book. He nodded wearily. "Are you in the custom of leaving this place unlocked?" he demanded.

Waite shook his head. "I must have been a bit flustered," he admitted. "What with everything that happened last evening. Usually I——"

"Not always?"

"Always I keep it locked," insisted Dr. Waite without conviction.

Cannon nodded. "All the same, Peter Noel got in here somehow and stole enough poison to kill everybody on shipboard. Was he in here, to your knowledge, within the last few days?"

"Since the death of the Fraser girl?" added Sergeant Secker softly.

Dr. Waite denied this. Then he added to his testimony. "The only time Noel was in my office was for a little while on the night that the Fraser girl went overboard," he declared. "Four or five of us were shooting craps in here. . . ."

"Craps?" inquired the chief inspector doubtfully.

"A dice game popularized by the American negro," the sergeant informed him.

"Gambling, eh?" Cannon seemed satisfied. "Well, that's it. Noel took advantage of your interest in the throw of the dice and stole the poison, substituting the nearest thing he could lay his hands on so that the cyanide would not be missed. Thank you, doctor."

But Doctor Waite was not satisfied. "Why, he couldn't have done that without my seeing him. . . ."

"May I ask a question?" said the sergeant. "Doctor, was Noel in your office before or after the hue and cry resulting from the Fraser girl's going overboard?"

Dr. Waite was positive. "Before," he insisted.

The sergeant looked at Cannon. "Then he couldn't have taken it then, sir, unless, as you say, he knew beforehand . . ."

The chief inspector grunted. "Or," added the younger man, "unless he stole it, not for himself, but to use in getting rid of the girl. And then changed his mind."

They went out of the surgery, leaving Dr. Waite shivering alone. He rubbed his shiny poll thoughtfully and then went over to his desk. A prescription of three fingers of brandy was indicated, he decided. From the top drawer he took a tall bottle and poured his much needed drink into a glass.

As he raised the glass to his lips, the outer door of the surgery was thrown suddenly open, and the pale thoughtful face of Sergeant John Secker appeared—so suddenly that the startled medico let glass and all go crashing to the floor.

"Sorry," said the sergeant. "But the chief said to tell you that the inquest will be tomorrow afternoon, and your presence is requested. In fact," the young man added as an afterthought, "your presence is jolly well demanded." The door closed.

Dr. Waite had planned upon utilizing his precious four days in London otherwise—a plan which included several bottles of brandy and a not-too-married lady who lived in Maida Vale. A thwarted and unhappy man, he put the bottle away and went disconsolately to his bunk.

Out on the promenade deck Chief Inspector Cannon was pacing back and forth, his heavy tread unmuffled for the benefit of any of the passengers who might be sleeping. Sergeant Secker paced beside him.

It was full morning now, and the river was coming alive. A string of coal barges went past, with a small dingy dog barking vigorously from the roof of a shanty. A rusty red freighter bearing the name *Inchcliffe Castle* steamed seaward, bound out on the tide for Africa, and a madly sculling fat man went upstream on a high-pooped dory which looked like a floating leaf. On either shore the city was arousing itself, but Chief Inspector Cannon did not pause to admire the scene.

Rapidly he ran over the case, as he knew it, more to refresh his own point of view than from hope of getting any help out of the young man who trotted along beside him.

"That's the story," Cannon finished. "Noel was sick to death of the girl. She was pleading with him, maybe threatening him, to marry her. He threw her overboard and then funked out."

"But you say the school teacher person was certain that the Fraser girl was alone at the rail? How could Noel throw her overboard when both exits from that stretch of the deck were covered—one by the drowsing school teacher and the other by the roommate who was coming in search of Rosemary?"

The chief inspector considered this an intelligent question and stopped at the rail to ponder it.

"Suppose she was leaning over the boat-deck rail, and Noel was up in the rigging somewhere? If he'd thrown something and hit her, she'd have gone right over, headfirst. . . ."

Cannon stopped and shook his head. "Too easy," he said. "He wouldn't have chanced a miss."

He looked up. "She must have been standing at the rail right over our heads," he observed. "It was somewhere amidships, anyway. This lower deck, we've found out, was deserted. Suppose Noel had been standing here and had reached up with a boat hook or something, and pulled her down?"

Sergeant Secker ventured to suggest that he had never seen a boat hook used on an ocean liner—not even on a half-pint vessel like the *American Diplomat*.

Cannon was forced to admit the justice of that. "Or even a walking stick," he went on. The rail of the boat deck was only a few feet above their heads.

"It would be easy if she'd worn a long scarf . . ." began the sergeant. He stopped short and nearly fell overboard as an acidulous voice cut in from a point seemingly just behind his ear.

"Rosemary Fraser *did* wear a long scarf!"

Both men whirled to see the New England face of a lean New England spinster, which had materialized miraculously almost between them. Miss Hildegarde Withers, her hair neatly braided, was leaning from her porthole.

"Don't look so indignant," she said. "If you're going to shout at each other outside my window all morning, you can't blame me for butting in."

"My dear madame——" barked the chief inspector.

But Sergeant Secker clung to one idea. "You say that Rosemary Fraser wore a scarf?"

"It was as characteristic of her as the coat she affected," said Hildegarde Withers. "All through the voyage she wore a gray squirrel coat and a long, dangling scarf, dark blue. When I saw her at the rail, she had no coat, but she was wearing the scarf."

"There you are," said Sergeant Secker to his chief.

Cannon was not sure just where he was. The young man plunged merrily on. "Noel had seen the scarf, hadn't he? He was carrying a dose of poison which he had stolen from the doctor earlier in the evening, wasn't he? Well, as he stood at the rail down here, wondering how he was going to get a chance to administer the cyanide, he saw the blue scarf dangling. On an impulse, he yanked at it—and Rosemary Fraser plunged past him—down into the water."

The chief inspector chewed this for a while, and Miss Withers very nearly clapped her hands in applause. Yet she realized immediately that some tiny detail, half remembered from the night when Rosemary Fraser disappeared, stubbornly refused to be fitted into the sergeant's ingenious explanation. It was temporarily lost in the bottom of her mind, and there was nothing she could do about it until she could remember just what it was. Something to do with the deck and the wind and the night—and the wind——

Chief Inspector Cannon, to do him credit, was not hesitant in his recognition of good work. He smote his assistant so heavily upon the shoulder that the young man winced a little. "Now tha's talking, lad!" He stopped suddenly and snapped his thick fingers. "It's my turn now." Forgetting that Miss Withers still formed an uninvited member of the party, Cannon went loudly on: "All along one thing has been bothering me—the splash!"

"What splash?" interrupted Hildegarde Withers from her porthole. "There wasn't any."

"Right you are! That's what bothered me. But I should have remembered a case that came up three or four years ago. Murders aboard the *Countess of Teal*—which was a dirty little tramp steamer anchored off Gravesend. Look it up in the files sometime, sergeant."

Secker interposed to say that he had read through the old files. "Captain and mate went overboard while the ship was at anchor, and the bosun swung for it, didn't he?"

"Right! Two men went overboard without a splash, because the bloody Lascar bosun strangled them and then lowered them gently into the water. Let go the rope—and that was that. Well, now you see how this Noel fellow got the girl into the sea without anybody's hearing a splash."

Sergeant Secker looked over the rail and down at the water, twenty feet or so below. "How long is a scarf, anyway?" he inquired.

That reminded Miss Withers of the ancient conundrum, "How long is a piece of string?" But she hurriedly withdrew from the porthole and tore open her battered suitcase. She threw almost everything she owned out upon her berth and came finally to the object for which she was searching. She thrust it out of the porthole.

"I'll loan you this old scarf of mine," she cried. "It's nearly as long as the one that Rosemary Fraser wore. One of you put it on and stand at the rail of the upper deck——"

Chief Inspector Cannon was not in the habit of receiving assistance from middle-aged school teachers, or for that matter from any of the general public. But this was an unusual situation. He accepted the purple wisp of silk and rubbed it in his fingers.

Then he handed it to Secker. "Tie it around your neck, sergeant," he ordered. "Then go topside and see if I can catch hold of it."

"Oh, I say," protested the young man. "What if anyone sees me? That—that's a loathsome color to go with my jacket. . . ."

"Wait a moment," gasped Miss Withers. "Let *me* wear it. . . ."

But it took her a considerable interval to change her dressing gown for a suit and hat. When she finally rushed out on deck it was only to see Chief Inspector Cannon standing at the rail, and stretching frantically in an attempt to grasp a wisp of purple silk which hung just out of reach.

"If you stood on the rail you could make it," she suggested. Cannon grunted inhospitably, but he followed her advice. He caught the end of the trailing scarf and gave a mighty tug.

Looking up, Miss Withers could see white hands grasping the boat-deck rail and a glimpse of the sergeant's face.

"Sing out if you feel that!" boomed Cannon, and tugged again. The sergeant did not sing out. Miss Withers craned her neck and saw that his face was of an extremely odd color. And he was leaning very far over the rail.

She was no respector of persons. The Yard official felt himself shoved aside, and a sharp command was snapped in his ear. "Let go, you fool!"

The chief inspector let go, but before he could give vent to the displeasure that filled his heart, he saw Hildegarde Withers running along the deck. "Hey!" he shouted, but nobody answered him.

He mounted to the boat deck as rapidly as he could and found the meddlesome school teacher kneeling beside the prone figure of a young man, who still kept his tense, desperate fingers clenched around the rail. Miss Withers was tearing at his throat, and as Cannon uncomprehendingly approached, the noose of silk came away.

Sergeant John Secker let go the rail and began to breathe again, shudderingly. Finally he could speak.

"A bit close, that," he said.

"Why didn't you sing out?" demanded Cannon.

"Why? Why didn't I sing out? With a blasted, bloody, bedamned snare around my throat? It was all I could do to keep from being thrown overboard, that's why."

"Oh," said the chief inspector.

"And now," Hildegarde Withers told him very sweetly, "*now* perhaps we know why Rosemary Fraser didn't scream."

There was something of a pause, after which Cannon picked up the purple scarf and handed it back to its owner.

"Much obliged to you, madam," he announced stiffly.

Sergeant John Secker smiled rather feebly. "I'm more than obliged," he said. "Thanks awfully." He dusted himself off very carefully. "Cheerio."

They moved away and left her there. "But——" began Hildegarde Withers. She followed quickly after them. "Can't I be of any further assistance? I've had a certain amount of experience at this sort of thing back in the States. . . ."

Chief Inspector Cannon was in a very bad mood. He felt that he had placed himself in an exceedingly unfortunate position. After all, if the young fool hadn't known any better than to tie the scarf in an ordinary slip-knot . . .

"This isn't the States," he said shortly. Then, to temper his gruffness: "You see, this completes our case. The rest is purely official."

"Oh," said Hildegarde Withers.

She watched them go forward, to where Captain Everett was issuing from his cabin, and heard the officer somewhat indignantly inquiring as to when he could put his passengers ashore.

"Sooner the better," she heard Chief Inspector Cannon say. And then she hurried aft and went down the ladder to the lower deck. She rushed rapidly toward her own cabin, but as she turned into the short passageway she saw that it was blocked by the well-starched back of Mrs. Snoaks, the stewardess. She was in hot argument with the Honorable Emily.

"I'll do it and keep me mouth shut," the woman was saying. "But two quid isn't enough, what with all the police hanging about. If your ladyship will make it four . . ."

"Done!" came the voice of the Honorable Emily. There was the snap of a handbag, and then the stewardess brushed past Miss Withers with four unmistakable pound treasury notes disappearing into her capacious bosom.

The Honorable Emily, still in the doorway, smiled at Miss Withers calmly. "The lower classes are becoming worse and worse every day," she observed. "Rank socialism, that's what it is."

She closed the door behind her, and the school teacher stared at it for a moment. Her brow was contorted with a frown. Was there an Ethiop concealed in the kindling? Certainly the Honorable Emily was the last person on board to be involved in anything which the police on board must not know—or was she? Was anybody, for that matter? By which you may rightly gather that Miss Hildegarde Withers was not inclined to agree with the inspector that the case had been completed.

While she repacked her clothing she attempted without success to imagine what had been the meaning of the interview which she had unwittingly overheard. Suddenly Hildegarde Withers kicked aside her suitcase and stood upright. "The simplest way to find out would be to ask!" she determined.

She moved toward the door, but at that moment there came a resounding knock. She opened it, and in came the Honorable Emily, monocle and all.

"I heard you talking with the detectives outside," said that tweedy lady. "I don't suppose they enlightened you as to the possibilities of our getting ashore sometime today?"

"As a matter of fact they did." Miss Withers sought for an opening. "We're to go ashore as soon as they can put the vessel in the dock. But, by the way, I would give anything in the world to know just——"

"We must have a good chat about it," the Honorable Emily broke in. "Come and have tea with me this afternoon at the Alexandria. Good hotel, that. I can't wait to drop into a good soaking hot bath instead of these lukewarm salt-water atrocities that they've given us aboard." She stopped short. "My word! The vessel is moving—I must finish my packing and get Tobermory and the bird ready to go ashore." She was gone.

There was the painful clatter of an upped anchor forward, and then the dingy waterfront of East London began to slide by again. Miss Withers, temporarily thwarted, resumed her packing. By the time she had finished, the little *American Diplomat* had miraculously eased herself through the bottle-neck of George V dock and was securely moored in her slip.

Miss Withers suddenly realized that she had forgotten to change her American money into pounds and shillings and rushed down to the purser's office. "Just enough for taxi fare," she implored.

Leslie Reverson, Candida Noring, and Andy Todd were ahead of her. Reverson was folding a small sheaf of treasury notes into his wallet. He left off bewailing the current exchange to answer a question of Todd's.

"Always go to the Alexandria," he announced. "Not too dear, and practically a skip and a jump to everything in London."

Andy Todd wanted to know if the Alexandria was near Buckingham Palace and the museums. "'Pon my word, I don't know," said Reverson. "I've never been to any of them. But it's a step from the Strand."

A steward broke in on the conclave to announce that everyone was wanted in the social hall to pass the immigration quiz. Miss Withers waited patiently for half an hour, and then swore faithfully before two weary young men in uniform that she was visiting England only for pleasure, that she was not a Communist, and that she had no intentions of seeking employment within the Realm. Her passport was stamped, and then, as she rose to go, a man in the uniform of a police constable halted her. He produced his notebook.

"You'll be wanted at the inquest upon the death of Peter Noel," he announced. "Your address in London, please."

"Address? But I haven't an address."

"You'll have to have an address," said the constable. "Everyone must have an address."

"Oh—Hotel Alexandria," said the school teacher impulsively. She watched him write down her full name— *"Hildegarde Martha Withers"*—and the name of the hotel. There were other names upon his list, but she was not adept enough at reading upside down to decipher the handwriting.

Then she was suffered to leave the social hall, which had such unpleasant associations for her. As she watched her baggage being hurtled down the corridor by white-clad stewards, she saw Candida Noring coming toward her. The girl's face was wan.

"Something has happened!" said Hildegarde Withers to herself. She had known that they would not leave this ship without another untoward event. Then she caught the distraught girl by the arm.

"Whatever is the matter, child?"

"Matter?" Candida was shaking. "Everything is the matter. I'm so frightened!"

"Frightened of what, pray?"

"If you want to know, I'm frightened of everything and everybody. I'm frightened of you and all the rest!" Miss Withers shook her head and then pressed the icy palm.

"It's been hard on you, but it's all over now."

Candida caught her breath. "But it isn't over! I don't care what the police say. Rosemary was *murdered*—and the murderer isn't through yet. And—and there's somebody in my stateroom."

"What?" Miss Withers almost laughed. "Why, child, of course. The stewards are putting the baggage out on deck. We go through the Customs in a moment."

"My baggage was out on deck two hours ago and the police took Rosemary's away," said Candida insistently. "Just now I came to my door and found it ajar. I stopped, and inside I heard a soft rustling and then a little crash. And I ran. . . ."

"We'll soon settle that," declared the school teacher. She led the way fearlessly to the stateroom door and thrust it open. No one had had a chance to leave while they stood outside—but the little cabin was empty.

Miss Withers looked under the berth and into the high wardrobe. She found nothing more significant than an

57

empty packet that once had held brown-paper cigarettes and two clothes hangers.

"You see?" she announced. "It's all your imagination."

At that moment an unhuman, whiskered face projected itself from the top of the wardrobe, and Miss Withers leaped back almost into Candida's arms.

"Mowr!" said Tobermory. His back was arched, and every silvery hair stood out on end. "Mowr!" he repeated, and then spat fearfully at the two startled women.

Miss Withers caught him by the scruff of the neck and lifted him gently down. Out in the hall she saw the buxom figure of the stewardess and delivered him into her care.

The school teacher turned to Candida Noring. "Come on, let's face the Customs together," she invited. "Have you decided about a hotel yet?"

Candida hesitated. "We—Rosemary and I—had reservations for two rooms at the Alexandria. But now that she's—she's gone——"

"Nonsense. Come along. Perhaps we can share a taxi, I'm going there myself." They hurried aft to find that a gangway had been let down and that most of the ship's passengers were already on the dock. Ahead of them Dr. Waite hurried, a smile of anticipation lighting his face. In his hand was a small kitbag. On the dock Andy Todd was taking a snapshot of the vessel he had just left.

"Good-bye, *American Diplomat!*" said Miss Withers with heartfelt relief. Candida Noring did not bid the staunch little vessel any good-byes, but she ran down the gangplank as if all the devils of hell were after her.

CHAPTER V

*

The Letter Edged in Black

Amazed and considerably ruffled, Miss Hildegarde Withers emerged from the Customs shed. Her modest baggage, which was now being wheeled after her in a creaking barrow, had been torn to pieces and scrutinized as if she had been suspected of being nobody less than Mamie the Queen of the Dope Smugglers. Long as the ordeal had taken, she was among the first of the passengers to have the blue chalk X marked on her bags.

She had hoped to share a taxi with Candida Noring, but this wet bleak doorway was no place for waiting, so she gave up the idea and hailed the nearest Jehu. She had her first glimpses of London Town through the murky windows of a vehicle which looked as if it might have carried Gladstone or Disraeli. They meandered through the East End, usually hemmed in by a slow dray or lorry. Miss Withers afterwards had confused recollections of countless bicyclists, midget automobiles, and of dray horses with sleek fat sides and many whiskers around their hooves.

After some hours the taxi swooped down upon Trafalgar Square, which Miss Withers haply recognized by the towering shaft in the center. She gave the English credit for a grim sort of humor in placing atop such a giddy pinnacle the statue of the famous admiral who, if history is to be believed, could not stand at his own masthead without intense weakness of stomach.

The taxi continued for half a block, and drew up before a vast stone mausoleum which was the Hotel Alexandria.

A dignified personage wearing handle-bar mustaches and three row of medals across his chest approached to greet her, carrying an umbrella, although it had ceased to rain. Lesser persons seized her baggage, and she was ushered

59

into a foyer almost as large as Madison Square Garden. The place was filled with marble pillars, deep-piled rugs of a bright carmine hue, many shining-topped tables and red-plush lounging chairs. Miss Withers was able to make out, after a time, that four or five human beings were lurking in the vastness, dropping cigarette ash upon the tops of the shiny tables or sipping from tiny glittering glasses.

On her right was an open doorway displaying a desk and the familiar pigeonholes of mail cubicles. Miss Withers entered, in a properly hushed manner, and heard the clear voice of Candida Noring, who had evidently drawn a more modern taxi than her own.

"But I *did* have a reservation!"

The two clerks conferred and then brightened. "Oh, yes! Two adjoining rooms with bawth for Miss Fraser and Miss Noring. Guinea and a half per day without breakfast."

Candida wrote her name on the card presented to her. Another was placed before Miss Withers. "And this is Miss Fraser, I presume?"

There was one of those silences, during which a white-faced Candida whirled to notice who stood beside her. Miss Withers nodded to her casually and wrote her own name in flowing script. "I am not," she told the clerk. "Something a little less expensive," she added. The clerk understood. There was a very nice room on the same floor with the two young ladies for eighteen shillings.

"Then Miss Fraser will be along a bit later?" he inquired politely. Candida turned away.

Miss Withers, who had a distinct feeling of chill along her spine, shook her head. "I'm afraid not," she informed the clerk.

Both women were entrusted to the guidance of a page boy who looked as if he had been manufactured to fit one of the more compact British automobiles, and were led across the foyer and down an interminable hall. They passed a pair of scrolled elevator doors marked "Lift Out of Order," but finally found an open door and were wheezed upward by fits and starts to the fifth floor. Candida was deposited in a surprisingly cheerful room in which a coal grate was merrily blazing. "I'll see you later?" Candida asked hopefully as if afraid of being left alone.

Miss Withers smiled and nodded, and was led onward to a door almost at the end of the hall. Her room was a little smaller than Candida's, and its window looked out on a brick wall instead of on the street. A mammoth mahogany wardrobe loomed beside the high brass bed, and the mirror of a dressing table mercifully shut off most of the window and its view of red brick. Here also was an open fireplace, but in it was only a lonesome festoon of red crêpe paper.

While Miss Withers was depositing a silver sixpence in the hand of the page boy, a porter appeared with a cartful of baggage. Then she was left alone. Hastily she began to unpack, pulling off her well-worn blue serge suit with the intention of slipping into something a bit gayer. She was interrupted by a faint knock on the door. Before she could answer, two maids marched in bearing scuttles and pails. Entirely ignoring her startled dishabille, they proceeded noisily and quickly to fill the room with smoke and coal dust. Then they departed.

Miss Withers found that the massive door between her room and the corridor had a keyhole but no key. She looked for a telephone, found none, and then discovered a bell push at the head of the high bed.

As soon as the uniformed man arrived, she ordered him to procure for her a key, at once.

He looked at her unhappily. Then he shook his head. "There's no need to lock your door in this hotel, mum. We never gives keys to the guests, because the maids don't like to find the doors locked. Makes trouble for them about their work, mum." He departed.

"The *maids* don't like it!" repeated Hildegarde Withers blankly. After the chamber of horrors aboard ship, this sudden plunge into Gilbert and Sullivan was a little too much for her. She sank down into an enfolding and comfortable armchair beside the rousing fire and laughed until she cried. "All that's left to come is a warming pan," she told herself feebly.

She got up again and attacked the remainder of her baggage. There was one small black bag too many. Since it bore the initials "C-N" it must be Candida's.

Miss Withers put on her coat and hat, resolving to drop the bag at the girl's room on her way out to take her first independent view of the city. She knocked on the door of

61

Candida Noring's room—Number 505—and received no answer. Knocking again, she pushed the door open and entered.

Candida was sitting at the dressing table, her head buried in her arms. "Heavens, child!" cried the school teacher. "Is anything wrong?"

The girl looked up and motioned toward a pile of mail which lay around her. "They just sent it up," she said falteringly.

Miss Withers understood. "Of course. Cablegrams from Rosemary's people, no doubt. You must be frightfully upset."

But Candida Noring shook her head. "Oh, it isn't that!" she said haltingly. She extended a black-bordered envelope, torn across one side. Miss Withers saw that it bore simply the name, "Miss C. Noring" written in round, vague letters, and that no stamp was affixed.

"This," explained Candida, "was in the box with the rest. The man said he didn't know how it came, but he thought it was by messenger. Read it—and then tell me I'm going mad."

Miss Withers took the single sheet of notepaper from the envelope and gasped.

She was staring at a message which, after the fashion customary among our grandmothers for funeral announcements, had been bordered with black—black which in this case covered all of the sheet except for a space in the center in which had been pasted an irregular-shaped scrap of cream-colored paper—paper with a faint blue line running through it.

Across that cream-colored scrap, in handwriting not too familiar to the keen eyes of Miss Withers, ran as follows: "*I hate you, and I shall go on hating you after I am dead and after you are dead. . . .*" That was all.

The school teacher sniffed and handed the thing back. "A very bad joke," she said. She tried to keep her voice from being doubtful.

Candida Noring was uncomforted. "You see," she explained, "that's Rosemary's writing. . . ." Her voice died away into a whisper.

"Who do you think sent it?" Miss Withers inquired casually.

Candida shook her head. "I don't know! I don't believe in ghosts, do you?"

Miss Withers did not, particularly in ghosts that stooped to use notepaper and cheap theatricalism in their messages. "More likely," she decided, "this is another offering on the part of the practical joker in our midst. Why don't you confront Mr. Andy Todd with that letter?"

"What good would that do?" almost wailed Candida. She drew away, and on an impulse turned and cast letter and envelope into the blazing grate behind her. "There's been too much trouble and unhappiness already. That's where anonymous letters belong!"

"In most cases," said Miss Withers with a faint sniff, "I should be inclined to agree with you. But right now I should like very much to know who was responsible for sending you that cruel and nasty note."

"He would only have denied it," said Candida.

"True enough. But Andy Todd is not as deep as a well—nor as wide as a church door, for that matter. It seems to me that a clever young woman could find out, in an hour's conversation, the truth—if he should happen to know it. My advice to you, young woman, is to try trapping flies with honey instead of vinegar." Miss Withers showed her interest a little too plainly.

Candida looked dubious and thoughtful. Then suddenly her eyes narrowed. "You think there's something more in this than a practical joke! Then—then you don't believe, as the police do, that Noel was the one who killed Rosemary, and that his suicide was a confession. You think that someone . . ."

"I haven't come to the thinking part yet," said Hildegarde Withers. "I'm simply wondering."

The two women stared at each other for a little while. Candida broke the silence: "I'm wondering too."

Miss Withers nodded. "And now, if you'll excuse my interfering, I suggest that you comb your hair and slip on your prettiest dress and come down and have late luncheon or early tea or whatever it is. I'll meet you in the lobby—I have an errand to do first."

Candida hesitated, but Miss Withers was firm. After winning a reluctant nod from the distraite young woman, the school teacher marched out into the hall. Oddly enough, her errand took her to the desk downstairs in the lobby, and then to a room at the end of the third-floor hall.

She knocked, receiving no answer, and then knocked again. She was just about to try the knob when a cheerful voice sounded behind her.

"Hello there!"

It was Andy Todd himself, wrapped in a heavy flannel bathrobe and with his hair plastered over his eyes. In one hand he bore a towel, and in the other a large bar of hotel soap.

"Just having a bit of a soak," Todd continued, giving Miss Withers a chance to compose herself. "Er—won't you come in and have a drink or something?"

He was fairly oozing friendliness. Miss Withers saw him holding the door invitingly open. Inside she saw three bottles of Scotch on the bureau, one open.

"I just came down to ask you," she improvised, "if you've received one of the anonymous letters that are going the rounds."

Andy Todd was either amazed or a better actor than Miss Withers had thought him. "What? Why—is the mystery of the *American Diplomat* still running wild? I thought it was all quiet now. No—I haven't got any letters, anonymous or otherwise."

"Thank you," Miss Withers told him, preparing to back out of the door. "Sorry to have disturbed you."

"Not at all." Todd brightened. "Say—that Reverson chap and his S.P.C.A. aunt have rooms down the hall. You might try them."

"I might," said Miss Withers. But she stared very intently past the looming young athlete. Beside the bottles of whisky on his bureau was a little heap of letters.

Todd turned and saw them. "Say! They must have just been brought up, while I was across the hall in the tub. Didn't expect any yet—but of course, the *Bremen* and the *Île de France* did pass us on the way over. . . ."

"I think you have one letter that didn't come to London by fast mail," Miss Withers advised him. She passed out into the hall again, leaving Andy Todd holding in his large wet hands a white envelope. It bore only his name, in a vague round handwriting—and it was bordered with a neatly inked black band.

"How in blazes did that get here?" Andy Todd inquired very loudly. Miss Withers heard his tenor through the door, which she had softly closed behind her. But she did not see another emotion replace the look of friendliness on his face.

Miss Withers plodded down the long hall, past the elevator doors with their "Out of Order" placard, and finally descended to the ground floor, where she made the long trek back down the hall and found Candida Noring waiting for her in the foyer.

At least, it looked like Candida Noring. Except that this vision wore a neat and very feminine fur-trimmed suit, and even a splash of red across the lips. The long ordeal that Candida had gone through was no doubt responsible for the becoming thinness of her cheeks, and the added shadows above her eyes. "Rosemary cast her into the shade," Miss Withers told herself. "But now she's opening up her petals a bit. It's an ill wind . . ."

The two women had hardly greeted one another before they were interrupted by a cultured, eager voice. "I say!"

Behind them was Leslie Reverson, beautifully attired in a soft heather lounge suit. "Thought it was you!"

He almost stared at Candida. "Hello," she said coolly. "This seems like Homecoming at college."

"What? Right-oh. But I thought—I mean to say, there's a ripping American cocktail bar here. Won't you pop in and have one, as old shipmates together and all that rot?" He smiled at Miss Withers. "You too, of course."

"I'm sorry——" began that lady. She made an abrupt *volte face*. "Thank you, we will," she told the young man. "If I can get an orangeade."

It was after hours, but as guests of the hotel the barman could serve them, even to a tall orangeade, for which Leslie Reverson paid—or signed for—the sum of two shillings and six.

Candida downed a Martini. "Have another, do," urged Leslie, delighted at playing host. "It goes on my aunt the Honorable Emily's bill, y'know. Dear lady, she's upstairs luxuriatin' in a hot tub, and reading all the back numbers of the *Times* since we left England."

Miss Withers sipped her orangeade and made a polite inquiry as to the health of Tobermory and the bird.

"Toby's not here yet," Reverson chatted on. "But the robin's not doing so badly. Aunt's named him Dicon, after King Henry the Eighth or somebody——"

"Wasn't it Richard?" Miss Withers interposed.

"Right you are. Anyway, he's hopping around in his new cage in grand style, though he won't sing."

Candida suggested that robins or other wild birds rarely were songsters in captivity, and the conversation languished. The three of them received freshly filled glasses from the obliging barman and sank into tremendous leather chairs around a richly carved table with a somewhat unstable top.

"I feel very wicked and ribald," observed Miss Withers, taking a deep pull at her orangeade. "So this is London!"

The girl beside her shared a smiling look with Leslie Reverson. If the two of them had known the mind of the eccentric spinster they might not have smiled so easily.

"Oh, there's that Todd fellow," said Leslie after a moment. Andy Todd was coming down the hall. He paused in the doorway of the American Bar, half nodded at the three of them, and fumbled with his cigarette case.

"Why don't you ask him to join us?" suggested Miss Withers mischievously. Reverson brightened, being slightly warm with two gin-and-its.

"Of course," he said quickly, "if Miss Noring doesn't mind."

"Call me Candy," said Miss Noring evenly. "Why should I mind? I'd like it."

So it was that a rather ill-at-ease Andy Todd made a fourth in the party, knocking over the table and Miss Withers' orangeade as he sat down. He ordered a rye and sat brooding over it.

"Staying in London long?" asked Candida brightly.

Todd for the first time noticed that there had been something of a transformation in one who had been on shipboard just another girl. After all, Candida Noring's features were more even than Rosemary's, though a bit less piquant. And this was a becoming suit that she wore.

"I'm afraid a couple of days—I hope," he garbled. "I'm supposed to be up at Oxford now, but the police told me not to leave London until after the inquest. Sorry, I didn't mean to mention——" Candida's pale face became a little paler.

"Never mind, we're all in the same boat," Miss Withers comforted the Rhodes scholar.

The barman collected the glasses somewhat ostentatiously, and Reverson overruled Todd and ordered another round.

"As long as these are going on my bill," said a pleasant, brisk voice behind him, "suppose that you count me in?"

The Honorable Emily was herself again, after an hour in the tub. She only needed one thing to make her perfectly contented, and that was due to happen soon. She polished her eyeglass vigorously.

Outside the twilight deepened, and the roar of traffic on Trafalgar Square increased. Miss Withers realized how typically American she was in seeing London through the bottom of a cocktail glass.

The Honorable Emily, amiably conscious that she was in the presence of three strangers to the city that she considered almost her own property, became at once a combined guidebook and char-a-banc lecturer. "You simply must see the changing of the guard tomorrow morning," she said. "And tonight—you ought to have your first view of London night life at the right place. Not a night club or a variety show."

Leslie Reverson nodded. "Dinner at Lyons Corner House and an educational cinema," he whispered to Candida. He had had bitter experience of his aunt's ideas of a gay London evening.

"After all, there's no place like London," the Honorable Emily continued.

"Then why do you always insist on dragging me back to Cornwall?" demanded Leslie. "If it wasn't for this bloody inquest . . ."

Miss Withers sat watching them, filled with a premonition that fate had brought them all together with some definite purpose in view. She saw Andy Todd, ill at ease and trying to cover it with too many ryes. She saw Leslie Reverson, for the first time making a definite protest at his aunt's calm management of his life, and waxing bolder and bolder under the calm gaze of Candida. It was the girl, rather than Reverson's drinks, who was making him become somehow older, more a man than a boy.

Miss Withers purposely engaged the Honorable Emily in a discussion of the relative merits of the Victoria and Albert and the British museums. The three younger persons drew a little apart.

"Say," began Andy Todd, in his high tenor voice. But as Candida turned toward him, Reverson spoke quickly in her ear.

"Wouldn't you let me take you to the Trocadero or somewhere this evening?"

"That's what I was going to say!" Andy Todd objected. The two young men glared at each other.

There never was a woman who disliked such a scene. Candida by this time had quite lost her hunted look. She smiled happily. "Then why don't you both take me?"

"Say——" began Todd again. "That's not so good."

"I've got a better one than that," said Reverson. "Let's leave it to chance." He produced an American quarter from his pocket. "Heads you have the honor, and tails Miss Noring——"

"Candy, please," said Candida.

"And if it's tails, Candy goes with me. Bargain?"

"Sure," said Todd. Reverson sent the coin spinning in the air and caught it neatly on his wrist. He showed it, in obvious triumph, to them both. "Tails!"

Andy Todd looked like a small boy who has been told that he may not go to the circus. "But I wanted to talk to you," he began to protest to Candida. "I wanted to explain about what happened on the boat. . . ."

Miss Withers was staring over the Honorable Emily's shoulder and was surprised to see Candida, with a motherly tact which the school teacher had never imagined she possessed, lean towards Todd and touch his lapel. There were understanding and forgiveness in that touch, and in the smile with which she whispered something in his ear that made Andy Todd brighten. He had instantly regained, Miss Withers thought, his air of having swallowed the canary. Buoyed up by some inner secret, he mumbled a farewell to them all and swaggered down the hall.

"Nasty bounder," was the murmured verdict of the Honorable Emily.

"If I'm going out to dinner with you I shall have to get a gown pressed," Candida told Leslie. "I'll rush and dress, and meet you here in an hour."

The others rose also, and Reverson gave the barman what he thought was a shilling. Miss Withers, who was last to go, saw the man scrutinize it and grin. Leslie took it back, replacing it with another coin, but not before the school teacher had noticed that the quarter dollar bore, surprisingly, the American eagle on both sides.

She nodded to herself. Evidently Leslie Reverson had seen something at the Chicago Fair besides the fan dancer and the Hall of Science.

He hurried on ahead to dress and left his aunt and Miss Withers to stroll together down the long red carpet of the hall. The Honorable Emily suddenly clutched Miss Withers' elbow.

"Wasn't there something you wanted to ask me on board ship?"

The school teacher, who had been trying to lead up to an opening during the last half hour, took the plunge.

"There was," she admitted. Then she felt like hedging. "Oh, I know it isn't any of my business. Don't mind me, I'm just a self-appointed busybody. But I'm not as satisfied as the police seem to be with the murder-suicide theory about those deaths on board. And I can't help wondering . . ."

"Quite right, too," said the Honorable Emily. She looked at her wrist watch. "Can you come up to my room for a few minutes? I might have something to show you."

They crossed the foyer and proceeded silently down the long hall, past the out of order elevators, and finally were lifted to the third floor. The Honorable Emily had a room facing the street, of the same general design as Candida's. Miss Withers took a chair near the blazing hearth, near where a bright new cage dangled containing the somewhat bedraggled form of the robin. Dicon showed no inclination to sing, and his manner showed very clearly that he still expected to be eaten at any moment.

"Poor Dicon-bird," said the Honorable Emily comfortingly. Then to her guest: "I had to smuggle him off the boat wrapped in a handkerchief in my pocket. We have a strict quarantine on incoming livestock, you see. . . ."

Miss Withers felt ill at ease. "I came up here to find out why you bribed the stewardess," she said softly.

Something flickered unpleasantly behind the monocle of the Englishwoman. Then she smiled, very warmly indeed.

69

"I was about to say——"

At that moment there came a knock on the door. The Honorable Emily answered it and admitted a solid person in a ratty fur coat, who turned out to be Mrs. Snoaks, stewardess of the *American Diplomat*. In one hand she bore a case of imitation leather. Miss Withers stared blankly at both stewardess and case. The woman set it down with a defiant "Here 'e is, the howling brute," and fled.

The Honorable Emily was on her knees, fumbling with the catch. The case opened, and Tobermory emerged as if shot from a gun. As his mistress tried to clasp him to her bosom he slashed in the general direction of her hand with a vicious uppercut, and leaped to the bed, from which vantage point he proceeded to stare fixedly at the caged bird. Tobermory was not a cat who easily forgot.

"You see?" said the Honorable Emily.

Miss Withers did not see.

"Tobermory is a home-loving cat," explained the Englishwoman. "He is dying to get back to my place in Cornwall, where he has a whole island to himself. He'd have died of boredom if I'd put him in quarantine for six months, as the law insists. He was too large to go in my coat pocket, so I paid the stewardess four quid to smuggle him off the ship for me. Members of the crew of a ship that docks here regularly every four weeks never have to worry over Customs."

Miss Withers made a note of that. She felt that she had made a fool of herself. "I see," she said. "Please understand that I didn't . . ."

"Of course not." The Honorable Emily was fairly purring now. "No offense meant, none taken, I always say. By the way, don't feel that you must rush off. I'm all alone tonight, since my nephew has taken it into his silly head to turn Lothario. Though I suppose it's only natural at his age. He's twenty, and I can't keep him in an Eton collar forever. But if you'd care to join me in dinner at the Corner House and a movie afterward?"

Miss Withers was still too conscious of the fact that she had made a mountain out of a molehill. She declined, pleading a headache, a previous engagement, letters to write, or some similar excuse, and edged toward the door. She glanced down at the leatherette case as she passed it, noticing the lining of newspapers and silver cat-hairs.

The Honorable Emily shoved the case beneath her bed. "Poor Toby does hate it so!" she said. Some inner amusement showed itself in her face. "Do drop in again if you have any more questions," she finished quite cordially.

Miss Withers was back in her own room again before it occurred to her that there very well might have been something besides newspaper and silver cat-hairs in the bottom of that imitation leather case. And then, of course, it was too late.

She had dinner brought to her room, and spent most of the evening in making meaningless little marks upon a sheet of notepaper. Once or twice she was very nearly at the point of sending a cablegram to her old friend Oscar Piper, inspector of the New York homicide squad, but she resolutely thought better of it.

At nine o'clock the maid entered, rattled at the fire, and turned back the bed. Miss Withers admitted, upon being pressed, that she would like to be called at ten o'clock in the morning.

The hotel, quiet enough at any hour, gradually took on the stillness of the grave as the few other guests retired. Yet Miss Withers could not bring herself to go to bed.

Somehow she felt in her bones that the events of the day had not been brought to a close. She left her door ajar, and shortly after eleven she heard voices in the hall. Peering out, she saw Candida Noring, chaste and resplendent in a white dinner gown, silhouetted against the dark of Leslie Reverson. Their soft laughter chimed in oddly with the trend of Miss Withers' thoughts, and she drew quickly back. But they did not notice her. After a moment she heard the door close, and peering forth again saw Reverson, walking very proudly erect, as he departed in the direction of the only working elevator.

Well, that was that. Miss Withers no longer had any excuse to spy on the corridor, though she would have given a good deal to know just how Andy Todd had spent his lonely evening.

Placing a chair against the door, she prepared to retire, a feeling of anticlimax still possessing her. She had a long search for her nightgown, which ended by her lucky discovery that it had been wrapped around a hot-water bottle and tucked in at the foot of her bed.

71

She turned out the light and tried to sleep, annoyed somewhat by the bright fire which, after an evening of sulking, had chosen this moment to blaze merrily, sending dancing shadows over walls and ceiling. The shadows took fearful shapes and pursued the nervous lady until she woke suddenly to hear a determined pounding upon her door, and to see feeble daylight trickling in between the heavy curtains.

She rose wearily and slipped on a bathrobe and slippers. Then she glanced at her watch and became very wroth. The knocking resumed.

She opened the door and spoke sternly to the maid. "I asked to be called at ten o'clock—not at seven-thirty!"

The maid's voice was oddly perturbed. "I know that, mum. But it's a gentleman from the police, mum."

Miss Withers looked out upon the bland young face of Sergeant John Secker, who looked unwontedly wide-awake and excited. "I'll dress in ten minutes," she promised, and closed the door firmly.

Clothed and in her right mind, she emerged with several minutes to spare. "Well!" she greeted the young detective. "Do you want to borrow my scarf again?"

The sergeant shook his head. "Sorry to trouble you, but there's a question or two. You see, there was an accident here at the hotel last night. . . ."

Miss Withers had a sudden flash of intuition. "It's Reverson!" she gasped. "Something has happened to young Reverson!"

The sergeant blinked and then shook his head. "Barking up the wrong tree, I'm afraid. Nothing wrong with Reverson. But you know the lift shaft up the hall—the one marked 'Out of Order'? Your recent shipmate Mr. Andy Todd was found at the bottom of it a little while ago."

Secker paused for effect. But even now Miss Withers did not completely understand him. This most emphatically did not fit in with the framework that she was painstakingly building.

"Todd? But what was Andy Todd doing there?"

"Shuffling off this mortal coil," said the sergeant. "When found an hour ago, he had completely shuffled. Popped off, y'know. Passed on, Gone West, *and* expired."

"Andy Todd *dead*?" said Miss Withers idiotically.

"Quite," said the sergeant.

72

CHAPTER VI

*

The Death of the Party

Miss Withers had started swiftly down the hall, but the sergeant touched her arm and shook his head. "Better not," he advised.

"But I must see for myself. . . ."

"They've taken the body away, what they could scrape up of it. The lift car is being held for repair at the top of the shaft, and so he struck on the concrete floor. It wasn't a pretty sight, my dear lady. When a man falls that far and strikes stone . . ."

Miss Withers nodded impatiently. "I know, I know. But how did it happen? Accident, suicide or . . ."

"That I don't know," admitted Sergeant Secker. "Area Superintendent Filsom is in charge. But dear old Cannon told me to toddle over and see if it had anything to do with the deaths on board the *American Diplomat*. Filsom thinks it's suicide, or death by misadventure. The lift was out of order and plainly marked so. Door was locked and supposedly could be unlocked only from the shaft. Although——"

"Did you make an attempt to unlock it from this side?"

The sergeant grinned. "I did. And—I succeeded. Though it couldn't have happened accidentally, even if the fellow had mistaken the lift for one of the automatic ones that you work yourself. It was a business of squeezing my hand through a narrow grating and fumbling for the catch."

"Then why the death by misadventure idea?"

"You see," explained the sergeant, "this Todd chap seems to have been jolly tight when it happened. The police surgeon is at his autopsy now, but he smelled the schnapps when he took his first look at the corpse. And an American dead drunk is likely to do anything."

"Um," said Miss Withers doubtfully. She proceeded slowly along the hall until she came to the first elevator rank. "Is this the one?"

"Right."

She peered at the latched door, shook it carefully, and looked dubious. Then, as the sergeant pointed out how he had put his hand through the grating, she tried, and found it a narrow squeeze. By dint of much forcing, she got her long thin hand through and opened the door. She looked down the dizzy shaft and saw the bright glare of a light at the bottom. Men were doing something to the place . . . she swung the door shut and heard the catch click into place.

"He'd been dead about five hours when the surgeon looked at him," went on Secker. "That sets the dive at approximately two o'clock. Though no one heard anything."

"I see," said Miss Hildegarde Withers, who as yet saw nothing at all.

"Filsom thinks that young Todd drank himself into a state of melancholia and then decided to kill himself this way," went on the sergeant.

"Melancholia fiddlesticks," Miss Withers retorted. "Why should he be melancholy when he drank? Todd was more the type to get hilariously gay. He was no old souse, you know. From what I understand, he's been spending his last four years or so in hard work and athletics, a regular grind, and that this was a vacation for him, in a way."

"Right you are. But I understand that something happened on the boat——"

"Yes—Andy Todd played a mean practical joke and caused infinite unhappiness to several people. He was what we call the Life of the Party, an obnoxious type. But I can't imagine his developing remorse."

"That's what I wanted to ask you about," the sergeant admitted. "You see, there was a letter——"

Now Miss Withers knew. "A letter with a——" she stopped.

The sergeant produced from his pocket an envelope bordered with black. There was an unpleasant brownish stain on one corner. He drew from it a sheet of notepaper, covered with black ink except in the center, where had been pasted some scraps of cream-colored paper, paper with a blue line running through it. "This was in his pocket when he fell," said Secker. "Ever see anything like it before?"

The message was short. "*And as for you, cruel silly fool whose hurt vanity made you crucify one who hardly knew you existed, I only wish that when death finds you, you will be as glad to die as I shall be. . . .*"

"Woman's writing," said the sergeant. "Ever see it before?"

"I never saw that letter before," Miss Withers assured him, not without guile.

She was thoughtful for a moment. "So Mr. Filsom of the Yard thinks that this note shamed Todd into jumping down the elevator shaft?"

Secker nodded. "It's Rosemary Fraser's writing. We've checked up on that. Or a better imitation never existed. She must have sent this to Todd before her death. Though, of course, that presupposes that she knew Noel was going to kill her, or at least suspected it."

"Not necessarily," said Miss Withers tartly. "Let me see. Do you have apples in England?"

"Eh? Why—of course, russets, pippins . . ."

"Well, we have an American expression which means a lot," she told him. "It's 'apple-sauce.' And you may quote me." She led the way toward the near-by stair. "Todd's room is on the third floor, you said?"

"I didn't say," the sergeant admitted. "But it is. Superintendent Filsom is down there now, watching the fingerprint men trying to get something off the lift door. But there doesn't seem to be much there."

"I don't suppose there's any use trying any other door?" asked Miss Withers casually. "After all, this hotel has six floors, each with doors opening into that shaft."

"He'd hardly climb up the stairs in order to do a longer dive," said Secker with a smile. "Besides, that lift door on the third floor was open wide. The maid noticed it this morning, and that's how the body was discovered."

They came down to the third floor, where three men with rusty brown cameras were puttering about the elevator door. When the sergeant inquired for Superintendent Filsom, one of the print men gestured down the hall.

They found Filsom and an inspector engaged in rifling the room of the dead Rhodes scholar.

The door was ajar. Sergeant Secker pushed it open and cleared his throat. But Superintendent Filsom was sum-

75

ming things up for the benefit of his aide. "It interlocks perfectly with the information in Cannon's memo on the Noel suicide," he declared. "Before she died, and while either in fear of death or considering suicide, the Fraser girl wrote a note to Andrew Todd, scoring off him for having made game of her. He brooded over it, and last night he emptied this bottle of whisky and then jumped down the unused lift shaft."

Filsom was holding a single empty quart bottle. He added it to the collection on the bureau, which comprised a few books, two cameras, and other odds and ends. Then he looked up and saw he had callers.

"This is the lady who was so helpful to Chief Inspector Cannon on the boat," said Secker. But the superintendent was unimpressed. He surveyed Miss Withers with a cold and fishy eye.

"Good of you t'trouble," he said. "Don't believe I've any questions after all. Just another case of a skylarking Yankee lad who went off his head."

"Of course," agreed the school teacher. "Excuse me asking, but you're sure that this was the bottle he drank from?" She pointed to the single "dead soldier."

"Eh? Of course. No other bottle of liquor in the room. One was enough to put him off his course, I'm afraid." As a sign that the interview was over, Filsom turned back to his examination of the dead man's effects. He picked up the smaller camera. "Remember to have these films printed in the lab," he reminded the inspector.

Miss Withers was turning away when she heard a sharp click. Filsom had touched the spring of the camera, and from where its lens should have been there leaped a rather lifelike imitation of a wriggling snake, which struck the inspector in the pit of the stomach. He did not flinch, but he turned two shades paler.

Sergeant Secker vented a small sound which was very like the choked-off crow of a rooster at daybreak. But Miss Withers only smiled, a little sadly.

"He was the Life of the Party," she said softly. "Poor Andy Todd—that should be his epitaph."

The two Yard officials were trying to get the serpent of wire and cloth back into its box. "If I can be of any further help——" Miss Withers suggested hopefully.

Filsom shook his head. "No, no, not at all. Sorry you were troubled. But it was the sergeant's idea. Secker here is a new man, and he doesn't believe yet that as far as the police are concerned two and two always make four."

The superintendent and his attendant inspector shared a booming laugh, and Sergeant Secker, flushing a bit, led Miss Withers out into the hall.

"Thinks I'll spread the story of his mistaking a jack-in-the-box for a camera," said the young man. "Well, just to pay him for getting so windy, I shall!"

"Never mind," Miss Withers comforted him. "I've learned that sometimes a detective has to make two and two into six, at the very least."

The sergeant stared at her. "Pardon? You've been mixed up in this sort of thing before, then?"

Miss Withers did not wish to enlighten him. "As an observer, you know. I rather enjoy the excitement."

"Then you don't blame me for dragging you out of bed before you've had your tea?" The sergeant was apologetic. "You see, perhaps I'm getting overanxious and all that, but Cannon has solved his Noel suicide and Filsom has solved his Todd suicide—and I'm left with the Rosemary Fraser disappearance. And I'm not so sure that it has been explained, in spite of what is happening. . . ."

"I could suggest one alternative," said Miss Withers wickedly. "Why not decide that Rosemary Fraser committed suicide, too?"

"And make it unanimous? I wish I could," said Secker sadly. "But somehow I feel that there must be a murder mystery mixed up in all these deaths. There's got to be!"

"Don't you worry," Miss Withers advised him as she prepared to take her departure in search of a belated breakfast, "there's murder enough hereabouts. I've been close to homicide before, and I can smell it."

The sergeant looked hopeful. "I don't suppose you can smell a murderer or so in the neighborhood?"

"Too many cold trails," Miss Withers told him. "But I'll make you a promise: if I strike a hot scent, I'll go into full cry."

"Bargain!" said the worried young sergeant. He was about to say something more when he heard his name bellowed from the doorway where Filsom lurked. He strode

77

away, whistling an old tune that Miss Withers recognized with a smile:

"Our feelings we with difficulty smother, when constabulary duty's to be done,
Ah, take one consideration with another—a policeman's lot is not a happy one!"

That afternoon saw the inquest into the death of Peter Noel, soldier of misfortune and bar steward. A police constable called upon Miss Withers shortly before lunch time to remind her that her presence would be necessary. She found that the court at which the inquest sat was far out in Stepney, and although she started out early enough, armed with a folding map of the city, it took her two tube rides, three buses, and finally a taxicab, to get to the ugly little red stone building, arriving just after the ceremony had begun.

She was buttonholed in the hall by Sergeant Secker. "I say," he greeted her, "you're late. Coroner Maggers'll be harsh with you. He's a great one for keeping up his dignity."

"Well, then, hadn't I ought to be getting in?"

Secker shook his head. "I've a message," he told her quickly. "From the D. I. Cannon tried to get this affair postponed, on account of the business that happened this morning. But Maggers wouldn't allow it. Necessary, he said, to get on with it before the *Diplomat* sails for the States on Friday. So I was told to ask you if the question should arise, as it probably won't, not to mention any more than you can help about the disappearance of Rosemary Fraser. And most particularly not to mention any doubts you may have as to Noel's killing her."

Miss Withers scrutinized his open countenance. "You mean that the Yard has doubts of its own in that respect?"

The sergeant shook his head noncommittally. "Very well," said Miss Withers. "I can guess as well as the Yard—perhaps better. But tell me one thing. You know of the pages that were torn from Rosemary Fraser's diary. You also know that they disappeared, supposedly carried along with her or destroyed by her. But was the terrific combing that the Customs gave my baggage an attempt to find those pages, on behalf of you people at the Yard?"

The sergeant put on a glazed and slightly worried look. But Miss Withers, who was a little nettled at discovering the London police more alive than she had imagined, pressed on.

"Tell me that, or I'll see that the coroner and the newspapers get all the facts and fancies that I have," she threatened.

"As a matter of fact," Sergeant Secker stiffly admitted, "we did request that the baggage of the passengers be scrutinized a bit more than usual. On my word, you got it no worse than the others."

"And you found——?"

"I say," protested the sergeant. "I can't spill things to you, you know." But, all the same, Miss Withers knew by the look in his face that in spite of the fine-comb treatment of the luggage, the police had drawn a blank.

"And the sheets torn from Rosemary's diary would have made a bulky packet in anyone's clothing, too," she thought aloud. "Yet—I'll stake my bottom dollar that they came off the ship."

The sergeant nearly nodded, but caught himself in time and tried to become very official indeed. "You'd better be getting inside," he advised her.

She found the small courtroom well filled with spectators, a crowded table for the gentlemen of the press, and on the front rows of wooden benches so many of her recent shipmates that a certain air of reunion and intimacy pervaded the grim occasion. The guardian at the door escorted her to a seat between Dr. Waite and the Honorable Emily.

The doctor looked more than a bit seedy, she thought. He was staring at Coroner Maggers, a rotund and Tweedledumish figure with a roaring voice, who just at the moment was engaged in giving Captain Everett a rather bad time of it.

"You haven't missed much," the doctor whispered to her as she sat down. "They're still arguing over the fellow's identity."

"Captain Everett," roared Maggers, "you have identified the body of the deceased as that of one Peter Noel, barsteward and assistant steward aboard your ship. Will you tell the jury just how long he has been in your employ?"

Captain Everett said testily that he did not "employ" the personnel of his crews. "Noel has been with the ship since early in January," he explained. "Making eight voyages in all."

"Was his conduct entirely satisfactory to his superiors and to you?"

The captain paused. "Yes," he said. "And again, no."

"What? What do you mean by that?"

"Satisfactory to me," said the captain. "But there was some trouble on our July voyage. We make the round trip between New York and the Port of London once a month, you know. On that trip, as I learned later, Noel became friendly with a passenger, a wealthy widow from Minneapolis whose name I would rather not make public. They became engaged, I understand, and since she had two grown sons of Noel's age, the family tried to make trouble. Lawyers got in touch with officials of the Line, and an investigation was made, during which time Noel was laid off from his regular duties."

The coroner seemed interested, if no one else in the room did. Miss Withers saw Candida Noring stifle a yawn at the end of the aisle.

"Aha!" cried Maggers. "But he was reinstated?"

The captain nodded. "Investigation showed that there was nothing to show that he had done anything discreditable. The lady involved was certainly old enough to know her own mind." There was a murmur of laughter in the court, instantly hushed by the coroner, who liked to make all the witticisms that were made.

"And that lady, she was not a passenger aboard the *American Diplomat* on this present voyage?"

Captain Everett shook his head. "She's safe and sound in Minneapolis, surrounded by sons who are trying to make her forget her shipboard romance," he announced.

The coroner glared. "Please confine yourself to answering the questions." He consulted some notes. "Oh, Captain. Is it true that there is a rule in your shipping line that only Yanks—I mean, citizens of the United States—are employed?"

Captain Everett hedged a little and admitted that he believed so.

"We have shown that Peter Noel was born in Montreal, a British subject," said the coroner quickly. "How do you explain that?"

Captain Everett was unable to explain that and clearly thought it unnecessary. He gave it as his opinion that Noel carried an American passport.

"Then how do you——" began Coroner Maggers. He was interrupted by Chief Inspector Cannon, who had a seat at the inner table. They conferred for a moment.

"I understand," said the coroner testily, "that Noel carried British and American passports, as well as those of several other countries. Was this known to you?"

"It was not," Captain Everett snapped. "I am master of a ship, and haven't the leisure to rummage through my crews' duffle boxes, as your police seem to have."

He was told that he might step down but must remain for further testimony later on. Much ruffled, Captain Everett sank onto a bench so heavily that the floor trembled. He folded his arms and waited. The Honorable Emily turned to Miss Withers and expressed a fervent wish that "the man would get on with it."

A dour and elderly police surgeon was called, very evidently a man to whom inquests were an everyday occurrence. He testified that he had made an examination of the body of Peter Noel and had found that the deceased came to his death through the absorption into his system of more than six grains of potassium cyanide, taken through the mouth. Such a death would be practically instantaneous.

Said Coroner Maggers: "In your opinion, was the poison taken in liquid or in powder form?"

The surgeon avoided an opportunity to plunge into abstruse and technical points. The poison had not been administered in liquid form, else it would have been found in the throat. Nor had it been in the form of an open powder, which would have remained in the mouth. "It seems clear that the cyanide was wrapped in a folded bit of paper and swallowed," he admitted.

"Was such a bit of paper found in the stomach of the deceased?" It was. The police surgeon stepped down.

Candida Noring was called. Miss Withers was interested to note that the transformation which had come over the girl still remained. She had dressed herself carefully and well for the ordeal, in smart woollen coat and tam, and she went to the witness chair without visible perturbation.

Coroner Maggers established rather quickly her identity, and the fact that she had had a room mate, one Rosemary Fraser, on board the vessel *American Diplomat*.

"On the morning of September 21st, did your room mate, Rosemary Fraser, disappear from the ship?" Coroner Maggers spoke with an unwonted delicacy, and Miss Withers wondered if he had not been coached a bit by the Yard official who sat just behind him.

Candida nodded, and then said "Yes" in a low voice.

"At the time of the ship's arrival in the Port of London, did you give certain information to Chief Inspector Cannon of the C.I.D. in regard to the disappearance of Rosemary Fraser?"

"I did," admitted Candida. "It was about——"

"Answer the questions, please. Did this information implicate Peter Noel, bar steward of the ship?"

Candida bowed her head. The jury was wide awake now, visibly stirring with uncertain suspicion. The young men at the press table began to make marks upon their blank white notebooks. Miss Withers leaned forward, intrigued and puzzled. But Candida Noring was permitted to step down. Cannon himself took the stand, made his oath with the ease that had marked the police surgeon before him, and sat down.

"Chief Inspector," began the coroner quickly, "you have heard Miss Noring's testimony. As a result of information given to you by her, did you arrest Peter Noel aboard the vessel *American Diplomat* shortly after midnight on the morning of September 23rd?"

"I made an effort to arrest him, yes," said Cannon. "I gave him the usual caution and was about to lay hands upon his person in formal arrest when he snatched something from his right-hand coat pocket and put it in his mouth."

"You made no effort to prevent him?"

The policeman paused. "It was too sudden," he said. "I moved toward him, and so did Captain Everett and his first officer, but the man collapsed as we reached him."

Coroner Maggers nodded, and as a little hum arose from the press table, he plunged on.

"Would you say that Noel's attitude was one of perturbation and excitement, in other words, that he was in a desperate mood in which he might have taken his own life?"

Chief Inspector Cannon was certain of it. "He seemed excited, surely," said Cannon. "And he had a sly look, as if he was pleased with himself."

"Did you see what he put in his mouth?"

The Yard man rubbed his wide chin. "It seemed to me like a bit of paper," he said finally. "But I would not take my oath to it."

"You made no effort to prevent him from swallowing the paper—or whatever it was? Or to apply proper first-aid treatment?"

Cannon looked annoyed. "I thought," he said, "that the prisoner was trying to destroy a bit of evidence against him. Then he went down as if struck by lightning."

Dr. Waite leaned toward Miss Withers. "Any fool knows that there is no first aid treatment for cyanide," he whispered. "Why, before——"

He was startled to hear his own name called out. After his oath, he was asked questions establishing his profession, and his billet aboard the ship. Then the coroner got down to brass tacks.

"Dr. Waite," he began, "as part of your equipment of medical supplies, was there a bottle of cyanide of potassium in your sick bay?"

"There was."

"When was that bottle filled?"

Dr. Waite wasn't sure. But he had inspected all the bottles in the cabinet at the beginning of the voyage in question.

"Tell the jury what you found when, at the instigation of the police, you looked in that poison bottle some four hours after the death of Peter Noel?"

Dr. Waite sniggered. "I found it full of Epsom salts," he said.

"There was no way in which the salts could normally have been in that bottle?"

Waite shook his head. "None whatever."

"Unless someone removed the cyanide and poured them in its place?"

"No. I mean, that would be the only way."

83

"Who, in your opinion, made that substitution?"

Dr. Waite protested that he could not swear as to that. He would rather not say.

"Very well. Was Peter Noel in your office, where the medicine cabinet was kept unlocked, on any day immediately preceding his death?"

Waite nodded. "On the night that Rosemary Fraser jumped overboard——"

"Please!" cried Coroner Maggers. "We are not hearing that case. Answer the question." Cannon leaned back in his chair.

"On the night of September 20th," Dr. Waite corrected himself, "Noel dropped into my office, where a number of us had congregated for a friendly game of craps."

"Craps! Craps! Please confine yourself to the English language, which has proved extensive enough for the courts of England these hundreds of years." Maggers grew oratorical. "Craps! What do you expect the jury to understand by that American slang expression?"

"*Craps!*" reiterated Dr. Waite. He looked bewildered. "Is there any other name for it? You play the game with a pair of dice, win on seven or eleven first throw, lose on——"

"Never mind! The jury will understand that you refer to a Yankee gambling game. Who were the participants?"

Waite thought a moment. "Besides Noel, who stayed only a little while, there were Mr. Hammond, Mr. Reverson, the purser, the third officer, Mr. Healey, First Officer Jenkins until his watch came at midnight, and Colonel Wright."

Maggers nodded. "You were much engrossed in the game? So much so that it would have been possible for an onlooker to open the cabinet and swiftly make a substitution of salts for the deadly poison?"

Dr. Waite admitted that it might have been so. He stepped down gratefully and mopped his brow beside Miss Withers, who was shaking her head rather dubiously.

Coroner Maggers looked at his notes. Then he consulted his watch and had a brief word with Cannon.

Then he turned toward the jury. "It seems to me that this hearing could be brought to a close without further delay," he said.

"Hear, hear!" said Hildegarde Withers under her breath. Maggers went on.

"I had planned to call a dozen other witnesses, but their testimony could do no more than corroborate what you have heard. It is rather late, and we shall have to adjourn within half an hour. In spite of the unfortunate and regrettable circumstances under which it appears that Peter Noel was able to cheat justice, the case seems to be very clear."

Maggers glared at Cannon, who smiled sleepily. "A girl, with whom Peter Noel was implicated, disappeared from the *American Diplomat*. When the ship arrived in port, a high detective official went on board to make inquiries and was given information implicating Noel. While placing Noel under arrest, the man swallowed a packet of paper and immediately fell dead. We have shown that he died of potassium cyanide poisoning, and that he was in a position to have secured a supply of the poison from the medicine cabinet of the ship some time before.

"Understand, gentlemen," continued Maggers, who dearly loved summing up, "that in this case there can be no question arising out of the hour of death, the means used, or the method of application. I submit to you that Noel, fearing arrest for his implication in the death of Rosemary Fraser, supplied himself with poison as a last resort. It is within your power to bring a verdict against a person or persons unknown, or against any particular person, who may have administered poison to him. However, let me point out to you that there can be little question in this case of anyone administering the poison to the deceased, as cyanide is almost instantaneous in its action, which means that Noel could not have drunk or eaten anything beforehand which resulted in his death at the moment of arrest, and also let me point out to you that he was seen to place a bit of paper in his mouth and swallow it.

"In other words, you will concentrate upon a decision as to whether or not Peter Noel met his death at his own hand or through misadventure. You will also consider the fact that Noel had already been in difficulties with his employers over an affair with a woman passenger, and that he may very well have feared final suspension over the Rosemary Fraser affair."

Coroner Maggers beamed on his jury. "Gentlemen, do you think that you can arrive at a verdict from the evidence brought before you?"

Somewhere in the rear of the room, a woman snorted. It was not a loud snort, but it was a snort nevertheless. Miss Withers turned suddenly and saw Tom and Loulu Hammond. Loulu did not look like the type of person to snort, yet Miss Withers stared at the young wife very intently indeed.

The jury was in a huddle. They had not left the courtroom, and the foreman, a thick and stolid person with watery eyes and a dirty white scarf around his throat, was haranguing his mates.

He stood up. "Hi say . . ." The courtroom became tense and silent.

"Gentlemen, are you ready to return your verdict?"

The foreman nodded vigorously. "Has I was saying . . ." He nearly choked himself with his scarf. "We 'old that the deceased met 'is end through the neg—negligence of the perlice, while nervous-like on account of being arrested for murderin' Rosemary Fraser——"

"But you're not to consider——" interrupted Coroner Maggers. Yet Miss Withers saw that Cannon, who had risen to his feet, was moving his lips in what seemed to be "Let it stand, man!"

"And that he committed suicide, by his own 'and," finished the foreman. There was a moment of silence, and then a woman rose to her feet not far from where Loulu Hammond was biting her handkerchief.

"Stuff and nonsense," said a clear voice. Everyone in the room turned to see the sturdy figure of Mrs. Snoaks, the stewardess. "Peter Noel was not the one to take his own life by no matter of means. He had every reason to live, he had—we was to have been married come Christmas."

Candida Noring's soft laughter broke the spell, and then pandemonium reigned for a moment. Mrs. Snoaks was escorted from the court, proudly sniffling in a handkerchief. Coroner Maggers had several things to say, but before he could say them the crowd had risen, and the jury were fumbling with their hats.

Miss Withers found herself moving up the aisle next to Candida. The girl caught her arm.

"Do you believe what she said?"

Miss Withers bit her lip. "Mrs. Snoaks is a fine figure of a woman," she admitted. "But she's at least ten years older than Noel. I'm afraid she's letting her imagination run riot."

They passed a bluff and towering person who was struggling into his greatcoat. He bowed to Candida, who nodded, and then turned to Miss Withers. "That's Colonel Wright," she said, "and the lady helping him with his coat is his wife."

"Aha!" Miss Withers, owing to her being a poor sailor, had not become acquainted with all her fellow passengers on the voyage. "Colonel Wright—wait a minute. You mean he's the man that Rosemary feared would let her family know of the scandal on board?"

Candida nodded. "Wright worked for her father's firm," she said. "He left after some sort of an argument, Rosemary told me. And while she never had anything to do with him or his wife on board, she was positive that they would not let the occasion go by without carrying the bad news back to her people."

Miss Withers nodded absent-mindedly. "Excuse me," she told her companion. "I want to catch up with the Hammonds." They were ahead, arm in arm, at the doorway.

She had a very important question to ask, but it was not to be answered for many a day. Though she was without any intention of eavesdropping, she came up swiftly behind the young couple, and heard Loulu say in a hard and unfriendly voice:

"And this, my love, ends the play-acting."

With that phrase she left Tom Hammond's side abruptly and stepped into a waiting taxicab. She was whirled away, and as Miss Withers drew back beside Candida, she saw Tom Hammond holding a match several inches from the end of his pipe, with fingers that seemed to waver considerably. He gave voice to an epithet which has not been current in polite society since Elizabethan days, and sought another taxi for himself.

Miss Withers stood still, blocking half the doorway. Her nostrils were flaring.

Candida Noring was beside her. "You look as if you'd seen a ghost," said Candida wonderingly.

"I've smelled one," Miss Withers told her.

CHAPTER VII

*

Nails for a Coffin

Superintendent Filsom of C Division leaned back from his desk in a very squeaky armchair and stared out across the muddy Thames at the uninspiring bulk of County Hall. His large and well-shod feet were resting upon a sheaf of papers marked "Andrew Todd," and he drummed impatiently upon the arm of his chair and wished for tea.

But Sergeant John Secker lounged gracefully against the file cases, his rather handsome face lit by a mild inquisitiveness. The superintendent listened for a few moments.

"Ingenious, very ingenious," he gave as his verdict when the younger man had finished. "But, all the same, I'm inclined to take the black-bordered note at its face value. Rosemary Fraser wrote it, all right—and then doctored it up in a silly theatrical fashion. As I told you, I think she had a premonition of death. And from what I hear, she had reason enough to wish Todd all the bad luck in the world."

Secker nodded without enthusiasm. "That's what Inspector Cannon said, too. And yet, sir, I've been wondering——"

"You'll get over that," Filsom promised him. There was a knock at the door, and a somewhat doddering constable put in his gray head.

"Lady to see you, sir," he said. "Same lady as before."

"What? The Yankee schoolmistress again? Tell her——" he turned to Secker. "Sergeant, you turned her loose on me. Now it's up to you to go down and steer her off. I've got other things to do besides listen to amateur Sherlock Holmeses."

"Right," said the sergeant. He stood aside as the superintendent's tea tray was brought in, and then walked down one flight of musty and ill-lit stairs to the main hall of

Scotland Yard, where an angular and fuming Miss Hildegarde Withers was stalking up and down.

"I want to know——" she began.

"I'm with you there," said Sergeant Secker. He led her into a little waiting room whose single window opened out upon the Quadrangle, where a solitary officer was wrestling with a tire on the rear wheel of a Flying Squad Chrysler.

Miss Withers accepted a hard-backed chair. "I've come to make a trade," she informed him. "I tried to see Chief Inspector Cannon, and he seems to be out of his office. Superintendent Filsom is too elusive. But you'll do."

"Thanks awfully," said the sergeant. He took out his notebook. "You wish to give information?"

"Put that thing away," Miss Withers insisted. "I want to know three things. First, what did your experts find out about the letter edged in mourning which Todd had in his pocket when he died? Second, what fingerprints were found on the elevator door—I mean lift? Third, what was found at the bottom of the lift shaft beside the dead body of Andy Todd?"

"I'm sorry," said Sergeant Secker. "But really, you know, I haven't the authority . . ."

"You want to solve the disappearance of Rosemary Fraser, don't you? Well, young man, don't think for a minute that you will get anywhere without figuring out what is really behind the warning notes."

"Notes?" said the sergeant.

"You heard me correctly. Andy Todd was not the only person to receive a letter with a black band around the envelope and a message pasted against a blacked-in page. Whether it was an unhappy accident or not I do not know, but such a message presaged Todd's death, and it seems to me that the Yard had better look into the other person who got one."

"Meaning?" There was a new light in the eye of Sergeant Secker.

"Meaning Candida Noring, of course. She got such a letter soon after she arrived at the hotel, and threw it into the fire, thinking it a bad joke. But I'm wondering if it *was* a joke."

The sergeant was wondering, too. "Why—she'd better have a man stationed to look after her. She ought to have reported this herself. . . ."

"Had she? I think that she did the perfectly natural thing. Use the information as you see fit, of course. But—isn't it worth what I ask?"

The sergeant considered. "Strictly between ourselves," he confessed, "you aren't asking much. There was only some broken glass scattered around the body at the bottom of the lift. There were no fingerprints of any kind on the door. And—nothing has come to light about the message except that it appeared in Todd's mail box at the hotel—that it did not go through the mail—that the writing was very much like Rosemary Fraser's—and that ink, envelope, and paper were of the commonest, untraceable type. So you see, I've won on the trade."

"Have you!" said Miss Withers, arising.

The sergeant was thoughtful. "If you go back to the hotel, tell Miss Noring that, if she requests it, the Yard will put a man where he can prevent anything happening to her. We've got operatives who specialize in hotel work."

"I will," promised the school teacher. "But I don't think she'll ask it."

"Then you'd better keep an eye on her yourself," Secker suggested. "Though I still don't see how anything further could happen. Unless there's a madman loose—a madman who can work black magic. The Fraser girl was murdered, I'll admit that. But no one can make a man swallow poison, and no one can hypnotize another man into jumping down a lift shaft."

"I didn't say that anyone did," Miss Withers retorted. They were walking toward the door. "By the way, are we all to be kept in town for this second inquest?"

"Todd's? I don't think so. Filsom will take statements if he wants them. Everything thé coroner needs has been brought out in the investigation of the Noel case."

"Everything!" said Miss Withers, her voice full of meaning. "Mark my words, young man, there is something very askew with this so simple affair."

Sergeant Secker was beginning to agree. His lightheartedness had left him. "The case is out o' joint," he remarked sadly. He knew that, only a few hours from London, the Hunt was cubbing over his ancestral and much-mortgaged acres, while his own horse ate its head off in a stable. "Oh, cursed spite that ever I was born to set it right."

"Some people would call that egotism," Miss Withers told him, and swept out toward the Embankment.

There was a raw and chilly wind, and as the street lamps began to come on Miss Withers was impelled to think of the warmth and nourishment to be found in a cup of tea. Across from the Alexandria was a brightly lit Lyons, reminding her pleasantly of Childs back home. She stepped inside and sought for a table, but before she found one she was greeted by the Honorable Emily. Leslie Reverson rose swiftly to hold a chair for her, and she joined them.

"Been sightseeing?" inquired the Honorable Emily.

"Some of them," Miss Withers admitted.

"You may have the town," confessed the Englishwoman. "It's wonderful, I know—but I never come up to London unless I must. I've been taking advantage of this enforced visit to have some clothes made, and as soon as they're fitted properly Leslie and I shall dash back to Cornwall. Things like this—" she made a wide gesture which Miss Withers took to include the events of the past week or more—"never happen in Cornwall."

Leslie Reverson made his first contribution. "Nothing ever happens in Cornwall," he said bitterly. "Not since the Phœnicians came trading for tin, and they've done with it these thousand years or so." He rose to his feet.

"Mind if I dash along?" He got part way to the door and then returned. "Aunt, could I—I mean——"

The Honorable Emily arose, reaching for her pocketbook as she did so. Miss Withers sipped her tea and listened to Reverson's hurried voice. She did not catch the words, but what he said seemed to amuse his aunt.

"Don't be silly," the Honorable Emily said, in a clear loud voice. "Here's ten bob. Flowers will do just as well, and they're not half so dear." She returned to the table, closing her purse.

"The younger generation on the loose," she remarked. "Heaven knows what's got into the boy, he runs through his allowance in no time at all. Just one girl after another. . . ."

Miss Withers saw that her companion was in an open mood. "It seemed to me that your nephew took rather a shine to Candida Noring," she suggested.

The Honorable Emily nodded. "He could do worse," she observed. "Good sensible girl. A bit dowdy on the boat, but

91

she seems to have, as you say, snapped out of it now she's in London. Do you know—" she leaned closer—"I was worried for a time on the voyage coming over. Leslie was making calf's-eyes at that Fraser girl. But luckily he didn't get involved with her. He's only twenty, and his father and mother died when he was a child, so I'm responsible for him. I shall feel a great deal more comfortable when I get him safe back home."

"If you ever do," Miss Withers very nearly spoke aloud. They passed out of the tea shop and crossed over to the hotel. The Honorable Emily provided herself with all the afternoon papers and a comic magazine.

"My only vice," she explained. "I dearly love to curl up in a hot tub and read myself to sleep. And the papers come in handy afterward—for Tobermory."

Miss Withers wished her a pleasant soak and sought her own room, where she sat and stared at the red coals of her fire until long after the dinner hour. They presented innumerable fantastic pictures, but never did they suggest the clear and definite answer to this complex puzzle which the spinster wanted to see. Finally she took up a piece of hotel stationery. "I might do it by algebra," she thought. "X equals—that's the trouble. X doesn't equal anything. Nor, for that matter, does Y or Z." She swept away her meaningless figures and wished wistfully that she understood relativity.

Hunger drove her out of her room, and on an impulse she rapped on Candida's door. She found the girl dressed in a flannel bathrobe and munching on a bun. A bottle of milk stood on the dresser.

"Come in," she cried gayly. "Share my frugal repast—there's lots of buns."

Miss Withers accepted a chair and a bun. "Dieting?" she inquired pleasantly. Candida shook her head vigorously.

"Broke," she announced. "Or severely bent, anyhow. I was hoping for another invitation to dinner tonight, like a regular little gold-digger. Of course, I could have dinner sent up and put it on the bill, but I didn't want to go in any deeper than I must."

Miss Withers understood. "It's always a bother getting remittances over here," she said. "But I'd be glad to lend you a few pounds. . . ."

Candida's eyes warmed. "You're sweet. But it's not what you think." She hesitated, taking a big bite of bun, and then went on. "I wasn't going to say anything about it. But there's no harm in your knowing. You see—Rosemary was to have paid our traveling expenses. She carried the money—and took it with her when she went. That's how I know it wasn't suicide, because Rosemary would never have left me stranded. I didn't want to mention it, because it seems so petty. But now I'm left on my own funds, and they aren't worthy of the name."

Miss Withers digested this information. "Rosemary was banker, then?"

Candida took a deep breath. "It's a long story," she said. "But I want to talk about it, I've been silent long enough. You see, I've known Rosemary Fraser ever since she was a baby. Her people have a lot of money and move with the upper crust of Buffalo. . . ."

Miss Withers internally shivered at the thought, but the girl went on. "And I'm just Candy Noring, whose father died before she was born and whose mother tried to be a dressmaker and broke her heart at it. When I was in high school I used to earn a little extra money by minding babies, and Rosemary was my first charge. My mother died, and some of the people for whom she had worked sort of banded together to help me through school. It made them feel very charitable, and I suppose I wasn't so much of a burden at that. I used to slave at vacation times as a companion, and an extra maid, and a practical nurse, and anything else I was called on to do, but most times I went to take care of Rosemary. She was such a sweet little girl, and though she had the world handed to her on a silver platter, we were more like sisters than anything else."

Candida smoothed her fingers, as if drawing on an imaginary pair of gloves. "Then I got a scholarship at St. Andrews, one of the oldest girls' colleges in the East. For several years I nearly lost touch with Rosemary, although one summer as a special treat I was allowed to go up to their camp in Canada as a companion for her. When I graduated, I stayed on as an instructor. Then Rosemary came to St. Andrews, and we became close friends again. This was to have been her sophomore year——"

Miss Withers was computing years and other figures. "I see," she said.

"Not yet," Candida told her dreamily. "Then Rosemary got into a scrape this year at Bar Harbor, in Maine, where her family took her every summer for the hot weather. She's never told me what it was all about, but I presume that it concerned—a man. She was an unsophisticated, soft little thing, romantic as they come. She wrote sonnets and tore them up all summer, but when fall came she refused to go back to school. She wanted to go around the world, she said. Well, she always had her own way. Her family only stipulated that I must go along to take care of her—as I've always taken care of her. All I was to get were my expenses—but what half-starved college instructor wouldn't take a trip around the world just for the ride? We were to have sailed next Monday on the *Empress of Siam.* . . ."

Candida broke off and sniffled at a handkerchief. "I've tried not to think of myself. But it's hard, when all your life you've been sitting on the outside looking at the good things through a pane of glass—and then to have a wonderful trip dangled before your eyes and snatched away!"

Miss Withers agreed. "But something was snatched away from Rosemary, too. Her desire for life—or else her life itself. Tell me, do you honestly think that she was capable of committing suicide?"

Candida shook her head wildly. "How do I know? Rosemary was capable of anything. She dramatized herself and everything that happened to her. She might have been driven to take her own life by the cruel, thoughtless laughter of the people at that captain's dinner. But it would have been more like her to get hold of a gun, somehow, and blaze away at the whole lot. She——" The girl stopped short. "I'm not going to talk about her any more."

"One thing I'm as sure of as I'm sure of anything," Miss Withers remarked conversationally. "And that is that Peter Noel did not kill Rosemary Fraser."

Candida's eyes opened very wide, but she did not say anything. She produced a paper bag. "Have another bun?" Her voice trembled a little.

Miss Withers declined. "The best thing for you to do, young woman, is to put all this unhappiness out of your mind. Don't stay here in your room by yourself: get out and play. Think of something cheerful. . . ."

She placed her hand on Candida's shoulder, and found her tense as a coiled spring. Then the girl suddenly relaxed.

"You're very wise and kind," she said. "I'll snap out of it. I've got something nice to think about, anyhow————" Suddenly she jumped to her feet and ran over to the dresser. From the top drawer she took a tremendous black ebony box and displayed it proudly to her guest.

"This came for me just before you dropped in," said Candida. "Wasn't it sweet of him?"

Miss Withers surveyed the tightly packed and aromatic contents—five hundred fine Turkish cigarettes, with tips of straw and cork and gold and silver and many-colored silk. The cover bore the name of one of England's foremost tobacconists—Empey's—and lying on top of the highest tray was a neatly engraved card, "Leslie Pendavid Reverson."

"It's better than an invitation to dinner," Miss Withers assured her. "Why, the box will be a treasure even after the cigarettes are gone." She closed the lid and surveyed the finely cut black wood with approval. The bottom bore a strip of pasted felt, so as not to mar a table-top. Miss Withers noticed that a careless salesperson had forgotten to remove the tiny price sticker and saw upon it the neat notation "£2."

"You'll have a coffin nail with me, won't you?" said Candida eagerly. "Try one of those tiny Russian ones, or the perfumed ones with silk tips. . . ."

"Mercy sakes no," said Hildegarde Withers. "I should be terribly ill. I know that most women smoke today, but when I was a girl we were taught that tobacco was physically and morally wrong—for girls."

Candida shrugged and took up one of the scented cigarettes with delicate fingers. Miss Withers sensed that here was a girl who appreciated the luxuries, the fine and tangible things of life, perhaps because for so many years she had seen them only at a distance. "They look so perfect in the box that I hate to take this," Candida remarked. But she struck a match and held it to the tip.

"I must run along," Miss Withers told her. "Now, keep a stiff upper lip, and if you receive any more anonymous notes, bring them to me as quick as you can."

Candida took the cigarette from her mouth. "But—there won't be any more notes with a black border now that Todd has killed himself, will there?"

Miss Withers realized that Candida did not know of the black-bordered missive which had gone down with Andy Todd to his death.

"I hope and pray not," she told the girl, and took her departure. When she looked at her watch she saw that it was almost ten o'clock. In spite of her tea and the buns she had shared with Candida she was very hungry.

"I'll just drop down to the grill and have a bite," she decided. "After all, Candida has cigarettes to take the edge from her appetite. But I need to keep up my strength."

She was surprised to notice that all the way down the hall in the direction of the lift she had been talking to herself. A maid, bound on some errand involving two pillows, looked at her suspiciously, and the school teacher pretended to be humming.

But she only talked to herself when something in her mind was clamoring for attention—something in her subconscious which raised its hand, like one of the pupils back in the third grade of Jefferson School, when it wanted to speak. The talking, she knew, was an effort to ignore that signal . . . because it meant bad news.

As she stepped into the elevator she began systematically to search her mind. Some thought, some word, had started a train of the sort of guesswork which she had learned to heed. What had it been—black-bordered letters, Reverson's card, buns, cigarettes—coffin nails? *Coffin nails!*

The elevator was at the ground floor, and in a daze she followed the other occupants out into the hall. Then she stopped short and was about to implore the man to take her back to the fifth floor in a hurry when she caught a glimpse of the Honorable Emily, resplendent in a dinner gown of modest crimson, moving across the distant foyer.

Down the corridor Miss Withers went, swooping like some grim, ungainly bird of prey. She came upon the Honorable Emily just as that lady was settling herself beneath a potted palm and preparing for an hour with a brandy-and-soda while the orchestra played its evening rounds of Strauss.

So suddenly did the school teacher materialize before the Honorable Emily that the Englishwoman very nearly went over backwards into the potted palm.

"Eh?" she demanded.

But Miss Withers had no time for explanations. "Important!" she gasped. "At tea-time—didn't your nephew ask you for money?"

"Why——" The Honorable Emily looked ruffled.

"Life or death," Miss Withers said melodramatically. "Tell me!"

"Why, yes, as a matter of fact, he did. Said he was flat broke and wanted to send Miss Noring a present of some candy or something."

"And you gave him . . . ?"

"If it's really a matter of life and death," the Honorable Emily confessed, "I gave him ten shillings, though he wanted more. He said——"

"Lord God Almighty!" said Miss Withers reverently. She turned and sprinted for the elevator. The Englishwoman shook her head in amazement. Then, on an impulse, she rose and followed. She moved with more grace than Miss Withers, but they arrived at the elevator door neck and neck.

"Are you all right?" inquired the Honorable Emily as they were hoisted upwards. "You look as if you'd seen a Boojum." But Miss Withers was demanding more speed from the bewildered operator.

"Can I do anything?" asked her now thoroughly worried companion.

"I'm afraid that no one can do anything," Miss Withers told her. They were at the fifth floor and hurrying down the hall. At Candida's door Miss Withers burst in without hesitating.

A tremendous surge of relief came over her as she saw that Candida Noring was sitting in a big chair which faced the fireplace, staring at the coals, and that from beside her a trail of blue smoke still rose toward the ceiling.

"Excuse me——" she started to say. Then she sniffed and ran forward.

"Candida!"

But Candida Noring did not answer. Her head was bent forward at an almost impossible angle, and the smoke at her

97

side arose from a smouldering circle where her cigarette had burned its way down into the arm of the chair.

"She's asleep!" hazarded the Honorable Emily. But Miss Withers caught the girl by the shoulders. Her head rolled to one side horribly, and then, in spite of everything that the school teacher could do, Candida Noring slid from her chair in an untidy tumble of bare thighs and crumpled bathrobe and lay woodenly on the floor.

CHAPTER VIII

*

The Doctor's Stirrup-Cup

Instinctively the Honorable Emily turned to Miss Withers for guidance. "What must we do? Police?" Her eyeglass slipped, and she caught it in midair.

"Of course. But—wait a moment." The school teacher knelt by the body, and it was limp and warm to her touch. She deftly pulled back one eyelid and then pressed her fingers to the temple.

Her voice was incredulous. "Quick—she's not gone yet! Help me get her on the bed!"

They managed it, not without difficulty, for Candida Noring was heavier than she appeared to be. Miss Withers searched her memory for information she had read regarding poisons. Then she ran to the dressing table. "If I only had some sal ammoniac!" She saw nothing but a trumpery japanned powder box.

The Honorable Emily tore open her handbag. "I always carry smelling salts," she said. "To sniff when I have my heart seizures."

Miss Withers was already wringing out a washcloth beneath the water bottle. She applied it vigorously over Candida's face and the back of her neck. Then she snatched the smelling salts from the trembling fingers of the distrait Englishwoman and held the little bottle under Candida's nose.

There was a faint widening of the nostrils and a movement of the head. "Run for a doctor," Miss Withers ordered. "And the police as well. Scoot, now!"

The Honorable Emily scooted. Almost immediately she was back, hustling along an elderly gentleman with sideburns. He introduced himself as Dr. Gareth, resident physician of the hotel. "What's the trouble here?"

"Trouble enough," Miss Withers snapped at him. "Inhalation of prussic acid, I think."

Dr. Gareth sniffed. "Right you are. Room's full of it. Open the window, somebody."

He busied himself with his kit, and Candida moaned and tried to sit up. "I'm all right," she said weakly. "It was—only the cigarette. It was too strong."

"Lie down and drink this," he said. Candida coughed at the taste of the neat spirits, but they gave her a new flood of strength.

The doctor bent and listened at her breast. "Heart is satisfactory—breathing nearly normal. You must have got a very light touch of it, young woman. We shall have to give you a hot-water bottle for your feet."

"I'll get the maid," Miss Withers offered. Then she saw that, luckily, the maid stood in the doorway, where a uniformed police constable was barring her path.

"I only came to turn down the bed for the night . . ." the woman began. Under her arm was a rubber bottle filled with hot water, and Miss Withers seized it. "You can't go out, ma'am," the constable told her. "Nobody but the doctor leaves or enters this room until the chief gets here!"

Miss Withers didn't want to get out. She looked inquiringly at the Honorable Emily.

"I asked at the Yard for Chief Inspector Cannon," said that lady. "He lives close by, in Kensington, and he's on his way."

"Splendid," said Miss Withers.

"But I don't understand!" Candida was protesting in a rather weak voice. "I just sat down to have a cigarette before I went to bed, and then all of a sudden everything went black. . . ."

The doctor nodded. "I'll just have a look at that cigarette." He went over to the chair before the fire and stared for a long time at the burned hole in its upholstery. He could see nothing but charred cloth and gray ash.

Then he crossed over to where the ebony gift box was lying on the dresser. He sniffed again. "Um," he said. "Brand-new—and only two cigarettes missing." He closed the box, and placed it under his arm. "I'll just take charge of this," he said.

Candida protested weakly. "But—there can't be anything wrong with it—a friend sent it to me."

Miss Withers made frantic signals to her, but Candida did not see. "And just who was your friend?" inquired Dr. Gareth casually.

"Why—Leslie Reverson—that woman's nephew." Candida pointed at the Honorable Emily. "A messenger brought it up at just about dinner time. Leslie's card was in it."

Candida subsided on her pillow. The two older women looked at each other, while the doctor measured a few drops of reddish liquor into a glass of water. "Take this when you wake up," he advised Candida. "You've had a very narrow escape—you're a lucky young woman."

"Thanks to you," said Candida, looking toward Miss Withers. "If you hadn't come back . . ."

"But I did come back," the school teacher announced cheerfully.

"I'm terribly grateful, at any rate. You—you seem to know everything."

Miss Withers smiled grimly. "I don't—but I intend to."

There was an interruption. Chief Inspector Cannon, with his tie under one ear and his spats half buttoned, came into the room. "Who knows everything about what?"

Dr. Gareth gave the detective a résumé of the situation. "Light case of prussic acid poisoning," he said. "No danger now—I'll arrange for a maid to sit in her room for a few hours." He handed over the box of cigarettes.

"This is a new one," decided Cannon. "I never heard of poison administered in a cigarette before."

"Cyanide in any form is a pretty mean thing," declared the doctor. "I must rush along now—but I'll look in again during the night. I'll leave it to you, inspector. And I hope that you'll be able to keep the name of the hotel out of the papers."

"I'll keep the whole thing out of the papers if I can," promised Cannon. He was engrossed in the box of cigarettes. "Easy to trace," he announced softly. "Dipped in poison and then dried, eh?" He sniffed and made a wry face.

"If you'll excuse me," Miss Withers put in, advancing from the corner where she had remained with the Honorable Emily, "I don't think the cigarettes were dipped in poison. And if you value your health I advise you not to get your nose so close to them."

"Eh?" The inspector recognized her with a start. "You here again?"

His tone lacked geniality. "Yes, I'm here again. And a lucky thing that I came at the right moment," Miss Withers retorted. "I've just been making a little experiment."

She showed him one of the perfumed, silk-tipped cigarettes, which she had snapped in the middle. A little cascade of white powder fell to the floor, and Cannon gasped. "Loaded, eh? Tobacco drawn out, and then replaced. Why, this is a new exhibit for the Black Museum."

The room smelled more strongly of bitter almonds. "Don't you think we'd better continue our conversation somewhere else?" Miss Withers gestured at the girl on the bed.

"Don't mind me," Candida told them. "I'm all right now." But Cannon nodded, and ushered the two women toward the hall. The Honorable Emily put her hand on Miss Withers' arm, when the Yard man stepped back into the room for a moment.

"You don't think Leslie——"

"I do not," said Miss Withers comfortably. But she was frowning.

Cannon joined them in a moment, replacing a small white envelope in his pocket. "Scrapings from the burned chair," he enlightened them. He produced his notebook. "And now, if you ladies will give me your statements——"

The maid who was sent to sit with Candida arrived and entered the room. "Suppose we go down the hall to my room," suggested Miss Withers. "I'll tell you all I know."

She told him—not all, but enough. "I suppose that you know about the anonymous letter Candida received?"

"Just like Todd's? Yes, Secker sent me a memorandum. We work together at the Yard. It looks like a nasty bit of business." Cannon turned to the Honorable Emily. "Where is this precious nephew of yours?"

"My nephew will be on hand when he is wanted," said the Honorable Emily stiffly. "I give you my word—and since you seem ignorant of the fact, let me inform you that I am the daughter of the late Earl of Trevanna."

Cannon was polite but not too impressed. He had seen earls and earls—one or two of them had come under his official scrutiny.

"I doubt very much if the boy would be foolish enough to enclose his card in a poison package—even if for any reason he desired to put an end to a young lady whom he admires very much," Miss Withers suggested.

"Oh, yes," said the Yard man. "The card—where is it?" He opened the ebony box and searched diligently. "It wasn't on the dresser, either. . . ."

He faced Miss Withers. "Did you pocket that, too?"

She said nothing, but stared at the Honorable Emily. That lady flushed. "I don't suppose you would care to have *me* searched?"

"Hand it to him," said Miss Withers kindly. "You're not doing Leslie any good by keeping it."

"How did you know?" gasped the Honorable Emily. But she produced the card. Cannon took it gravely.

"Leslie Pendavid Reverson," he read aloud.

"You have our statements," Miss Withers told him. "Wouldn't it be fair of you to ask young Reverson about this, instead of beating around the bush?"

"Yes," put in the Englishwoman, arising. "I'll go and fetch him."

But the inspector halted her. "Where's his room?" he demanded. "I'll have the constable go, if you don't mind."

Leslie arrived, in dressing gown and slippers. He was too bewildered to say anything more than, "Oh, I say!"

"Did you send a package to Miss Noring today?" demanded Cannon.

"A package? No, of course not. Why yes, but it wasn't a package. I sent her some chrysanthemums by a page, just before dinner."

"Chrysanthemums, eh? Well, she never got any chrysanthemums. Was your card attached?"

"Why, yes. Yes, of course. I met the boy a few minutes afterward and asked him what she said when she got them." Leslie was blushing furiously. "He said that nobody was in the room but that he'd put them on the dresser."

"She was out—to buy buns and milk," said Miss Withers softly.

"It's a good story," Cannon told him. "We'll soon see if it'll wash." He put down his notebook and produced the ebony box. "Ever see this before?"

Leslie shook his head.

Cannon nodded. He opened the box and extended it. "Care to have a smoke?"

"Don't care if I do." Then Leslie drew back his hand. "I don't care much for that kind," he said. "Too sweet."

"Much too sweet," agreed Cannon. He put the ebony box away again. "That'll do for you. But mind, you're not to leave town."

Leslie Reverson grinned at his aunt. "I'm doing my best not to," he said. Then suddenly the smile was wiped from his face. "Oh, I say! Nothing's wrong with Candy, I mean Miss Noring, is it?"

"Nothing serious," he was told. "She'll be all right in the morning. But somebody made a jolly good effort to put her to sleep everlasting. Any idea who might have done it?"

Leslie Reverson looked as if he hadn't an idea in his head. "That'll do," said Cannon impatiently. "Come on downstairs and point out that page boy to me. If he bears out your story, that'll give us something to work from."

Miss Withers and the Honorable Emily were alone. "Don't look so worried," said the school teacher.

The Honorable Emily tried to smile. "But Leslie is such an odd boy sometimes," she said. "That's why I was pleased to see him interested in Candida Noring, she seems so sensible. You don't suppose he would possibly be capable of——"

"He's not the masked marvel who's behind all this monkey business," said Miss Withers absently. "At least, I don't see how he could be." She began to stride up and down the room. "No, the Leslie Reverson I've seen isn't the type to carry on in such a dime-novel fashion. But it's all such a puzzle. . . ."

"I feel considerably more confident with you around," confessed the Englishwoman. "The police are at such a loss, and you seem to take hold of things."

"To use an American expression, I'm afraid I've bitten off more than I can chew," Miss Withers admitted. "As you may have guessed, I've had experience with homicide before. Wherever I go I seem to run into it."

She wanted this woman's confidence and on an impulse went over to her suitcase and drew out a silver badge. "I'm not just a snoop," she explained. "I was given this some time ago—by the New York police. It's purely honorary, of course."

The Honorable Emily leaned back in her chair. "Tell me!" she begged. And for more than an hour she listened, engrossed, while Miss Withers recounted some of her adventures. "And so they hung both of them at San Quentin," she finished. "I'm afraid it isn't a very pleasant bed-time story."

"You've given me something to think about," said the Honorable Emily, and hurried off to bed.

Miss Withers slept, and was awakened shortly before noon by a crash of her door against the chair which she had placed as a barrier. She rose sleepily and found the maid standing outside.

"Excuse me, mum——"

"Never mind. It's high time I was up. Send a waiter with some breakfast, will you? I'm starved." Miss Withers had a sudden doubt. "I don't suppose I've slept two nights and a day, have I?"

"This is Thursday, mum."

"Then it's all right. By the way, how is the young lady down the hall? The one in 505?"

"Her that was sick last night? She's peaked, mum. But she ate a good breakfast. The police was up to see her, and just a few minutes ago I saw her going downstairs with a young man."

"A young man? A policeman?"

The maid was loquacious. "No, mum. The handsome young man down on the third floor."

Miss Withers heaved a sigh of relief. "All right, you can go. And tell the waiter I want two eggs this morning."

She had finished the eggs when she had another caller. Sergeant Secker knocked on her door.

"Good-morning," she greeted him. "Going to accept me as a consultant?"

He declined a cup of tea. "As a matter of fact, I came on such an errand. You can help us, if you will. I'm not giving away any secrets when I tell you that we've traced that box of cigarettes."

Miss Withers had not expected this. "You know who packed it with poison?"

"Well, not exactly. Our laboratory expert, Sir Leonard Tilton, had a look at it this morning and found that only a dozen or so of the topmost cigarettes were doped. The prettiest ones, as a matter of fact. And he's still trying to figure out just what the effect would have been if the girl had finished smoking one. He never ran up against cyanide used as incense before."

"Yes," urged Miss Withers. "But who sent it?"

"That's what I'm here to ask you," said the sergeant brightly. "You see, the box was sold by the main store of the manufacturer, Empey's, of the Strand. It was ordered by telephone and sent C.O.D. to a Mrs. Charles at the Norwich Hotel. That is a little lodging-house place, full of transients, on an alley off Charing Cross. Mrs. Charles only booked her room for a few hours, it seems. All the record they had of her—she hadn't even registered, unfortunately—was that she wore a gray fur coat."

Miss Withers dropped her teacup. "A *what*?"

"Not a what. A gray fur coat. The people who run the place have their own reasons for not being too friendly with us at the Yard."

Miss Withers was staring at the wall. After a moment she said, "Did they mention a long blue silk scarf?"

"They didn't mention anything," said Secker. "We dragged it out of them. No, I heard nothing of a scarf." The sergeant cocked his head. "I came over to ask if you knew any woman connected with this case who has such a coat?"

Miss Withers shook her head absently, more at herself than in answer to his question. "Tell me," she demanded. "Did you have sense enough to search the room of this mysterious Mrs. Charles?"

The sergeant nodded. "The room was without personality," he said. "Just a bed and a chair and a bureau. One of those gas heaters that you put a shilling in, you know."

"But there was *nothing*? Not even a pin or a scrap of paper?"

The sergeant fished in his pocket and brought out a racing form, two lottery tickets, and finally an envelope. "Only this scrap of paper," he said. "It was with some ashes underneath the gas heater."

Miss Withers saw, as she had feared to see, a tiny bit of charred paper, paper of a cream color and bearing a faint blue rule across it.

"I see," she said. But she most emphatically did not see.

"I'll be running along," said the sergeant. "Oh, by the way. No need to worry over young Reverson. His story about the chrysanthemums seems to be truthful. The florist remembered him, and so did the page boy. Somebody must have thrown away his flowers and stuck his card in the poisoned cigarettes."

"As simply as that, eh? So the chief inspector has it all figured out."

Sergeant Secker looked at her. "Don't you underestimate old Cannon," he said. "He's a real bloodhound. And you know, he's been handed over this whole affair to sort out—Noel, Todd, and the attempt on Candida Noring's life. Me, I'm still stuck with the Fraser suicide, and messenger-boy errands in between. Which reminds me that I'd better get back to my sleuthing for a lady in a gray fur coat."

"Good hunting," Miss Withers wished him.

She spent the rest of the day at the British Museum, buried in a heap of voluminous tomes in the reading room. When she came out she knew a great deal about the properties and effects of cyanide of potassium in its many forms, but nothing more about the series of mysteries and suicides which was beginning to prey upon her mind to an uncomfortable degree. "And I took this trip for a rest!" she said sadly to herself.

Returning to the hotel, she met Candida and Leslie Reverson, dressed for the evening and headed for a taxi.

"You children seemed undaunted," she remarked.

"Oh, quite," said Leslie Reverson.

Candida drew closer. "We're going out because I'm too nervous to stay in my room," she confessed.

She seemed paler than ever. Miss Withers wondered again at the way in which she had lost the tanned look of out-of-doors healthiness which had been hers on the boat.

"How do you feel after your narrow escape?" she inquired.

"Shaky," Candida confessed. "But Leslie thought I'd feel better if we went out to dinner and a variety show. And I feel safe with him."

"Safe as a vault," said Leslie gallantly. Miss Withers thought of some vaults that she had seen, and smiled wryly.

She touched Leslie's sleeve, drawing him aside. "Watch over her," she whispered.

"Nothing else but," said Leslie Reverson. It was a phrase that he had learned in Chicago, and he was proud of it.

The young couple rolled away in a taxi, with Miss Withers staring after them. They made a good pair—the new Leslie and the new Candida. After all, their ages couldn't be so very unlike. Candida, who had had no youth, and Leslie, who had had too much. . . . "She has strength enough for both of them," said Miss Withers to herself.

She dined in solitary splendor in the hotel dining room, and then, feeling very much at a loose end, decided to forget the problems which beset her and follow the example of the younger set. A vaudeville show, she thought, might be just the thing. It was true that her old friend and one-time fiancé, Oscar Piper of the New York police, had dragged her against her will to the Palace on several occasions, but this was England, and besides, she did not feel up to a play or concert.

She bought a ticket at the hotel desk for the Palladium, and then walked northward through the bewildering little streets of London. After a certain amount of wandering, she found the theater and sat through a show comprising most of the best vaudeville acts she had seen in New York at the Palace in the past two years. She came out onto Oxford Street, hurried along by the crowd, and sought for a bobby to ask how to get back to Trafalgar Square. Strangely enough, there was no stalwart figure in black rubber cape on the corner—but she did glimpse a familiar form which made her start.

She saw Tom Hammond aiding a rather garishly dressed young woman to board a bus marked "Marble Arch-Edgware Road." He stood back as the vehicle rolled away, waved his hand rather casually, and then started back across the street.

It had not been Loulu Hammond, that girl. Miss Withers was positive of that. There were many questions she would have liked to ask Tom Hammond. For lack of anything better to do, she followed him down Oxford Street, keeping a discreet distance behind.

He rounded a corner, and when she came after him he was out of sight. Miss Withers found herself standing beneath a canopy marked Oxford-Palace. Peering inside, she saw Hammond at a hotel desk. He accepted a key and moved toward the elevator. She would have liked to follow, but she noted that the time was nearing midnight. "At least I know where the Hammonds are staying," she told herself. "Tomorrow will do just as well."

But tomorrow was Friday, the day set for the inquest into the death of Andy Todd. She had forgotten that, until she was reminded by a telephone call in the morning from Sergeant Secker.

"There may not be anything to it," he said. "But you'd better be there. At any rate, you won't have to go away out to the East End. It's being held just off Drury Lane."

She found the place without difficulty, but was disappointed in the ceremony. Here was not even the modest drama of the other inquest, though many of the same people sat on the wooden benches.

Chief Inspector Cannon sat at the table behind the coroner, and evidently the sergeant was telling the truth about his being handed over the whole case, for there was no sign of the heavy-handed Filsom. There was a sketchy identification of the body, mostly from Todd's passport photograph, and testimony from a police surgeon who seemed to have been poured out of the same mold as his fellow medico at the other inquest. He told the jury that the deceased had met his death as the result of a fall of four stories—three floors and a basement—and that the autopsy showed an excessive amount of alcohol in the brain.

"The body was badly injured in the fall," finished the surgeon.

"Would you say unusually damaged?" inquired the coroner.

The doctor wouldn't say that. He had seen worse. But not from a fall of that distance. If the man hadn't been drunk he might have got off with only some broken bones, but as it was he had been unable to catch hold of anything or to land on his feet and had struck head first, with the natural result.

"Were the circumstances such as to impel you to a belief that death was by suicide?" inquired the coroner.

The police surgeon nodded, but before he could speak Chief Inspector Cannon had risen to his feet.

"I should like to request that this hearing be postponed, sir," he said. "For reasons satisfactory to the police."

This remark did not seem to surprise the coroner in the slightest. He was of a somewhat milder temperament than Maggers, Miss Withers decided.

"Very well," he decided. "I shall adjourn this hearing until Monday week, at the request of Scotland Yard."

"And that's that," Sergeant Secker greeted Miss Withers as she hurried out of the place.

"It certainly is," she told him cryptically. She did not care to linger, for she had something on her mind.

It was shortly before twelve o'clock, and she hoped to catch the Hammonds before they went out for the day's sightseeing, or whatever it was that they had come to London for. She took a taxi and was whisked away to the Oxford-Palace.

She marched up to the desk, across a foyer all in glass and silver—a modernistic scheme of decoration which reminded her, by contrast, of her own hotel. She asked the clerk for Mr. or Mrs. Hammond.

"I'll see if they're in," he promised. He reached for a desk phone and dialed a number.

"No answer." But he was anxious to oblige. "If you'll wait a moment I'll find out if they left a message."

He darted away and was gone for some minutes. Then he came back, shaking his head.

"That's odd," he remarked. "They've gone."

"Gone?" Miss Withers looked puzzled.

"Yes, madam. I was off duty yesterday. But it seems that Mrs. Hammond left yesterday morning, and Mr. Hammond very late last night. I was sure that they were here, because there's some mail in their box."

"Oh?" Miss Withers concocted an artifice. "I'm a close relative. Can you give me their address?"

The clerk shook his head. "Only that their mail was sent here from the American Express, and I suppose that we shall have to send it back there."

Miss Withers nodded. "And Master Hammond?" she asked.

By the expression of distaste on the clerk's face she knew that he had had experiences with the terrible Gerald. "Master Hammond left with his mother," he said.

Miss Withers thanked him and then displayed a half crown. "It's a little unusual," she explained. "But I wonder if you would mind looking in the Hammonds' mail to see if they received a letter I sent them yesterday. It's quite important."

The young man declined the half crown magnificently. "I understand," he said. He reached behind him and took from an upper box a little sheaf of letters. "All from the States," he said. "Except this." He showed her a letter with a border inked with black. It bore the brick-colored penny-ha'penny stamp of the Royal Mail.

His voice took on a note of polite respect. "A death in the family?" he said. "Unfortunately, they left before this arrived."

Miss Withers had also left, leaving the half crown behind her. She ordered lunch at a near-by restaurant, but had little appetite for it. She could not help thinking of another table at which she had lunched—a round table in the dining saloon of the *American Diplomat*. There had been Rosemary Fraser—she was gone. Andy Todd had likewise departed, willingly or unwillingly . . . after the receipt of a black-bordered letter. Such a letter had come to Candida Noring, and she had escaped death by the skin of her teeth, as Miss Withers would have put it.

That left the Honorable Emily, Leslie, the Hammonds, and herself of the group who had sat at the doctor's table.

"I ought to do something," Miss Withers told herself. But she wasn't sure just what she must do. There was no use warning the Honorable Emily or Leslie: they had had warning enough. The Hammonds, in spite of the black-bordered note, were out of reach—both of the murderer and of herself. If she could not warn them, it seemed likely that the murderer could not reach them.

Just to calm her conscience, Miss Withers dispatched a telegram to Tom Hammond, care of the American Express, and telling him to take his wife and child as far from London as he could possibly manage. "Though he'll only think I'm crazy," she admitted to herself.

Then she stopped short. She had forgotten one person who had been at the table—the doctor himself!

The ship sailed on its return journey to the States today, she knew. But there was still time and to spare before half-past two. She paid her bill in the restaurant and hailed a taxi outside. "Pier seven at George the Fifth dock," she told the driver. "And try to hurry."

He did his best, and better. They wound through the interminable streets of eastern London and drew up at the waterfront shortly before two o'clock.

Miss Withers gave the man a generous tip and then bustled through long and strangely vacant piers until she came out on the open dock.

There were a few broken bits of paper ribbon at her feet, but the slip was vacant.

"Isn't this where the *American Diplomat* sails from?" she demanded of a solitary person in a blue coat who was sweeping up.

He stared at her dully. "She'll be back again three weeks from Monday," he informed her. "Went out hours ago."

"But I thought she sailed at two-thirty. . . ."

"Eleven in the mornin', mum. They has to go out with the tide, y'see."

Miss Withers noticed a strip of glistening wet along the bottom of the cement pierhead. The tide was going out—and the *American Diplomat* was somewhere off Gravesend.

On board that trim little cabin-class vessel, Dr. Waite was just rising from the table over which he presided. There was a pleasant crowd on board, mostly American students driven home by the fall in the dollar, and the genial doctor anticipated a pleasant cruise. This would not, he was sure, turn out like the last trip over, with suicides and investigations and such. But he mentioned only pleasant topics.

"*What* a crowd and a voyage that one was," finished Dr. Waite. "Dancing until eleven or twelve every night."

There was no Loulu Hammond to be sweet and sarcastic about the pace that kills. Feeling a tremendous sense of relief, Waite walked back to his sick bay and seated himself at the desk.

The vessel was beginning to roll in the Channel swell, a comforting rocking motion. The doctor rubbed his bald head with the palm of his hand, loosened his vest, and leaned back in his chair. The world wasn't so bad, after all. What if he had come off rather badly with the not-too-married lady who lived in Maida Vale? There would be other weeks in London, and in the meantime he had one faithful mistress.

He reached in the drawer of his desk and took out a glass and a tall bottle. He poured himself out six fingers of the brandy and then held up the rich dose to the light which streamed in his port.

"Here's to a smooth voyage," said Dr. Waite to himself. He stopped suddenly and squinted at the glass. There was, instead of the fine clear glow of the brandy, an oily cloud of something heavy and dark at the bottom of his glass.

"Now what in the devil's got into that?" he asked himself. He sniffed, almost tasted, and then set it down with shaking fingers. Hastily he fumbled in his medicine cabinet and made a laboratory test that he remembered from dim distant days at Rush Medical.

When he had his result, he was shaking all over. "Good God!" said Dr. Waite. "It's loaded with cyanide!"

He took the bottle, holding it at arm's length, and dropped it out the porthole. Then he went to his medicine cabinet, found a small bottle of whisky, and though it smelled perfectly as it should, he put it away again.

"I'll be damned!" he assured himself. "Completely damned!"

There was a knock on his door, and fat, cheerful Sparks entered, smoking a new curving calabash which he had bought in London to add to his growing collection. The wireless operator took the pipe from his mouth. "Message for you," he said. "Figure it out if you can."

He handed over a yellow sheet of paper upon which he had typed out the words:

SUSPECT WHOLESALE MURDER PLOT TAKE CARE OF YOURSELF. HILDEGARDE WITHERS.

For the first time the bald and sniggering doctor realized that the black-bordered note which had awaited him when he came back on board was not simply a bad joke.

"I'll be thoroughly and completely damned," he said.

CHAPTER IX

*

Whom God Hath Put Asunder

"I may need your support," said Hildegarde Withers. "Come on in with me, and be surprised at nothing."

The Honorable Emily and Miss Withers had been taking a pleasant stroll on this bright and windy Saturday morning, and now they stood outside that Mecca of tourists, the offices of the American Express. Around them the busy Haymarket roared and boomed.

"But for what?" demanded the Englishwoman.

"Never you mind," Miss Withers told her. "Just look like the daughter of a hundred earls and say nothing."

They went inside, and after standing in line for a few minutes, stood before the mail desk. The young man at the counter wore very thick eyeglasses and peered through them dubiously.

"Anything for Mr. or Mrs. Thomas Hammond?" inquired Miss Withers. She spoke firmly, with an air of uprightness and authority, in spite of the fact that she was planning a bare-faced robbery of the Royal Mail.

It was all too easy. The young man at the counter reached behind him and then handed her a sheaf of letters. Most of them were from New York, and one was forwarded, with the old address, "T. H. Hammond, Advtg. Mgr. Pyren Extinguisher Co., N. Y. C." The women turned to go.

"Just a moment," said the clerk, staring over his eyeglasses with a cold appraisal. "Are you Mrs. Hammond?"

"Er—no," Miss Withers admitted.

"Well, I can't let you have mail addressed to anyone else unless they identify you and you register here," he told her. "I have Mr. Hammond's signature in the book, and on a written order from him I'll be glad to——"

"Go jump in the Thames," Miss Withers remarked in a very low voice. She smiled brightly. "I'm sorry—I didn't know the rules," she said.

She handed back the sheaf of letters and then stalked out of the place, with the Honorable Emily in tow.

"Well, whatever you were trying to do, you didn't do it," said that lady drily.

"Didn't I!" Miss Withers well concealed any feeling of chagrin that might have filled her maidenly bosom. "At least I've discovered that no package of poisoned cigarettes or gumdrops or bath salts is waiting for the Hammonds. There was nothing but letters and postcards."

"Was that what you had in mind?" The Honorable Emily looked incredulous.

Miss Withers smiled and patted the crinkling envelope—with a narrow inked border of black—which reposed snugly in her sleeve.

"Of course!" she answered, and they walked back toward their hotel in silence. They parted in the elevator.

"I'm alone a great deal now that Leslie has set about paying court to Candida Noring," said the Honorable Emily a bit wistfully. "Would you care to have tea with me around five?"

"I should love to," Miss Withers told her. "But I'm afraid I shall be very, very busy around five o'clock."

As soon as she was in her room she got down to business. From her sleeve she took the black-bordered letter which she had first seen at the mail desk of the Oxford-Palace and which she had chased all the way down to the express office. For a long time she studied it. No doubt there were fingerprints on it—prints which might solve the whole mystery of this wholesale chain of murders—or what she was beginning to suspect must certainly be murder on a wholesale scale.

Yet heaven only knew how many other persons beside the sender had touched the envelope. There was certainly herself, the man at the desk in the American Express and the hotel clerks at the Oxford-Palace, together with whoever had sorted and handled the mail in the post office. Besides, the police had one of these fantastic messages intact, taken from the pocket of dead Andy Todd. They would find whatever was to be found in the line of fingerprints. Miss Withers had no facilities for such work, and, moreover, she had learned from her friend Inspector Piper that few juries on either side of the Atlantic will accept fingerprint evidence even in this advanced day and age.

"Bother the prints," she decided. She turned her attention to the envelope itself. It told her very little at first glance.

It was squarish and white—of a rather cheap grade. The stamp was affixed on a slight angle, and the postmark read, "London—8 A.M.—26 SEP—1933." Beneath the date was a single letter "C" which she took to represent the post office at which the stamp had been canceled. That would mean more to Scotland Yard than to her, and probably very little even to them. Yet, after all, it meant something to know that this was the first of the murder messages that had gone through the mails.

The address was written in common blue-black ink, in a roundish hand from which most of the personal characteristics of the writer had been removed. It was the same writing as the other letters edged in black, Miss Withers was quite sure of that. Yet as an intelligent, if rather elementary, student of handwriting through the treatises of such experts as the famous Gypsy Louise Rice, she knew that very little indeed can be done with so limited a sample of handwriting as the address on an envelope. This white square bore only the words "Mr. and Mrs. Tom Hammond, American Express, London." There were also scribbled forwarding notations—to and from the Oxford-Palace—but they of course meant nothing.

It was certain, then, that the writer of that address had been almost without emotion. Only someone impassioned and cool could have kept personality so hidden. There was nothing more, except that the black border had been hurriedly inked.

Without a second's hesitancy Miss Withers inserted a hairpin in the flap and opened the message.

As she had known, it consisted of a few scraps of cream-colored paper glued upon a blacked-in background. The handwriting was, if not the same, very similar to that on the envelope, yet it seemed a bit more definite, more natural and human and intense. The writer of this message had been inflamed with passion.

"And you, you superior self-satisfied fools, one of these days you'll learn that the people around you aren't just puppets to laugh at. . . ."

"Never end a sentence with a preposition," Miss Withers told herself absently. She was disappointed, having hoped for something definite, something pointed, in the message. It was like all the rest, showing a very real malice which almost reached hatred, and which still did not seem quite in tune with the doom which had descended upon at least two of the recipients of these letters. It was not until months afterward, when it was all over, that she knew that Dr. Waite had been added to the list.

She sat and stared at the black-framed message for a long time, but no further inspiration came to her. The whole affair seemed essentially childish and almost ridiculous—and yet three persons had died exceedingly unpleasant deaths, and one more had come so close to the scythe of the Grim Reaper that she would sleep ill o' nights for many and many a month.

"I wonder," Miss Withers asked herself, as she put the purloined letter carefully away, "I wonder just what it was that Peter Noel was throwing into the sea that morning?" There had been the cryptic letters "osem" on the one scrap she had found. That might, of course, be part of the word "Yosemite." It also fitted into the name "Rosemary." Miss Withers inclined very strongly to the latter possibility. Then had Noel, also, received a warning note before his death? If so, what about his suicide?

Supposing it wasn't suicide? And then how on earth could anybody make a man swallow a dose of poison, in full view of the police, against his will? Miss Withers was back where she had started.

She ordered tea sent up to her room, and tried to put the whole affair out of her mind for the time being. But it was no use. She felt herself in the middle of the second act of a mystery melodrama, stuck in the center of the stage before a crowded house, and without the vaguest notion of what her lines and business should be.

"For the last three years," she scolded herself, "you've been wishing for a chance to tackle a murder mystery without Oscar Piper and the police to back you up. Now you've got it and you don't know what to do with it."

On an impulse, she went downstairs to the lobby and telephoned to Scotland Yard, asking for Chief Inspector Cannon. She learned that he was not on duty. "He'll probably ring in after the football game," said the man at the desk. "Shall I give him a message?"

"Never mind," Miss Withers answered wearily. She asked for Sergeant Secker.

"He's not available either," she learned. "He usually goes up to his home in Suffolk over the week-end."

"I only hope that the criminal world observes its holidays as carefully as the police in this fair land," Miss Withers remarked acidly, and hung up.

Driven by sheer necessity to the company of the Honorable Emily, Miss Withers went down to the third floor and rapped at her door. But there was no answer.

She continued on down to the foyer and asked at the desk if the Honorable Emily had left any message.

"Her ladyship is, I think, having a guest for tea in the lounge," the clerk told her. "Shall I have her paged?"

"No, thank you." Miss Withers gave it up. She went out to the nearest newsdealer, and bought an armful of American newspapers and magazines, with which she proceeded to stupefy her intelligence through the evening and through most of the following Sunday.

She took a long walk in the Sabbath afternoon, strolling through the Embankment Gardens. In spite of the mist in the air, and a chill wind which swept up the Thames, the place was filled with young men and women, paired off two and two, most of whom were happily courting in the English fashion, which consists of striding under a load of heavy tweeds in no particular direction but with a great deal of energy. "No doubt until they finally drop in each other's arms of sheer exhaustion," Miss Withers decided.

She saw one couple who, instead of striding vigorously forward, were strolling idly along the walk above the river, and now and then stopping to toss chestnuts to the screaming gulls over the water. As she drew closer she saw that it was Leslie Reverson with the Noring girl again. They were walking very close together and laughing at nothing at all. At least, Reverson was laughing.

Miss Withers, with an unwonted delicacy, withdrew down a side path before she met them. "Love!" she remarked softly to herself. "It goes on at the brink of a volcano, and on the deck of a sinking ship, and in the shadow of the gallows."

Then she caught herself short. "At my age!" she said. All unbidden the gay chorus from *Patience* came to her mind:

> *Twenty lovesick maidens we,*
> *Lovesick all against our will,*
> *Twenty years hence we shall be*
> *Twenty lovesick maidens still. . . .*

She went back to her hotel, feeling very much alone, and wrote a long and very caustic letter to Oscar Piper, back in New York—a letter which made the worthy inspector suspect that English cooking did not agree with her. Hardly had she affixed the stamp when there came a tap on her door.

It was Leslie Reverson. "I say, is my aunt here by any chance?"

Miss Withers shook her head and knew at once that there was something else the young man had to say to her.

"Won't you sit down?" she invited. Reverson entered and leaned against the dresser.

"I say," he began once or twice. But that was all.

"What's the matter?" Miss Withers prompted him. "Course of true love a bit bumpy?"

"Eh? No, no, not at all." He grinned pleasantly. "But what I wanted to ask you—you see, Aunt Emily thinks you're the real stuff, all wool and a yard wide, and all that sort of rot, you know. It's an odd thing to ask, but I wish that if you get a chance you'd put in a good word for Candy—Candy and me, you know."

"Why, I——"

"Aunt isn't the easiest person in the world to get around," Reverson went on. "Until she dies I haven't a penny except what she gives me, and she makes me toe the line, you know. If you'd just say a word . . ."

"Of course, if the opportunity arises. But I don't understand. I thought that your aunt approved of Miss Noring?"

Leslie nodded emphatically. "Quite. Oh, she does. But it's more than approval I want. And Candy is so outspoken. We all had luncheon together, and Candy got a bit under aunt's skin. She ragged us about not having serviettes at table unless you order them specially, and about the warm cocktails and the duty on cigarettes and no central heating. . . ."

Miss Withers smiled. "Candida Noring is suffering from an attack of Homesickness Americana," she informed the young man. "The best remedy would be to show her something of the real England, that lies outside your smoky old London."

"Oh!" Leslie understood. "You mean the country! Never cared for it myself." He snapped his fingers. "Wait—I've an idea! Marvelous idea! Aunt will be insisting on our leaving for the old ruins in Cornwall in a day or so. She's been eating her heart out in town, mostly because she worries over silly old Tobermory. I'll get her to invite Candy down to stay for a few weeks!"

He hurried toward the door. "Thanks awfully for the suggestion," he said. Miss Withers, who felt a natural desire to keep the characters in her pet mystery play together until she could at least cast them in their proper rôles, was mildly protesting.

"But I didn't suggest——"

Young Reverson, jubilating over the new inspiration, was gone. Miss Withers shrugged her shoulders and went back to her magazines.

Bright and early next morning she set out for the Haymarket. There was a goodish crowd around the mail desk this morning, for the *Europa* had come in on Saturday. Miss Withers lurked about on the fringes of the crowd, trying to think of a dodge to secure the information she needed.

Unfortunately the same clerk, with the same thick glasses, was at the counter. He seemed to see more through the thick lenses than one would imagine. Miss Withers saw him look toward her and his gaze fix itself for a moment before it passed on. He was talking to a young man in a gray checked topcoat, who turned suddenly and strode toward her.

It was Tom Hammond—and a Tom Hammond that Miss Withers had never seen before. He was wearing a blue tie that went very badly indeed with his green shirt, and his eyes seemed slightly reddened around the rims. He was very angry.

"See here!" he began. "The clerk tells me that you've been——" He stopped short. "Oh, it's you, is it? Would you mind giving me some explanation . . ."

"Not at all," said Miss Withers coolly. "I've been trying to find you for days. But you moved out of your hotel, leaving no address but this."

"I'm staying at the Englamerican Club," he said shortly. "But what that's got to do with your trying to wangle my mail away from the desk——"

"Young man," said Miss Withers sternly, "be still for a few moments and I'll enlighten you." She drew him into a corner and produced an envelope bordered with black. Then she told him what it was necessary that he should know and very little more.

"Now you understand," she finished. "I felt it my duty to warn you and your wife, in case this insane chain of murders is scheduled to continue. Since I couldn't get in touch with either of you, I took the liberty of scouting around a bit, to make sure that nothing had been sent to you in the mail which might cause another tragedy."

Tom Hammond was holding the black-bordered letter which she had returned to him. "This is all a lot of nonsense. I'm going to turn it over to the police."

"The police have one of those letters and haven't found out anything more about it than have I. Perhaps not so much. If you take my advice, you'll take your wife and child and pack out of England just as fast as you can. This was to have been a vacation trip, wasn't it? Well, you can vacation somewhere else—where it's healthier."

Tom Hammond gave her a queer sidewise look. "It's easier said than done," he remarked casually.

"What is?"

"Packing up my wife and child. You see, I haven't laid eyes on either of them since the day of the Noel inquest."

"What?" Miss Withers had not expected this. "You mean . . ."

"I mean that Loulu walked out on me," he said stiffly. "God knows why." His voice had raised a little, and almost against his will the words came tumbling forth. "After she left me at the inquest I came back to the hotel and found her packed and gone, Gerald, bags, and all."

"But didn't she leave a note?" Miss Withers was properly sympathetic.

"She left nothing. I don't know what's got into her. She ought to be examined by a lunacy commission. She's been

121

strange all the way over on the boat, and stranger since we got to London. If you ask me, I think she's gone stark staring mad!"

"Now, now," said Miss Withers commiseratingly. "It's not as bad as all that. Perhaps I can help you find her." She peered at him. "You do want to find her, don't you?"

"I should dearly love an opportunity," said Tom Hammond, "of being alone for ten minutes with my wife." His voice was very intense.

Miss Withers hoped that she understood this as it was meant. "She can't have disappeared into thin air," she told him. "If I'm to help you, you must tell me one thing. Did you give her any reason for going?"

Tom Hammond glared. "No! No reason at all!" He was unnecessarily definite about this, the school teacher thought. "Though why I'm telling all this to you I haven't the slightest idea!" he finished belligerently. "I didn't ask you to interfere."

"But you want me to," Miss Withers told him gently. "You want me to find Loulu and your son Gerald——"

"Never mind Gerald," said Tom Hammond. "He can stay lost."

"——and give you two young things a chance to make up your quarrel," Miss Withers went on. "No doubt you have hurt her feelings in some way without knowing. I suggest that you be very sweet when you see her again. You might smooth things over with a new wrist watch or a fur coat or something. . . ."

"Great idea," sneered Tom Hammond. "I did buy her a fur coat, as soon as we got here. I thought it might break the great silence. Paid sixty guineas for the best squirrel coat at Revillon's, and got a chilly thank you. She only wore it once or twice, and left it behind when she moved out of the hotel."

"Dear me," agreed Miss Withers. "This is serious—and more serious still when you realize that your wife is alone in London with a murderer very probably lying in wait for her. And we can't even get a warning to her."

"If I can't find her," pointed out Tom Hammond sensibly, "I don't see how the mysterious murderer can find her."

"It might happen, all the same," Miss Withers insisted. She had an idea. "There's one quick way to find her," she said. "You have a photograph of your wife?"

Hammond hesitated. "Had," he said. "Tore it up."

"Well, what about your passport? Don't married couples share a passport?"

He shook his head. "We have separate ones. Loulu's been over once or twice without me. Of course, she took it with her."

"Well, if her passport picture is like most of them it wouldn't help. I was going to suggest that we have the police and newspapers search for her as a person suspected of suffering from amnesia."

"She'd thank you for the publicity," Hammond said drily.

Miss Withers bit her lip. "Perhaps she can be found without publicity. It oughtn't to be easy for a young woman and a child to disappear. Did she take—I mean, was she in funds?"

"Loulu has her own money," Hammond informed her.

"Good! Then we can trace her through her bank. Let me have, also, a list of her friends in London."

Hammond gave the information requested. "By the way," he asked, "if you do find her, don't let on that I'm looking for her. I wouldn't give her that much satisfaction. Just tip me off to where she is, and I'll do the rest."

"Naturally," agreed Miss Withers. She glanced at her watch and realized that she had been standing in this draughty corner of the express office for more than half an hour. "I'll get in touch with you at the Englamerican Club if I find out anything. And in the meantime, if you should receive any samples of bonbons, restrain your appetite, young man."

She nodded brightly and left him there. As she hurried down toward the Mall, serenely unconscious of the fact that a very dark-browed young man was staring dubiously after her, she congratulated herself. "A very neat bit of business," said Hildegarde Withers.

She spent the rest of the morning in a vain attempt to extract information from the impassive officials of the bank through which Loulu Hammond was supposed to receive funds. The affairs of its clients, she learned, were a matter of the utmost secrecy.

"Well, would you give the information to Scotland Yard?" she demanded at last.

"If the police can show us a proper order of the court, very possibly yes," she was told. "And perhaps not even then."

Shortly before dinner time that night Miss Withers walked wearily in through the doors of the Hotel Alexandria. The Honorable Emily and Leslie Reverson were sitting at a little table in the foyer, behind two tall glasses. They waved, and she sank wearily in a chair that the young man sprang to hold for her.

"You look a bit seedy," the Honorable Emily told her. "Better have something to warm you up. Been sightseeing?"

Miss Withers glared at her. "Sightseeing! I've been walking my legs off trying to find Loulu Hammond, who seems to have disappeared in thin air. I got nothing from her bank, and none of her friends in London have any idea where she is. I suppose that I'll have to appeal to the Yard."

"That ought to be easy enough," the Honorable Emily told her. "That young sergeant from the Yard has been here twice looking for you this afternoon. Seemed to have something on his mind, didn't he, Leslie?" Her nephew nodded.

"Good heavens!" Miss Withers started. "I wonder if anything has happened to Mrs. Hammond already?"

"It's happened very recently then," said the Honorable Emily. "Because she had tea with me here Saturday, the afternoon when you locked yourself in your room to think, and she also rang me up a few hours ago to thank me for some advice I'd given her."

"Advice?" Miss Withers was incredulous. "You mean, about going back to her husband?"

"Her husband wasn't mentioned in our conversation," said the Honorable Emily. "She called on me—and at my invitation stayed for tea—to ask my advice about a school for her son."

"Filthy little bounder," put in Leslie Reverson and then subsided.

"She said that she had decided to send him to school in England and asked if I would be willing to recommend one. I told her about Tenton Hall—located down in Cornwall a few miles from our home. The headmaster is Starling, a very sound person who used to be Leslie's tutor——"

"He spoke softly and carried a big stick," said Leslie reminiscently.

"—and so she decided to follow my advice. She called up today to tell me so." The Honorable Emily tossed off her drink.

"But where is she? From where did she telephone?" demanded Miss Withers.

"I haven't the slightest idea in the world," said the Honorable Emily. And that was that.

"Well," decided Miss Withers, "I'm going to snatch an omelette and then see what sleep will do for my problems. The farther I go into this muddle the thicker it gets."

"Must you?" asked the Honorable Emily. "Go into it, I mean?"

"'One who never turned his back but marched straightforward,'" quoted Miss Withers.

"Of course, you're right," agreed the Honorable Emily. "None of us is safe until this mystery is exposed. All the same I was thinking that you might like to get out of London for a while. We're going down to Cornwall tomorrow—if my dressmaker fulfills her sworn oath and gets my new suits over here tonight. Leslie has persuaded me to ask Candida Noring down—the poor girl needs a bit of fresh air after her horrible experience the other night—and I thought you might like to come along and have a look at Dinsul, the oldest inhabited castle in England." The Englishwoman hesitated. "As a matter of fact, I'd feel ever so much safer if you were there!"

"Many thanks," said Hildegarde Withers. "But duty before pleasure, you know. The heart of this maze I'm following lies right here in London, and here I must stay until I reach it." She was thinking, oddly enough, of Loulu Hammond.

The Honorable Emily stood up and held out her hand. "Cheerio, then," she said. "We're taking the Cornish Riviera express at ten in the morning, and with impedimenta consisting of Tobermory and the bird and—and all the rest, we'll leave rather early for the station."

Miss Withers wished them *bon voyage* and went upstairs. But much as she had hoped for an early bedtime, it was not to be. Sergeant John Secker tapped at her door while she was attacking her omelette.

"I've got a very important question to ask you," he announced. "I want you to make an addition to your statement about the night when Rosemary Fraser disappeared."

Miss Withers motioned him to a chair. "Yes, yes, go on."

"When you were sitting in the deck chair, and noticed Rosemary Fraser leaning over the rail, just what were the weather conditions? The sea and all that?"

"It wasn't rough enough so that the splashing of the waves could drown out a splash or scream, if that's what you mean," Miss Withers said thoughtfully. "There was a light mist, and a rather chilly breeze."

"Sure of that? The breeze, I mean?"

Miss Withers was positive. "I think it was what sailors call a head wind."

The sergeant showed his delight. "I've got old Cannon," he announced. "Don't you see? If there was a breeze, particularly a head wind pushing past the ship, how in the world could Rosemary's scarf dangle straight down so that a man standing on the promenade deck just below her could catch it? It would whip back along where she was standing!"

Miss Withers nodded. "That's just what it did. I remember now."

"At last we're getting somewhere!" said the sergeant.

"After a restful week-end?" inquired Miss Withers a bit sarcastically.

"Perhaps. But the wires were humming and the wheels turning," he insisted. "It wasn't such a barren period at that. I've been in touch with the States."

"Yes?"

"Yes, madam. Trying to dig up a motive for these blasted crimes —if they are crimes. I'm not bothering so much with the Noel case, or the death of Todd. It all radiates from Rosemary Fraser, and that angle of the case is the one turned over to me. I've been looking for a motive."

"What," inquired Miss Withers sweetly, "did you find out about Candida Noring?"

"What?" The sergeant looked up quickly. "How did you know?"

"It was only natural that you'd suspect her, as Rosemary's only friend on the boat. Shipboard acquaintances don't usually have time to develop homicidal motives."

126

He nodded. "I got in touch with the Buffalo police. Had an idea that perhaps Candida would inherit some money from her friend, or that perhaps they were both interested in the same boy-friend, as you Americans put it."

"And you found——"

"Candida Noring got nothing from the death of the Fraser girl," went on the sergeant. "As a matter of fact, she lost considerably from the death of the girl. Her heart had been set on a trip around the world, and Rosemary was taking her as a companion. No Rosemary—no trip. As far as heart interest is concerned, Rosemary had the reputation in her home town of being a little in love with every good-looking man she met, but never anything too serious. Candida Noring just the opposite—strictly hands off with the boys and waiting for the grand passion."

"Interesting, if significant," Miss Withers admitted. "What's your theory? Don't tell me you haven't got one."

"I have," said Secker. "Somebody killed Rosemary Fraser—God only knows how. And either that somebody has been killing off the possible witnesses, first sending them a warning note made out of scraps of the dead girl's diary, in order to throw suspicion in the wrong direction and otherwise confuse the issue——" He stopped short. "Or—somebody who is not the murderer of Rosemary is trying to avenge her, and in order to make sure of getting her murderer is knocking off, one after another, the persons on board who might conceivably have done it. How do you like that for a theory?"

"Ingenious," Miss Withers granted. "What have you decided about motives for the original murder?"

"Candida—none, unless they had a quarrel we know nothing about. Besides, since girlhood they have been together more or less, and probably had quarreled and made up dozens of times. The Honorable Emily—none that I can see, unless she was trying to protect her nephew against a designing woman, which seems doubtful. Mrs. Hammond—possible, if she had suspected her husband was the man involved with Rosemary in the famous blanket-locker affair. Only we know from Candida that Noel was the man in that."

"You're sticking pretty close to one sex," pointed out Miss Withers.

The sergeant nodded. "You forgot that the mysterious Mrs. Charles, who almost certainly sent those messages edged in black, was a woman."

"Not necessarily," Miss Withers said. "Did you ever hear of Mask and Wig, or Haresfoot, or any of the hundreds of other college dramatic societies in the States, in which young men play the parts of girls?"

The sergeant looked blank. "You mean, that under the fur coat Mrs. Charles might have——"

"Might have worn trousers, actual or figurative." Miss Withers nodded. "You'd better keep on with your list of motives."

"Peter Noel—he might have killed Rosemary. Possible motive, since he had been involved with her and wanted to keep his rich and susceptible gold mine of a widow in Minneapolis. But he certainly didn't send any letters, nor kill Todd and attack Candida and the rest of it. Because he is quite dead."

"Go on," said Miss Withers. "Take the rest of the table group."

"Well, there's Andy Todd. He had his feelings very badly hurt by Rosemary, who was snobbish to him. But if he killed her, what about Noel? And how could he perpetrate further monkey business after he lay squashed at the bottom of the hotel lift?"

"Right," agreed Miss Withers.

"There's Reverson. He made eyes at Rosemary, somebody said. But it never got any farther than that, as far as we can tell. Then, last, we have Hammond, who might very well have had an affair, or tried to have one, with Rosemary, and then killed her for some motive arising out of it, perhaps having to do with his wife. I'm leaving out the doctor on board, because no matter who else was in and out of his office that night, we know that he stayed in the dice game. He has an alibi, almost the only one."

"You're leaving out somebody else," Miss Withers reminded him. She wore a very cryptic smile.

The sergeant frowned, and then his face cleared. "Righto! You mean yourself? That's ridiculous, of course. I've checked up on who you are."

"Nothing is ridiculous in a case such as this," she told him sharply. "But if you want to know, I was not referring to myself."

Long after the ambitious young detective had taken his departure, Miss Withers lay in her bed thinking over the list that he had roughly sketched in. "It would be so much easier if Rosemary had been an aquatic star," she decided. "Or if I knew the meaning of what Loulu Hammond said after the inquest. . . ."

She was to have an answer to her last question sooner than she expected. At eleven o'clock the next morning she was told that someone wanted to speak with her on the telephone, and she hurried downstairs. The voice was Tom Hammond's.

"Just wanted to let you know that you don't need to search any more for my wife," he said shortly. "No doubt your intentions were all right——"

"You mean she's come back?"

"No, I don't mean that she's come back!" Hammond mimicked. "I mean that just now I got a cablegram from Paris. Loulu is over there instituting suit for divorce."

"What grounds?" asked Miss Withers quickly, determined to extract the last morsel of information.

"I'm damned if I know," said Tom Hammond. "But if I had her here for ten minutes I'd give her some grounds, and I don't mean mental cruelty, either."

He sounded rather violent. "May I ask what your plans are?" Miss Withers requested.

"You may," yelled Tom Hammond into the telephone. "I am going out and get howling, stinking drunk!" He crashed the receiver.

"I don't blame him," said Miss Withers after a moment of deep thought.

CHAPTER X

*

The Scream of the Gull

Paddington Station has never been noted for being a place of rest and quiet, and the advent that morning of the Honorable Emily, Candida Noring, Leslie Reverson, together with their accumulated boxes, coats, and baggage, did not serve to make the hectic scene any more peaceful. Tobermory squalled shrilly and profanely from his carrying case, stretching a furious and gleaming-taloned paw from the opening and slashing at thin air. Dicon, the pessimistic robin, who was traveling in his bird cage covered with newspaper wrappings, vented a "cheep-cheep" now and then and jumped heavily from trapeze to floor and back again, beating against the newspaper with heavy wings.

The Honorable Emily, like all her countrymen, more at home traveling than otherwise, marshaled her forces around her. She dispatched Candida for magazines, Leslie to discover their reservations in the first-class carriage, and then stood guard over the tremendous mound of suitcases until a porter had splashed stickers marked "Penzance" over them and carted them away.

Candida returned with an armful of reading matter, and the two women marched on down the platform toward where Leslie stood waving his arms. He came forward to greet them. "This is the one," he said. "But we've got to change to another compartment. That loathsome fat Hammond child is in there——"

"Oh," said the Honorable Emily. "Didn't I tell you? When Mrs. Hammond rang me up to say that she was following my advice and sending her son to Tenton Hall today, I thought it would be kind to offer——"

"Offer?" said Leslie bitterly.

His aunt looked away. "As a matter of fact, she did hint at it herself. But it's only for a few hours, you know. He's too young to take the trip by himself, and his mother couldn't take him herself because she had an engagement somewhere and had to leave London yesterday. She said she thought she could arrange with her hotel to keep him last night and send him over here this morning."

"Ugh!" said Reverson "Well, there he is—cutting his initials in the windowpane with a glass-cutter or something."

"He's only a child," said the Honorable Emily. She turned to Candida. "You won't mind his being with us?"

"Not at all," said Candida Noring. "It ought to be jolly."

Jolly wasn't the word for it. They were finally arranged in the compartment, Leslie and the terrible Gerald next the windows, the Honorable Emily and Candida facing each other next the corridor, and Dicon hanging from the luggage rack. Tobermory made valiant swipes at Candida's stocking from where his case had been placed on the floor, but for the time being she was just beyond the reach of his claws.

The Honorable Emily, feeling the duties of a combined hostess and tour manager resting heavily upon her shoulders, attempted to start things off on the right foot by making introductions all around. "Treat children as adults and you win their everlasting confidence and esteem," she had heard somewhere. But it did not work with Gerald.

"This is Miss Noring, and this is Mr. Reverson, Gerald," she said sweetly.

The boy grunted unpleasantly and went on scraping at the window glass. He had already cut his initials, a dimly recognizable horse, and an unprintable four-letter word.

He turned suddenly to Candida, who was laden with the magazines. "Did you get any candy?" he demanded.

"Why, I don't believe I did," said that young lady. For the benefit of Leslie she was endeavoring to be very kind to Gerald.

"Not even any chocolate?" pressed the child.

"Not even chocolate," admitted Candida.

"I thought you wouldn't," said Gerald. He took a bag from his pocket, removed four untidy looking caramels, and placed them in a row on the window sill. The other occupants of the carriage had a sudden fear that they were to be called upon to share in the unattractive feast, but they did not know Gerald. He put away the bag and stuffed the four caramels in his mouth. Then he went back to his glass-cutting.

The train was moving. Candida, used to American railways with their bumps and jerks, noticed with surprise that they had gotten well under way without any noticeable tremor. The view from the window consisted of fog and dingy tenements, but Candida was staring at, and not out of, the window.

"Why, that isn't a glass-cutter," she said suddenly. "That's a diamond."

Gerald concealed his tool and looked defiant.

"Let me see that," ordered the Honorable Emily. He extended it, in the middle of a murky palm. It was a diamond solitaire.

"Why," cried the Englishwoman, "how did you——"

Gerald concealed the ring again. "My mother gave it to me."

"Your mother gave you her engagement ring?" The Honorable Emily remembered that diamond upon the finger of Loulu Hammond, and so did Candida.

"That's what I said," reiterated Gerald, who was a poor liar in this instance. He saw that he was not believed. "Well, just the *same* as gave it to me. She threw it in the waste basket when we walked out on papa—and I hooked it."

The Honorable Emily looked blank. "Oh," she said.

"I won't give it to you, either," Gerald finished. He snatched the nearest magazine and immersed himself in a deep study of the illustrations.

"Thank heaven," said the Honorable Emily under her breath.

But heaven did not long deserve her thanks. Before the outskirts of London were reached, Candida found that her conversation with the attentive Leslie was being interrupted by the insane flutterings of Dicon, the robin. He had seemed at first resigned to the swinging of his uncovered cage at the train's movement, but now he was throwing himself frantically from one side of the barred prison to the other, cheeping shrilly.

The Honorable Emily stared over the top of the October *Strand*. "Poor Dicon-bird," she said reprovingly. "Is he train sick?"

But Dicon was not train sick. It was Candida who first noticed the cause of the fat robin's perturbation, and she leaned closer to Leslie. "Watch," she whispered.

Reverson watched, and in a moment he saw the terrible Gerald peep from behind his magazine to send a spit ball flying with deadly accuracy through the bars of the cage. It struck Dicon on his red breast and sent him into spasms.

"I say!" gasped Leslie. "Don't do that. Not sporting, you know. Potting a sitting bird and all that."

The pride of the Hammond household hastily sent another spit ball. "Mind your own business," he told the young man.

"I say——" began Leslie. But Candida, with the intellectual acumen of her sex, simply leaned over and took the magazine from Gerald's lap.

"I'd like to look at this," she said pleasantly. There was quiet for a few minutes, while the train slipped pleasantly along at sixty miles per hour. They had passed most of the suburbs now, and London's horrible appendages of villas and cottages were thinning out.

Candida got well into an interesting story before she discovered that the latter pages of it had been torn out to make ammunition for Gerald. The Honorable Emily was still buried in her magazine, and Candida felt that she might as well try to follow her example. There was no use trying to chat with Leslie in front of this wide-eyed monster who faced them.

Indeed, when Reverson returned from a trip to the corridor bringing her a glass of water, Gerald piped up, "He's sweet on you, isn't he?"

"Little boys shouldn't——"

"Well, he is! You can't fool me, you can't." Gerald swung his legs and looked smug. "I don't like girls," he informed the group.

Nobody seemed inclined to encourage a further disclosure as to his tastes. The London sky had disappeared, and the sun shown through patches of cloud, beaming down here and there upon a wonderful soft green countryside, cut chess-board fashion into little irregular squares lined by hedges. Here and there a wooded hill swept past . . . .

The Honorable Emily seemed visibly to expand. "Coming into Berkshire," she announced.

Candida, in spite of the natural tension under which she rested, could not resist an exclamation. "How lovely it is!"

The Honorable Emily raised her eyebrows. "Wait until you see Cornwall," she advised. But her eyes softened: Leslie could not help noticing that.

He leaned back and watched Candida covertly, wondering again as he had wondered so often these last few days just why it was that he had had eyes on the boat only for the shallower, more apparent charms of Rosemary Fraser. It wasn't that Candida had lost some of her tanned, boyish healthiness, but that she had gained something more, something deeper. Leslie would rather look at her than at the farmlands of Berkshire.

The terrible Gerald cared little for sylvan beauty. "Dirty old backwoods," he said. "We got farms ten times as big as these in America."

The train cut across a roadway where a fine pair of white horses waited with a load of rails.

"See the big horses," said Candida tactfully.

But she was no success as an arbitrator. "Dirty old horses," said Gerald scornfully. "Call those horses? We got horses ten times as big as those."

A conductor accepted the sheaf of tickets which the Honorable Emily had in readiness and passed on down the train. It was the signal for which the lady had been eagerly waiting.

For more than two hours poor Tobermory had been languishing in his box. Now that the conductor was out of sight, and no stop would be made until Plymouth was reached late in the afternoon, his mistress, as was her wont, opened his case in time to save it from being entirely chewed through and took the nervous and annoyed cat out on her lap.

He dug his claws ungratefully into her thigh and stalked down onto the cushions, curling up into a silver-gray ball of fur as soon as he had made certain that door and window were firmly shut against him.

The terrible Gerald showed interest. "Dirty ol' cat," he declared. "We got cats ten times as big——" He was edging forward.

"I firmly advise that you respect Tobermory's privacy," said the Honorable Emily sharply. Gerald slid back into his corner and stared morosely out of the window. They sped through the village of Pewsey.

"Dirty ol' town," said Gerald softly. As a matter of fact, he spoke the truth, but no one loved him the better for it.

The first call for luncheon was welcomed by everybody in the carriage, except Tobermory, who was forced to return temporarily to his case. The Honorable Emily, who still fancied that she had a knack with children, spoke kindly to Gerald.

"Hungry, little man?"

"Yaaa—" mimicked the child, "I'm hungry-little-man, you bet your life." He led the way to the dining car.

His order, given in strident tones to the waiter before anyone else had spoken, was for pudding, pie, ice cream, and meringue glacé—all the desserts on the menu.

"You'd better have something a bit more——" began the Honorable Emily faintly.

But the terrible Gerald stared at her. "I guess I can have what I want," he blurted out. "I guess my mother gave me money to pay for it. I guess——"

"But does your mother let you eat only sweet stuff?" he was asked.

He nodded. "My mother says that children's natural appetites should be encouraged. She read it in a book. She says it preserves the identity of character."

He spoke the phrases as one word. The Honorable Emily shrugged her shoulders. She gave her attention to a bit of cold lamb, and luncheon proceeded in a silence broken only by the loud gulps of the child.

Candida had come to the table with a good appetite, but the sight of Gerald's hasty absorption of pudding, pie, ice cream, and meringue made her pause. When he ordered a second round, and poured cream, sugar, and strawberry jam on his pudding, she rose hastily to her feet.

"I think I'd better—I mean, I'll just have a walk through the train," she said.

Leslie rose quickly, leaving most of his luncheon untasted. Food meant very little to Leslie Reverson these days. "I'll go along," he offered, and they passed on together.

Gerald spoke through a mouthful of meringue. "They've gone out to pet," he announced. "Like they do in the movies, I know."

135

The Honorable Emily sighed and thought that she might as well say nothing at all. She remembered that her nephew did not yet know that she had contracted to keep this child overnight at Dinsul and deliver him on the morrow to Tenton Hall.

There were dungeons somewhere cut into the solid rock underneath her ancestral home, and the Honorable Emily thought wistfully of what a good place they would be for Gerald to spend the night. "Preferably in chains," she added.

Leslie and Candida stood in the vestibule, sharing a cigarette. The green-brown slopes of Aller Moor were flowing past. "King Alfred's Fort," pointed out the young Englishman, as proud as if he had laid every stone.

"Beautiful, all of it," cried Candida ecstatically.

"You've seen nothing," Leslie told her. "Wait until you get to Cornwall. Big black cliffs above the sea, with little gray stone fishing villages——" He grew tired of landscape. "We've got a ripping golf course not far from Dinsul, and tomorrow morning we'll have a round. You play, of course."

"A little," Candida admitted.

"Well, I'm not so good myself," Leslie said. "I'll give you ten strokes——"

"I usually play with a five handicap," Candida told him gently.

Leslie whistled, and his eyes widened admiringly. His own handicap was twelve.

"You'll like it down in Cornwall," he repeated. "You know, it's very important that you do."

"Why?" asked Candida.

His answer was unwittingly to justify the evil guess of Gerald Hammond by taking Candida Noring in his arms and kissing her rather inexpertly on the side of the mouth.

Candida pushed him away, breathing rather hard. She was surprised, more at herself for liking it than at Leslie. After a moment she said laughingly, "It's a good thing for my honor that I didn't tell you I play tennis and ride, as well as golf."

Reverson looked blank at that. She took his arm. "Come on, let's go back and rescue your aunt."

They came into the dining car and had a long view of the terrible Gerald demolishing the last of another pudding.

"And not a bit of cyanide in it, I'm afraid," Leslie observed wistfully.

Candida said that he was heartless, but she gripped his arm a little more tightly.

It moved him to a tremendous act of self-sacrifice. "See here," he suggested, "I've got an idea. You and aunt have a good get-together chat in our compartment, and I'll take the demon-child into one of the other vacant ones for the rest of the trip. Manly influence and all that, you know."

"I'll try to make her like me," promised Candida.

But Leslie found that he had bitten off a good deal more than could be chewed. Gerald showed no disinclination to leave the ladies, but when they were alone the boy began afresh upon the window with his diamond.

"I say, the conductor will object to that," Leslie protested. "Not a very nice word you've scratched there. . . ."

Gerald protruded his lower lip, and continued. "If you keep on I'll take the bloody diamond away from you," said Leslie.

Gerald left off his engraving and began to slam his heels against the seat. On a lucky inspiration he began to sing, in a shrill and quite tuneless soprano, a song almost recognizable as "The Big Bad Wolf."

After half an hour of this, Leslie put down his newspaper. "I say, old chap, do you mind varying your repertoire?"

Gerald was growing a bit pettish. "Go to hell," he said.

"Now see here! Hasn't your mother taught you——"

"I live with my grandmother in Brooklyn, mostly," Gerald said. "She lets me do what I please." He cocked his head. "But I'll be quiet if you'll buy me some candy when the train stops."

They were not far from Plymouth. "Bargain," capitulated Reverson. Gerald left off his singing, and amused himself by scratching various parts of his anatomy in a noisy and vigorous fashion.

The train halted in Plymouth, and Leslie hurried off. He swung back aboard just as they began to move out of the station, rather out of breath.

"Where's the candy?" demanded the youth.

Leslie handed him a small packet. Either from haste at the candy counter or from a latent sense of humor, he had brought Gerald a box of Muggles' Digestive Yeast, chocolate

137

covered. But if it was a practical joke it failed utterly, for the boy crammed several pieces into his mouth and chewed happily.

He was in an expansive mood. "You like girls, don't you?" he inquired, as one man to another.

"Why, er——"

"You like that big Noring girl, anyway," prodded Gerald.

And then Leslie Reverson lost his temper. "Speak respectfully of Miss Noring, or I'll give you a caning that you won't forget for a fortnight!"

"Yaaaa," came back Gerald. "Try it, that's all. My father whipped me once, and I showed him, I did. I'll bet he wishes he'd never touched me."

"I'll bet he wishes he'd never begotten you," thought Reverson. Gerald finished the chocolate yeast, and they rode on across the river Tamar in silence. The hills and moors of the ancient Duchy of Cornwall, warmed by the rays of the afternoon sun, were around them—a different land entirely from the England they had left.

The Honorable Emily and Candida had been having, as Leslie had hoped, a very pleasant chat, during which the girl had learned something of her hostess' almost fanatical love for Dinsul, their destination. "It will be Leslie's when I die," said the Honorable Emily. "The estate was unentailed, you see. But I wish you could have your first evening with us without the company of that dreadful child."

The train slowed for Penzance, and the Honorable Emily began to fasten newspapers around Dicon's cage again. Tobermory watched from his cushions, impassive and waiting . . . but he did not purr.

Then Leslie and the child joined them, and there was much business of struggling into overcoats and gathering up magazines.

"What a trip!" the Honorable Emily thought wearily.

There was a sound of horrible shrieking behind her, and she very nearly leaped through the glass of the carriage. She turned, and saw blood streaming from the back of Gerald Hammond's hand.

Tobermory, arched and spitting, had backed into the farthest corner of the seat. His forepaws, talons extended, were held out like a boxer's.

"Damn ol' cat, he bit me!" howled Gerald. "I just touched his ol' tail. . . ."

Leslie and Candida smiled, and then the girl offered her handkerchief in a motherly gesture to bandage the wound. The Honorable Emily soothed Tobermory and put him safely away in his case.

"I warned you to respect Tobermory's privacy," she remarked sweetly. It was the only bright moment of the trip for the Honorable Emily. But there was to be another.

They alighted in an unbelievably dingy station. Then the Honorable Emily noticed a tall, spare man approaching. He had sandy hair and a determined expression of firm kindliness which the thin-rimmed pince-nez did not soften.

"Starling!" she called.

"Yes, my lady." The headmaster shook hands with her, and then with Leslie Reverson.

"But, Starling, I don't understand . . ."

"Master Leslie telegraphed me from Plymouth," said the schoolmaster. "He suggested that it might be well for the young man to begin his school life at once."

He beamed down at the terrible Gerald. "How do you do, Hammond?"

Hammond did not do very well. He refused to shake hands. "I'm not going to like your ol' school," he announced.

"I hope you are mistaken," said Starling gently. "But let me point out that it is not at all necessary that you should."

They departed, quietly and expeditiously.

"Leslie," said his aunt, as she led the way toward where a uniformed chauffeur was waiting beside a somewhat moldy Buick limousine, "sometimes I actually have hopes for you."

Leslie Reverson gripped Candida's arm. "If I have just the proper inspiration," he amended.

"Good-evening, Trewartha," said the Honorable Emily to the driver. "And how is the tide?" The tall, red-faced Cornishman smiled widely.

"On the ebb, milady. But I knew you'd not wait, so I told the boatmen to be ready."

They were driven through a mile or so of streets lined by houses that seemed cut out of the solid rock of Cornwall, and then along a winding and very vile road which skirted the shore of the bay.

Smells of pungent salt fish reached them, and the Honorable Emily sniffed eagerly. "Newlyn," she observed. "We're almost home."

They sped on, rounded another curve of the cliffs, and then plunged down into a tiny fishing village with streets so narrow that the foot passengers and cyclists had to dodge into doorways so that the limousine could pass. They went on through the village and down to a stone pier.

"Here we are," said Leslie. Candida looked out of the car window and saw a row of stone cottages and what seemed countless thousands of drying nets.

"Like the place?"

"I adore it," she said slowly. She was looking toward the village. "But I don't see——"

"You won't, unless you look around," Leslie told her. She turned, and saw that something less than a quarter of a mile out from shore a rocky island rose like a mailed fist from the water. It was topped by grayed and weatherbeaten ramparts.

"Simple little place," the Honorable Emily said. "But it's home."

At the foot of the pier four stalwart men in faded livery waited at the oars of a skiff. Breathless with astonishment, Candida suffered herself to be led into the boat and saw the baggage stowed away.

"There's a causeway and motor road," she was told. "But it's only uncovered at very low tide, and usually we signal or telephone for the skiff."

They skimmed over the surface of the bay, and the rocky mountain peak drew closer. Candida saw a tiny pier at the base of the hill. High above, the castle stood out grimly against the sky.

"It must be terribly old," Candida said.

The Honorable Emily nodded. "An ancestor of mine is supposed to have built Dinsul Castle. Man by the name of Uther Pendragon. He got to be a local king by selling tin to the Phœnicians and built himself a castle out of the profits. But he had no idea of bathrooms."

"What? Why—that's the father of King Arthur you're talking about!" gasped Candida. The Honorable Emily beamed and nodded.

They landed at a little stone pier, and the rowers began to wrestle with the baggage. Then the party began a climb up the longest flight of stone steps that Candida had ever seen.

"This," she said, "ought to be one place in the world where we'll be safe from—from the things that happened in London."

Leslie Reverson told her sadly that nothing had happened here in the last thousand years. "Until you came," he said.

They approached a magnificent stone doorway, above which hung a row of great spikes of ancient rusted iron, pointing downward like bared fangs.

Candida stopped and stared. "Whatever in the world——"

"When Dinsul was built," explained Leslie, "they sometimes needed something heavier than oak to bar the doors. You are gazing, my dear, upon the only working portcullis in southern England."

"Except," her hostess added, "that we don't show it off any more. It drops like a shot when you pull the big chain in the hall, but it takes four strong men a good while to get it up again. And heaven knows," she added, "it costs dear enough to pay the boatmen for our ferry service, without having them in to work the windlass, as we used to do when the tourists were allowed to pull the chain." She saw disappointment in Candida's face. "Well, my dear, perhaps once while you're here we'll show it off for you. . . ."

The great doors swung inward, and the Honorable Emily handed Tobermory's case to a smiling butler. She took the big cat out in her arms.

"Home again, Toby," she said. "And aren't we glad!"

Leslie moved to take Candida's coat, and from a pocket of his own topcoat something slipped to the floor.

He stared down, went white as chalk, and put his foot over it neatly. He smiled at Candida. "You'll want a wash before dinner—Treves will show you to your room. . . ."

Candida was hardly breathing. "What——"

But Leslie Reverson shook his head, with a quick glance at his aunt, who was graciously inquiring into the health of Treves and his family. He leaned down quickly and picked up the thing which had dropped from his coat. He slipped it into his pocket.

But Candida saw that it was a white envelope bearing a black-inked border. Outside the castle a herring gull, buffeted by the wind, gave a despairing cry like the wail of a soul lost in hell.

CHAPTER XI

*

A Trap Is Sprung

Chief Inspector Cannon of Scotland Yard took seven steps across his office to the glowing coal grate, and then seven back to the window with its excellent view of the river and the county buildings opposite.

Then he stopped suddenly and faced his subordinate. "All right, all right. I grant you that Rosemary Fraser wasn't killed by a jerk on the scarf, as I suggested. It was merely a hyph—hypo——"

"Hypothesis," contributed Sergeant John Secker.

"Yes, that's it. Supposing she was killed in some other way—I still maintain that for her to go into the water without making a splash that anybody could hear, she must have been lowered there. At the end of her scarf, or failing that, a rope."

"Wait a moment," said the sergeant. "Suppose she didn't go into the water?"

Cannon frowned. "She disappeared, didn't she? How else can you account for it? She didn't fly away in the air. She couldn't escape observation on that boat for two days, not with everybody looking for her. There's only one place where the Fraser girl could have gone, and that's Davy Jones' locker."

"Fair enough," said the sergeant. "But *when?*"

"Don't be a cryptic ass," said Cannon.

"Sorry, sir. What I meant to say was—supposing she was killed, and her body hidden somewhere for a few hours, and dropped overboard when the splash wouldn't be noticed? Or supposing she hid herself for some reason, and was killed at a later hour?"

"Supposing the moon was made of green cheese," Cannon remarked unkindly. "It's clear enough. Here's the

Fraser girl, at the rail of the ship, near a pair of lifeboats swung on davits, or whatever you call 'em. There's the deck house at her back, with a door leading into the radio operator's cabin, and two doors leading into cabins for the mates and captain respectively. Latter both locked. Forward of the ship is a ladder to the bridge, and one down to the promenade deck. Aft we have the old maid school mistress in a deck chair that blocks most of the passageway. Forward ladder blocked by the Noring girl, who is searching for her room mate. How could any of the business you suggest have happened?"

"Supposing," suggested the sergeant, "that there was a man concealed behind those lifeboats? Supposing he killed the Fraser girl, and hid her underneath the canvas cover of one of them, and then stole away after the two women were starting the search?" He paused. "Or supposing that she crawled in a lifeboat to meet this man and was killed there by him?"

Cannon pouted. "Won't wash, I'm afraid. When the girl was suspected to be missing, they of course searched the lifeboats."

"They did." The sergeant smiled. "But it was not until the next forenoon. You see, they were so sure she had gone overboard."

"What I don't see is——" began Cannon. A sharp knock had come at the door, and the doddering constable who guarded the main entrance looked in.

"Lady to see you, sir," he told the chief. "She was here before. Name's Withers."

"Oh, Lord," said Cannon. "The Yankee sleuthess. I suppose I'd better see her; sometimes she has an idea. You stay, Secker."

The sergeant had no intention of leaving unless he was thrown out. A moment later Miss Hildegarde Withers achieved her lifelong ambition and entered an office of the C.I.D. at Scotland Yard.

Cannon rose and politely offered her a chair. "I'm very busy," he said unpromisingly. "That's why I had you come here instead of to the reception room. Well?"

"First,"began Miss Withers, "I wanted to ask how you are progressing with the Fraser-Noel-Todd-etc. murder case? If it isn't entirely a dead issue I'd like to offer a suggestion."

"The case is still open," said Chief Inspector Cannon coldly. "But I might call your attention to the fact that in the year 1932 we had just one unsolved murder in England and Wales."

"Looks as if you'll have two or three this year, doesn't it?" Miss Withers said sweetly. "Or maybe half a dozen. Dr. Waite had a lot of cyanide stolen."

The chief took out his notebook. "If you have any additions to your statement, I shall be glad to take them down."

"I just want to ask a question," Miss Withers told him. "I have no facilities for finding out, but I'd like to know. Can you wire the Buffalo police back in the States and discover whether or not Rosemary Fraser was unusually good at water sports—swimming and diving and so on?"

The inspector laughed. "Swimming, eh? You think that she was good enough a swimmer to fight the waves six hundred miles or so to shore?"

"There are fishing boats which go out into the Gulf Stream beyond the Scilly Isles," suggested the sergeant. "Supposing——"

"We sighted no boats until off Land's End," Miss Withers told him. "No, I didn't mean that Rosemary might have swum to shore. Although, if she had been in London this past week or more, it would simplify this case tremendously."

"Here at the Yard we don't believe in ghosts," said Cannon heavily. "I don't mind answering your question. We got a full report on Rosemary Fraser, description, tastes, and past history. She was not an athletic type, according to the report."

"But she spent every summer of her life at Bar Harbor, Maine," put in the sergeant. "Isn't that one of your Yankee watering places? She'd pick up a good bit of swimming there."

Miss Withers thanked him. "I'll leave you to your labors, gentlemen. If I get any more ideas, or notice any more murders——"

"The cycle ought to be complete," said Cannon. He was friendlier than at the beginning. "The people concerned in the case seem to have scattered to the four winds. Of course, we're keeping an eye on their whereabouts. . . ."

"I have an idea that we're not anywhere near the end of the cycle, as you call it," Miss Withers told him. "And furthermore, how do you know just who among the many passengers and members of the crew of that ship are mixed up in this affair?"

Cannon smiled. "Easy, my dear lady. If you knew anything about criminology you'd know that in any case of anonymous letters—poison-pen letters as your yellow press calls them—the writer always sends one to himself or herself, figuring that that gives him a certain protection from suspicion. Therefore, the sender of those black-bordered notes has received one—and made a great to-do about it, most likely."

Miss Withers knew that as well as he, but she nodded. "I don't suppose you have looked into the affairs of the Hammond family, have you? They received a joint letter edged in black, you know."

Cannon looked at some papers in his desk. "The child was dispatched to a school in Cornwall. Mrs. Hammond is out of our jurisdiction, in Paris. And out of reach of the murderer, too."

"But Tom Hammond is right here in London," Miss Withers pointed out. "And from information received, as you people say, I understand that he is trying to drink himself to death. He'd be easy prey for somebody, in that dulled condition. Remember, Andy Todd was dead drunk when he fell to his death through an elevator—I mean liftshaft—door that was too narrow to let his hand through to the catch."

"Well?" Cannon was growing weary of this.

"I think Hammond ought to be warned to follow the example of the others and get out of London," Miss Withers announced. "For his own good. Or at least told to take care of himself and be on his guard."

The chief inspector rose to his feet. "Thank you for coming," he said. "I will consider the suggestions that you have made."

He was a human wall too thick and high for Miss Withers. "I know what you intend to do about this murder case," she remarked acidly. "You're going to wait until every person in the group has been killed but one, and then arrest that one, figuring that you can't make a mistake."

She swept from the room, and the sergeant looked at his superior. "At that, it wouldn't be a bad idea," said Secker.

"I detest amateur sleuths," Cannon complained. "If people want to be detectives, let 'em start at the bottom as P.C.'s."

Sergeant Secker smiled at the thought of a helmet atop the long and somewhat horselike visage of Hildegarde Withers. "I didn't mean her idea about waiting to arrest the last surviving member of the group," he continued. "I mean—she gave me an idea. Hammond has been marked down by this murderer—at least, he received a black-bordered letter. If he's seen about town drunk, that puts him in a dangerous position right now. . . ."

"We can't give him police protection unless he asks for it," cut in Cannon.

"I didn't mean that. Don't warn him. Let him go on as he is. And don't frighten off the murderer. But set a trap!"

"Eh?"

"A trap—with Hammond as the bait." The sergeant enlarged upon his plan, and Chief Inspector Cannon, a just man, considered it and found that it was good.

Miss Hildegarde Withers was writing a letter, back in her room at the Alexandria. She puzzled for a while over the proper manner in which to address the envelope. One couldn't begin "Dear the Honorable Emily." She finally sent down for a copy of DeBrett's, and discovered that her friend's name was not Reverson but Pendavid: "The Honorable Emily Pendavid, only surviving daughter and heir of the late Earl of Trevanna, title now extinct."

"Dear Miss Pendavid [she began], *I have been doing a good deal of thinking about the events of the past week and more, and I am more and more convinced that we have not reached an end to the tragedies. Scotland Yard seems at a complete loss. I feel it my duty to warn you to take the utmost precautions for your own safety. Remember that you and your nephew, besides myself, are the only members of the party at the doctor's table on board ship who have not yet been threatened. Place your servants on their guard, and see to your doors and windows at night. Be overly suspicious of everybody and everything, particularly of anything sent to you in the mail. And write to me, besides*

notifying the Yard, if you receive one of those horrible letters."

She signed "*Hildegarde Martha Withers*" in a large round script, and placed the message in a square gray envelope. "*To the Honorable Emily Pendavid, Dinsul Castle, Cornwall,*" she wrote.

The letter mailed, she turned her attention to the chase. For two days she divided her time between the newspaper files, the reading room at the British Museum, and a search for the mysterious Mrs. Charles—discovering no more about the latter than had the police. The mysterious young woman—if she was a woman—had taken cheap lodgings in several hotels in the neighborhood of Charing Cross, not far from the Alexandria. She had worn a squirrel coat, collar turned high. That was the sum total of her findings—except that one chambermaid, well tipped, admitted that "Mrs. Charles" had been seen smoking a cigar in her room. Moreover, she had been a person of strange nocturnal habits, staying out most of the night and returning in the broad light of day.

Once Miss Withers got in touch with Sergeant Secker, after much telephoning, and demanded to know what had been done with the torn diary and the other personal effects of Rosemary Fraser.

"They were sent to her people in the States, of course," she was told.

"Oh, I see," said Miss Withers, in a tone of distinct disappointment. She hung up the receiver.

She had done her best, but it seemed to be a cold scent and a lost trail. The school teacher took to wandering aimlessly about the fascinating old city of London, peering into the faces of passers-by and through shop windows as if there she expected to find an answer to the riddle which haunted her mind. Normally a person of regular habits and addicted to early hours, she upset her usual routine, sensing that she could never get the real *feel* of the city in daylight—or what Londoners know as daylight.

One night—it was the fourth since the Honorable Emily and her entourage had departed for Cornwall and security—she was walking aimlessly through the streets of Soho, taking a short cut from the shop windows of Oxford

Street back to the hotel. There, on the other side of the street, she saw Tom Hammond, walking very briskly and determinedly northward.

"Yoicks!" said Miss Withers to herself, and drew back into a convenient doorway. But he was too intent upon his destination to notice her.

"Now, I wonder where he is going!" she asked. With Hildegarde Withers, wondering was a prelude to the taking of definite steps toward finding out. Beset by curiosity, she followed the young man northward, keeping a discreet distance in the rear and ready to slip out of sight if he should hesitate or turn, which he showed no signs of doing. There were still a goodly number of people on the streets, for it was not yet eleven o'clock.

He turned down Oxford Street and then disappeared through the swinging doors of The King's Arms. Miss Withers took up a stand on the opposite corner, where she could command a view of both doors to the public house, and was hopeful that in spite of the fact that she leaned against a jeweler's window she would not be picked up as a snatch-and-grab suspect.

She looked at her watch—it was four minutes before eleven. Her wait was momentary, for almost immediately Tom Hammond reappeared, walking a little more unsteadily but with a continued air of definiteness. He was followed by the other customers of the place, for eleven o'clock is closing time on the south side of Oxford Street.

He turned and headed north along Tottenham Court Road. Miss Withers, who had read enough of the London newspapers to know that this unpromising section has outclassed Limehouse as London's center of crime and violence, clutched her umbrella the more tightly, and strode onward. There was never a bobby in sight, though buses swung past her at lengthening intervals. Young men walked by her in twos and threes, usually wearing soiled white scarves around their necks in lieu of neckties and shirts—and underwear, Miss Withers feared. But they paid her no attention.

Hammond turned down a side street. She followed, growing rather out of breath.

He knocked at an out-of-the-way door and was admitted to a murky hallway. Again Miss Withers waited, this time for more than half an hour. When Tom Hammond emerged he was rocking a bit, with his hat too far back on his forehead and his legs betraying him now and then. Miss Withers guessed that he had just visited one of the unsavory emporiums which in the not-so-golden yesterday would have been called "speak-easies" in her own country. The world, she observed, was a small place after all.

Tom Hammond proceeded northwards, pressing on into the narrow courts and alleys which cluster about Middlesex Hospital. He turned down a narrow passageway which led on into a more brightly lighted square. But instead of pushing on, he halted and consulted a slip of paper.

It was at this point that Miss Hildegarde Withers had a distinct shock. She realized that someone else shared her ideas about following Tom Hammond, for a swaggering idler in rough clothing and a dingy white scarf and low-drawn cap had halted, even as she, in order to keep from approaching too closely to the young man.

The quarry found what he sought on the scrap of paper and rang a bell. In a moment a door opened to cast a bright glow of light into the passage, and then closed again behind him.

Miss Withers could not make out the other watcher who waited, but she knew that he was there ahead of her, in the shadows.

Puzzled and at a loss, she stood and took stock of the situation for a few moments. Then she decided upon a desperate move. Hammond had been heading constantly northward. There was a good chance that he would continue to press onward into the sections where constables were few and far between and the possibilities, therefore, for acquiring unlicensed beverages at forbidden hours greater.

She turned hurriedly back, found a street cutting through to the right, and made a complete circle, coming out at last into Fitzroy Square and the opposite end of the passage. Here, at any rate, she was not entirely alone, for some distance on a man was tinkering with a stalled motorcycle, and beyond him a solitary taxicab was cruising slowly around the square.

She took up her stand in the shadows, where she could peer up the passage through which she confidently expected Tom Hammond, and the dark figure who pursued him so stealthily, would come.

Of course there was the danger that the mysterious one would choose this particular place to strike. Yet she thought not. If she knew anything about this particular series of murders, it was that the perpetrator was not addicted to man-to-man violence, and Tom Hammond was still well able to hear the tap of feet on the stone flagging behind him and put up a healthy resistance.

The whole situation was foreign to the conception which Miss Withers had developed concerning what she called the Fraser-Noel-Todd case. "Yet if a man can pass as a woman in a fur coat, then a woman could pass as a man in rough clothing and a cap," she reminded herself.

She waited impatiently in the cold London evening, clutching her umbrella and heartily wishing that Inspector Oscar Piper were here beside her, villainous black cigar and all—or else that she had taken up rock gardening instead of sleuthing as a hobby.

Then she got her signal—a flare of light in the darkened passage as a door opened and Tom Hammond emerged. He was definitely wobbling now—but he set his course in her direction. Miss Withers stepped down into a basement doorway and watched him come out into the lighted square, still hurrying as if he were trying to catch up with himself— or to leave himself behind.

She came out as soon as he had passed, and stood waiting. Had she made a bad guess? No—for soft footsteps were approaching. She caught a brief glimpse of a furtive, rather boyish figure in rough clothing and a low-slung cap—and went into action.

Holding her umbrella by the tip, she swung with all her force against the head of the furtive stranger as he slipped out of the mouth of the passage, at the same time shouting with the full strength of her lungs: "Help! Police! Help!"

The cap must have turned the force of her blow, for the dark stranger did not fall. He turned a dazed face toward her, and she redoubled her screams: "Help! Murder!"

There were the comforting sounds of running footsteps, and she left off swinging her umbrella and closed with her victim. She flung both arms around him and clung for dear life.

"Don't you try to get away," she warned. But he did not try.

To Miss Withers' combined amazement and delight, the man who had been tinkering the motorcycle turned out to be no less than Chief Inspector Cannon, and the cruising taxicab, when it drew swiftly nearer, she saw contained three constables in uniform.

"I've got him!" she announced as Cannon drew near. Tom Hammond also had retraced his steps and stood blinking at the scene.

Her victim went rather limp in her arms, and she had to let him fall to the sidewalk.

Cannon bent beside her quarry. "Haven't you!" he said, in a peculiar voice.

"I saw him creeping after Tom Hammond here, and I figured that the murderer would consider that a drunk was easy prey," she went on.

"Nobly done," the chief inspector said to her. He seemed unusually gentle with the captive. "That is just what we figured at the Yard, and we acted accordingly. We too were waiting for the murderer to strike." Cannon beckoned to one of the constables. "Get some water, man." He looked up at Miss Withers. "All the same, I'm afraid we were both wrong."

"Wrong? Why—I tell you this man was creeping up on Hammond."

"I know," said Cannon wearily. He tugged at the limp body and splashed the face with water provided by the constable from the nearest house. He tore away the dirty white scarf and the cap—and Miss Withers looked down on the peaceful, pale face of Sergeant John Secker of the C.I.D. A fine big lump, of the general dimensions of an egg, was rising on his forehead.

Secker opened his eyes dreamily. He stared at Cannon, Miss Withers, and then back at the umbrella with its heavy curved handle.

"Well batted," he said encouragingly. "Saw you an hour ago, but didn't dare warn you off. Hoped you'd get tired."

"Good heavens," said Miss Withers. "I'm so sorry! Not for the world——"

"I know," said the sergeant. "Best of motives. All the same, I feel terrible. Anybody got a drink?"

Tom Hammond produced a pint flask. "Bootleg, but it didn't kill *me*," he said, somewhat thickly.

"Thanks, old man. But won't you need it?"

Hammond shook his head. He looked white and almost sober. "Didn't know I was making a horse—a fool of myself and playing bait for you fellows," he said. "I think I'd better go on the wagon for a while."

"Wait," protested the sergeant feebly, struggling to his feet and avoiding the proffered help of his fellows. "The idea is still a good one. Won't you be sporting and go on—I mean, won't you play the drunk and let us lurk about waiting for the murderer to strike?"

Tom Hammond was completely sober now. "No," he said. "*Nein, non*, nix, no. What do you take me for? The only pleasure I have left is a good howling binge, and you have to spoil that for me."

He refused Cannon's offer of transportation home, and departed in search of a taxicab and in the keeping of two constables.

Miss Withers held out her hand to the sergeant. "Sorry," she said. "I wish I'd known what you were up to, and I wouldn't have interfered."

"Quite all right," said Secker, rubbing the lump on his forehead. "I'll take it in the spirit in which it was sent, as the vicar said to the old lady who gave him brandied peaches for Christmas."

"Well," observed Miss Withers, who was given an undeserved ride back to her hotel in the commandeered taxicab of the police, "thus endeth that lesson. The next step is up to Monsieur—or Madame—X."

"I have a few steps in mind myself," grunted Chief Inspector Cannon. She was deposited at the door of the Alexandria, and the taxi rolled away. She went wearily inside, feeling that she had done much tonight to destroy any feeling of comradeship that Cannon and the sergeant had been beginning to feel toward herself.

But she forgot all that when she passed the desk, for the night clerk who lounged there produced a telegram.

It was from Penzance, bearing the signature of Emily Pendavid.

HAVE JUST RECEIVED WARNING LETTER FROM LONDON. COME DOWN AT ONCE. TAKE CASE EITHER AS OPERATIVE OR

AS FRIEND. WILL GLADLY GUARANTEE MODERATE EX-
PENSES URGENT WIRE COLLECT DECISION.

Miss Withers did not even smile at the addition of the
cautious word "moderate." She turned to the clerk.

"Have you a time-table for the Great Western?" she demanded. "I am checking out in the morning, or
sooner. . . ."

"Ah, a trip to the wonderful Cornish Riviera," said the
man heartily. "Madame will find it the garden spot of England."

But, Miss Withers told herself, there was a flower growing in that garden which badly needed plucking—a poi-
sonous, luxuriant mandragore or nightshade. The seed of
murder had taken root there . . . and threatened to bloom.

"Leaves Paddington 5 A.M.—arrives Penzance 12:45
P.M." she read. "I'll do it. Heaven knows there's nothing
happening in London."

That night Miss Hildegarde Withers went speeding westward out of the city aboard the Great Western's second-best
train, just as the moon was setting. It was also then that the
body of Rosemary Fraser came floating up the Thames with
the tide.

CHAPTER XII

*

As the Tide Turns

That day was dismal and gray, with low-hanging clouds shutting away the sun even at noon. Miss Hildegarde Withers, who had managed to sleep very little on the train which bore her down to this farthest corner of England, stood alone upon an ancient stone quay, shortly after one.

"Tide's ebbing fast," the Cornish taxi man had told her. "Half an hour or so and you'll be able to walk across to the island."

The half hour had gone, but still great rolling swells swept in from Mount's Bay to splash across the black causeway. From where she stood, the gaunt castle-fortress of Dinsul appeared unreal and forbidding, reminding her of Arnold Böcklin's unforgettable masterpiece at the Metropolitan back in her own New York; *Totinsel—The Isle of the Dead*, he had called it. In that picture there had been great granite cliffs plunging down to the sea, against a sky of drifting dark clouds. . . .

She supposed that, if she only had taken the trouble to find out, there were means of communicating with Dinsul from the mainland. A telephone, perhaps—or some system of signals. Certainly she could have sent a message announcing her arrival, and there would have been someone to meet her. But she preferred arriving unannounced and unheralded, and thus receiving her impressions naturally.

Finally the slackening waters drew back from the causeway, and she gingerly set out across the wet passage, carrying her overnight case. It was not as long a journey as she had feared, and within a few minutes she had marched across (feeling somewhat like the children of Israel) and was mounting the interminable steps, cut in the solid rock, which led to the great door of Dinsul.

There was no bell and no knocker. She beat with the handle of her umbrella until Treves, the red-faced butler, appeared.

He took one look. "This is not a visiting day," he said shortly. "Monday, Wednesday, and Saturday only. . . ."

He prepared to close the door, but Miss Hildegarde Withers put her foot in it. "I don't care what day it is," she told him. "Take my name to your mistress. Say that Miss Withers is here."

He stood back, murmuring polite apologies, and she entered the hall. She shivered—not because the place, like all English homes, was several degrees colder than a tomb, but because there was an unmistakable atmosphere, an aura, so to speak, of things ancient and done and forgotten. It was the feeling, she thought, that she might have received at Stonehenge on a March day.

The warmth of the Honorable Emily's greeting did much to dispel her first impression. "Good of you to come," said the Englishwoman. "And damned silly of me to ask you. I mean—to think it necessary, you understand. I'm not the nervous type, usually, but that message rather gave me the muley-grubs for a time."

"Oh, yes, the message," said Miss Withers. "I'd like to see it."

"Afraid you mayn't," said the Honorable Emily. "I sent it off to Scotland Yard when I telegraphed you. But there was nothing much to see. Just a letter with a black border marked on it. Came yesterday afternoon, with the late mail. Postmarked London—and a very cruel and unkind message. Something about what a horrible laugh I have, and how the writer hoped I would laugh through hell . . . you can imagine."

"I can indeed," said Miss Withers dryly. "Let me see— yesterday, if I am not mistaken, was Saturday, the seventh of October. I don't suppose that you happened to notice the postmark date on that letter?"

"I noticed it most particularly," the Honorable Emily assured her. "It was dated two days after we left London to come down here—the fifth, to be exact. In case it makes any difference."

It made a tremendous amount of difference to Miss Withers, but she nodded slowly. "Then it must have arrived about the same time you received my letter?"

"Yours came in the morning mail, the black-bordered one in the afternoon," she was told. "But don't let's talk about it any more now. We have lunch in about an hour. Treves will show you to your room. . . ."

Miss Withers noticed that her hostess was clad in a lounging robe which appeared to have been hastily slipped on. "Never mind about me," she said. "Let your man take my bag upstairs, and I'll wander around and absorb the atmosphere of your charming old place while you dress. After lunch will be time enough to talk about things."

"Righto." The Honorable Emily gestured widely. "Make yourself at home, my dear. It's an old place, and the conveniences aren't what they might be, but I love it. My family has owned Dinsul for heaven knows how many years."

She dashed off, and, handing her bag to Treves, Miss Withers walked slowly down the great hall.

Room after room opened off it, each furnished with ancient and blackened pieces of oak and decorated with family portraits which stared down in unison and with a dignified disapproval upon the Yankee school teacher.

"Never mind," she told herself after a time. "You have just as many ancestors as anybody else, and what's more, I'll wager that they were a more prepossessing lot than these besotted Cavaliers."

She came past window after window, each of which looked out upon the sea. By craning her neck she could see the almost perpendicular cliffs beneath, and here and there a few trees clinging precariously to the slope, still green in this southerly latitude.

Then, at the end of the hall, she entered through wide double doors into what she knew must be a banquet hall. A refectory table at least thirty feet in length ran down the center. At one end was a raised balcony, doubtless for musicians, and around the walls was a painted hunting scene, still bright and cheerful, in which mounted lords and ladies chased deer, boar, stag, fox, rabbit, badger, and heaven knew what else, in a bewildering complexity.

Beneath the mural painting was a modest placard— "Please do not add your initials to the wall decorations"— which puzzled her a good deal.

She started suddenly as a cheerful young voice spoke up behind her. "Jolly, eh what?"

It was Leslie Reverson, in plus-fours. "Aunt said you were here," he went on. "Shall I escort you round?"

She could only say yes. "What a delightful old place," she told him.

"Think so? Seems a bit grim to me. I sometimes shiver at the thought of spending the rest of my life here, but you know the Honorable Emily. She's all for the moated grange stuff, you know. And while I'm a Pendavid only on the distaff side, I'm the heir, you know."

He led the way, chatting merrily, back down the hall, and then to a wide stone staircase. Halfway up he paused at a window and pointed upwards and out.

"St. Augustine's Chair," he informed her. "The legend is that the man or girl who sits there first will be top-dog in their married life."

Miss Withers peered out and saw a niche in the granite cliff at the end of a narrow and steep pathway. "He'd deserve to be," she commented. "If he lived."

Leslie laughed. "Right you are. It is a giddy thing, isn't it? That's why we tell the tourists that the famous chair is a crotch in the stone down by the pier. They fight to sit in it, and go away as happy as if they'd found the real one."

"*Tourists?*" said Miss Withers.

"Oh, didn't you know? Only way we can keep the old place going, you know. Three days a week we have open house, and the family retires into seclusion while the public tramps through—at half a crown a head."

"I see," said Miss Withers.

"Of course, there's been a lot of remodeling done in the place," Leslie went on. "We're coming into what used to be the chapel of the old castle. It was a monastery after the kings of Cornwall died out, you know. Aunt had it rebuilt into her private apartment, some years back. But she couldn't make it livable."

Miss Withers shared his viewpoint, but for different reasons. This hulk of stone was not livable simply because it had been lived in too long.

Leslie led her aside, down a smaller hall. "This wing opens off the hall where your room is—and mine and all the guest rooms, for that matter. Aunt has it for her very own, you know. That's the door of her sitting room, and there's her bedroom." He pointed to a door just beyond. "That little room was my own discovery," he announced proudly. "When I came home from school I was full of romance and all that sort of rot. Hidden treasure and so forth. I paced off the hall and found that it was a good ten feet longer than the rooms opening off it. We had builders tear into the wall, and they found a secret room. It was all written up in *The Times*—the only occasion in my life when I got into the papers."

Miss Withers admitted that she had not read of it. Leslie looked disappointed. "Oh, well, in the States, I suppose . . . but it was a great furor for a time, and it still brings the tourists. You see, the builders found a dried-up skeleton in the room, all covered with armor and gold lace and whatnot. There was an old story that in 14- something John of Pomeroy, a local baron, filched this place in the absence of Richard the First. When he heard that the King had returned to England, he knew that he'd be hanged for high treason, so he was supposed to have opened his veins and bled to death. Must have been true, for the armor and trappings bore the Pomeroy insignia. We gave the bones decent burial on the shore—but the real joke was discovering that Aunt had slept all her life next door to a walled-up skeleton in a secret room."

"I can imagine how she felt," Miss Withers told him.

"Of course. She was certainly delighted."

"Delighted?"

"Yes, naturally. It's hard enough to find a place to put bathrooms in a castle built with six-foot-thick walls, and here was one ready to hand." He opened the door and displayed a neat and almost modern bath, complete even to a large gas heater near the tub. "Aunt does love to soak, you know."

The door leading to the bedroom opened, and the Honorable Emily, neatly dressed in her characteristic baggy tweeds, appeared.

"Leslie, you may leave off the discussion of my personal habits and take our guest down to luncheon. And I suppose Treves is busy in the kitchen, so you'd better rap on Candida's door."

Candida seemed surprised and relieved to see the new member of the party.

They all of them went down together and, instead of losing themselves in the great dining hall, had a cosy and quite cheerful lunch in a little room which opened directly onto a balcony overlooking the sea.

Any misgivings Miss Withers might have had regarding ceremony and state were speedily dispelled. The butler served and waited.

"We have only Treves and his wife to cook," the Honorable Emily informed her. "Women come up from the village once a week to clean, and we manage. Though it's not easy in a place this size."

Miss Withers agreed. "It's because of the fact that we have almost no land tax to pay," her hostess went on, "that we can keep Dinsul at all. At that, every shilling has to be saved to pay the death duties, you know. One of these days this place will come to Leslie, and I don't want it to be sold to pay duties, like so many of our old homes in this country."

"Now, Aunt!" said Leslie uncomfortably.

"Well, we must look ahead," said the Honorable Emily. "One of these days my erratic heart will stop for good and all. I've known that for a long time. And a Pendavid belongs in Dinsul. I'm leaving it to you, but I'm going to make a change in my will so that in order to get anything you have to live here nine months of the year."

The trend of the conversation was definitely gloomy, and Miss Withers aptly changed it by asking Candida how the golf game had come out.

"I'm afraid I was lucky," said that young lady.

"She made a 76 to my 89," Leslie cut in proudly. "And the Penzance course is no slouch, either."

Candida gave him a motherly smile. "It's your wrist," she pointed out. "You're too nervous."

The conversation lapsed, while Miss Withers picked at an excellent Cornish pasty composed of meat, onions, apples, potatoes, and she did not dare to guess what else.

Then Candida spoke. "You're not down here for the trip," she said. "We may as well break the ice. Do you think the police are any closer to an explanation of the things that happened on the boat and in London?"

"I do not," said Miss Withers. "They're trying the process of elimination."

"What about yourself?" asked Leslie. "Getting warmer?"

"Do you know," said Miss Withers solemnly, "I've made up my mind to one thing. The mystery has been enclosed by a great deal of fuss and feathers. But I think it is as solved as it ever needs to be. The murder cycle seems to be at an end, and those who have been killed seem very easily spared. . . ."

Candida spoke quickly. "But Rosemary—?"

"Rosemary Fraser was not murdered," said the school teacher shortly.

Candida gasped, and Leslie Reverson's hand reached for hers under the table. He found it cold as ice and rubbed it.

"Cold hands—warm heart," he whispered solemnly, and she laughed.

At that moment Treves arrived, announcing that Mr. Starling was on the telephone for his mistress. The Honorable Emily rose hastily.

"That Hammond child has no doubt set fire to Tenton Hall," she observed.

But it was not as serious as all that. Starling's voice was its usual crisp self.

"Excuse me, my lady, for troubling you. But there is a gentleman here in my library, a Mr. Hammond. He is very excited and seems a few sheets in the wind, if you'll forgive the expression. He says he is the father of the pupil you brought me last Tuesday and insists upon taking him away. I'm not sure just what I ought to do."

"Hm," said the Honorable Emily. "I'm not sure either, Starling. What do you wish to do?"

"Give up the youngster and say, 'Thank God!'" said Starling. "But his mother placed him in my care, through you. I understand the parents have separated, and I'm naturally hesitant——"

"I suggest that you go on hesitating," said the Honorable Emily shortly. "Tell the man to come back tomorrow, and notify the mother."

"Thank you, my lady. She's in Paris, I understand. I'll write her at once." He rang off, and the Honorable Emily returned to her guests. "I can't imagine what it means," she said.

Miss Withers rose to her feet. "I can imagine," she said. "You'll have an irate father on your hands one of these days. Where is this school for boys?"

"Tenton Hall is a few miles this side of St. Ives—about six miles from Penzance," she was told. "But why——"

"I'm going over there, that's why," Miss Withers announced. "Now, this very minute. Because I think I see a streak of light."

"Why, I—of course." The Honorable Emily started back for the telephone. "It's low tide—I'll ring up the man who drives for me and have him bring the limousine. Lucky that we have this under-water phone cable to shore."

"You made fuss enough when I insisted on having it put in," said Leslie. "Aunt, you're weakening in spite of yourself. One of these days you'll let me have a wireless installed."

"Never!" insisted the Honorable Emily. "And now, you two children amuse yourselves as best you may while I try to catch up on the thousand business details that have accumulated during our trip to the States."

She followed Miss Withers into the hall. "They make a nice couple," she admitted, when she saw that the school teacher was looking back. "Of course, she's a bit older than Leslie. But he needs someone with some stamina."

"Napoleon was younger than Josephine," Miss Withers reminded her. "I think it was Josephine. Although," she added, "Napoleon didn't need stamina, did he?"

An hour later she was closeted with Mr. Starling, of Tenton Hall. He read through the letter which the Honorable Emily had given her.

"So you want to see Gerald Hammond?" he inquired wonderingly. His tone implied that there was no accounting for taste. "Are you a relative, perhaps?"

"Perhaps," agreed Miss Withers cryptically. "A sort of aunt."

"Very well." He rang a bell and spoke to the young man who appeared. "Bring Hammond here, will you?"

He rose. "I'll turn over my office to you, madam, for half an hour. And—if you need help, just call loudly." He smiled and withdrew. A few moments later the terrible Gerald was ushered in, and the door closed firmly behind him.

"You're a liar," said that fat-faced urchin. "You're not my aunt. I haven't got any aunt."

"Well, I'll do until an aunt comes along," Miss Withers said. Her tone was somewhat stern, and young Hammond left off scratching himself to stare at her. He saw the lady cross over to the master's desk and take down a light cane which hung above it—mainly for moral significance, let us add.

"Hey!" cried the terrible Gerald. He backed swiftly toward the door, but Miss Withers was swifter. She turned the key in the lock and then took the pride of the Hammond household firmly by the nape of the neck.

She led him to a chair near the window. "Young man, sit down." He sat, aided by a shove. "And now you and I are going to have a very pleasant little chat. At least, I hope it will be pleasant."

Gerald had his doubts. "I don' wanna chat—I don'——"

"Quiet," Miss Withers advised. "Gerald, do you see this cane? Do you know what it is for?"

Gerald knew. He had felt it, or a similar one, twice already since his stay at the school—once for swearing and once for teaching a smaller boy to sing "Down in the Lehigh Valley."

"Yes," he admitted sullenly.

"Good!" Miss Withers smiled. "Then you and I will be able to come to an understanding. You said just now that I was a liar, which we shall let pass. I am not your aunt, nor did I say that I was. But a lie has been told—a lie which has done a good deal of harm."

She swished with the stick so that it whistled in the air. "Gerald, I want you to be frank with me. Just what lie did you tell about your father?"

"I didn't tell any lie—an' if you lick me I'll pay you back good and plenty."

"I have switched larger boys than you," Miss Withers told him. "And they lived to thank me for it." Gerald showed natural skepticism at that statement.

"Well, are you ready to answer me?"

"I didn't tell——"

Smack! The light cane caught Gerald Hammond on the ankles, and he opened his mouth to let forth a tremendous howl. But Miss Withers spoke calmly.

"If you cry out, Mr. Starling will come, and as he is stronger than I am I shall turn the stick over to him."

Gerald closed his mouth. "Answer me," said the school teacher. "You may as well get out with it."

Gerald flushed and stammered, and then suddenly poured forth a torrent of words. Yes, he had told a lie, and it was good enough for his father, too. His father had licked him for cutting a teenty-weenty notch in the leg of the ship's piano, licked him with a slipper. "And I—I told Mama that Papa was the man who was necking that big Fraser girl on deck," he blurted. "I told her that I'd got out of the cabin where Mama locked me, and was playing Trap the Neckers with Virgil and his flashlight, and that I saw Papa and the Fraser girl get into the blanket locker box. . . ."

"Aha!" said Hildegarde Withers. "And it wasn't true?"

"N-no. But it served Papa right for licking me. I guess Mama was good an' mad."

"Did she mention this to your father?"

Gerald laughed scornfully. "Not her! She wouldn't even speak to him, hardly, for days. She was good an' mad, she was."

"But you didn't think of admitting the truth?"

"I'd have got another licking," said Gerald simply.

Miss Withers stared out of the window at a peaceful landscape of rolling green hills and little pearl-gray cottages covered with vines. Her mouth was drawn rather tightly.

"Gerald, who was the man who got into the blanket locker?"

The youth frowned. "I don' know his name. It was the guy who sold drinks and candy and stuff in the bar. An' another man said he would give me a dollar if I could catch the big Fraser girl up to anything so he could have a laugh on her, and I saw them get into the locker, and I went down and told him and got the dollar. And I spent it," he added.

"On yourself, of course?"

He shook his head. "I had to give Virgil a dime because he owned the flashlight."

Miss Withers stared at him. "Young man, when you grow up you'll probably be a bandit."

Gerald sniffed. "I don' wanna be a bandit. I wanna be a gangster."

She nodded. A great many blanks had been filled in by this somewhat unwilling interview.

Gerald rose, very hastily. "Wait a moment, young man. Do you realize that you have perhaps wrecked your parents' lives by this wicked lie? Your father is coming back tomorrow—will you tell him the truth about it all?"

"No," said Gerald. "He might lick me."

"He might," Miss Withers agreed. "And in case he shouldn't——"

There ensued a very unpleasant ten minutes, in which Miss Withers had her coat torn at the hem, and in which a howling urchin received a healthy warming upon the portion of his anatomy set aside by tradition for the express purpose.

Miss Withers hung up the cane and unlocked the door to find Starling outside. The headmaster looked perturbed.

"Really," he began, "I had no idea . . ."

"I don't approve of corporal punishment as a regular thing myself," said Miss Withers. "But there are times . . ."

Gerald was sniveling behind her. "Hammond, go to the dormitory," said Starling.

"Yes, sir," said Hammond, and went.

The headmaster stared after him wonderingly. "Do you know, that's the first time that Hammond has said 'sir' to me without being reminded at least twice?"

"Strong medicine," said Miss Withers. "Repeat in small doses as needed." She paused. "I happen to be a friend of his mother," she explained. "It would be a distinct mistake if the boy were taken out of your hands, I'm convinced. In spite of what the father may say, keep him here."

Starling nodded. "I intend to," he said. "But the father was a little—unpleasant. I had to tell him that the Honorable Emily Pendavid had advised me not to accommodate him. That seemed to quiet him."

"Did it!" Miss Withers said, and took her departure.

She rode back through the country lanes of Cornwall without noticing one of the sylvan vistas which opened up on either hand. Ancient stone fences, with stiles of granite slabs already worn thin when the Normans invaded England, slipped past unnoticed and unadmired.

As they came down the long slope leading to the little old town of Penzance, Miss Withers saw a white curl of smoke against the sky.

"The express from London," explained the chauffeur proudly. It was five o'clock in the afternoon.

They drove onward, at a moderate rate of speed, and crawled through the town behind a truckload of market vegetables, which remained obdurate before repeated hoots of the horn. They stopped at the post office while the school teacher composed a cable, and then went on. Miss Withers was impatient to get back to Dinsul, very impatient indeed—yet she was to change her mind in the next few minutes.

At length the town was behind, and they passed into the huddle of fishing cottages that is Newlyn. Streets so narrow that the limousine almost grated on either wall—turns so sharp that the corner stones of the houses had been chipped away to form a rough curve—and then it happened.

A man, riding away from them on a bicycle, failed to duck into the nearest doorway with his wheel, in spite of the hoot of the horn. There was hardly time to stop—Miss Withers was thrown forward as the brakes screamed, and the rider leaped clear just as his machine was smashed under the tires of the limousine.

"Heavens above!" said Miss Withers. Then she noticed that Sergeant John Secker of the C.I.D. was clinging to the running-board.

He looked in at her, smiled rather feebly, and brushed the dew from his forehead. The sergeant was getting used to narrow escapes.

"Close, but not a hit," he observed.

"Get in, get in," she urged.

The driver was surveying the wreck of the bicycle. "Let it go," said Secker. "I left a two-quid deposit on it, and that's more than it was worth." He turned to Miss Withers. "Glad to see you," he said. "I was just trying to think of a way of getting word to you at the mausoleum without the others knowing."

"But how did you know where I was?"

He grinned. "When you try to escape the Yard, don't hail a taxi and go to Paddington," he said. "Your trail was as clearly marked as an elephant's."

"Thank you," Miss Withers remarked coldly. "And might I inquire——"

"Why I came. Surely. It was easier for me to come down here and take depositions from you and from some of the others involved than to have the provincial police attempt it, or to ask you to come back to town. There are a lot of loose ends to this case still——"

"Loose ends? It's completely at a loose end, isn't it?"

The sergeant laughed. "Was," he admitted. "Though I've had a suspicion all along. But it was impossible until this morning."

Miss Withers had a sudden fear that her own rapidly developing theory was being stolen from her. "You're not going to tell me——"

"I'm going to tell you that we've got the murderer of Rosemary Fraser and Peter Noel and Andy Todd." He beamed. "Guess who?"

Miss Withers was keeping her own counsel. "Well?"

"Rosemary Fraser herself!"

"You've what? Arrested Rosemary Fraser? You mean her suicide was faked?"

"Not faked," said the sergeant. "Just predated a bit. You see, about six o'clock this morning two boatmen saw something in the Thames that didn't look right. They investigated, and then called the river police: Rosemary Fraser's body—or, at least, I was lucky enough to identify it when the word came through. You see, she was addicted to that long blue scarf, and shreds of it were still wound around her throat. Right off I saw the whole thing."

Miss Withers felt a little ill. "Yes?"

"It's clear enough, all but the gaps. And they're small ones. La Fraser decided to die, that night on the ship. But she didn't want to go without getting back at the people who had been so cruel and unkind to her—as she saw it. She was quite off her base, of course. She wrote all the unpleasant things that she could think of in her diary, but that didn't satisfy her. She hid herself in a lifeboat while all the hue and cry went on, and next morning, when they were making a thorough search, she kept out of the way of the searchers—probably by slipping from her refuge into another one that had already been searched. Sounds a bit thick, but stowaways have done it before."

"Um," said Miss Withers. "Go on."

"The ship comes up the Thames, and she overhears that the police are to make an investigation about her own disappearance. She hates Peter Noel, because it was her—er—her association with him which started everything. She knows he'll be questioned and probably searched, so she writes a note to him and slips it where he'll find it at the last minute. The note, you see, is soaked first in poison that she's lifted from the doctor's medicine chest. That would be easy late at night—the watchman makes his rounds very seldom and very regularly, I'm told. Noel has told her one of his cock-and-bull stories about swallowing evidence when he was a spy, or something similar. Well, he is arrested, and the note which is in his pocket would incriminate him and at least make him lose this widow in Minneapolis. He swallows it, thinking to beat the police, and the cyanide soaked into the paper finishes him as it hits his stomach. Remember the report that there was paper in his stomach?"

Miss Withers remembered. The sergeant went on. "Still hiding out, the girl slips ashore, perhaps disguised as one of the crew. It wouldn't be hard late at night, and the ship stays in port for five days. She had no clothes, but she had money and purchased another outfit."

"Including another squirrel coat?" Miss Withers suggested. "Go on."

"She hid out in cheap lodgings, spying on the members of the passenger list of the ship. She had a real grudge against this chap Todd, because it was his misguided wit that exposed her own petty scandal. He went on a terrible binge, you remember, the night that Candida Noring turned him down and went out with Reverson. He had a terrific inferiority complex, which accounts for his virulence about the slight Rosemary gave him on the ship. But he paid for it. She slipped into the hotel—it's a big place, and she wouldn't be noticed—and found him dead drunk in his room. No locks on the doors in that place, you know. Well, she dragged him, or else carried him, to the lift shaft, opened the catch by reaching her small hand through the bars, and dropped him down."

"Throwing the booze after him," put in Miss Withers. "Which accounts for the broken glass around him. Clear as crystal."

"In the meantime she'd been dodging from one cheap room to another, and sending those silly black-bordered notes right and left. Pure mania is the only explanation. She wanted to throw a scare into all the people at that table on the ship."

"Except me," said Miss Withers.

"Yes, except you. She had a particular hate against her best friend on board—the Noring girl. Another sign of her being clean off her head. Or perhaps Candida had given her a tongue-lashing over the Noel affair. Anyway, she sent a box of poisoned cigarettes to Candida Noring, hoping she'd smoke one and die—though our laboratory men say cyanide wouldn't be apt to kill that way—and her work was finished. She jumped into the Thames."

"Aren't you basing a good deal," suggested Miss Withers, "upon the mere fact that a victim of the Thames was wearing a few scraps of blue silk around her neck?"

Secker shook his head. "I'm not that stupid. This morning I wired the States a complete description of the dead girl's teeth made by our expert in such matters, and in half an hour we got an answer from Buffalo. The family dentist of the Frasers said that beyond doubt it was Rosemary."

Miss Withers felt a distinct jolt. "About this body," she began. "What was the cause of death?"

"Drowning, of course," said the sergeant. "She'd been in the water a good bit, and Sir Leonard Tilton is making an autopsy now. Like many of the bodies who go into the river, she'd been sucked in by the propeller of a steamer, and the body was terribly cut up. Clothes mostly torn off, and——"

"What was she wearing, beside the scarf?"

"There was little enough of the dress," said the sergeant. "What there was seemed to be a white silk gown. You saw her last in such a garb, didn't you?"

Miss Withers admitted that she had.

"Well, what do you think of it?"

She hesitated. As a matter of fact, she thought a good deal of it. "Young man," said Hildegarde Withers, her voice tense with a difficult determination, "I take off my hat to you. By the living God that made you, and so forth, Gunga Din. You've solved your own case, and also those handed over to your superior. I must revise my opinion of the Yard. And now, what do you want of me?"

It was already dark and rather chilly when the limousine had set them on the quay. "I want to get you, and the others at the castle if possible, all together and try to piece out the holes in my case," said the sergeant. "I know it's got holes—big ones. But Rosemary was the only person with a motive to kill Noel and Todd—don't forget that."

"I haven't," said Miss Withers. "I agree with you on that point. And I congratulate you exceedingly. By the way, what about the cigar that the maid saw the mysterious 'Mrs. Charles' smoking in her room?"

"At first I thought it meant that a man was disguised as a woman," said Secker. "Then I remembered that Rosemary Fraser was addicted to brown-paper cigarettes. She carried some of those with her."

Miss Withers nodded. "You've got it all explained, haven't you?"

He grinned. "And a very good thing for you that we have. You remember that warning letter that Miss Pendavid received?"

The school teacher leaned forward eagerly. "Yes?"

"We tested it at the Yard for fingerprints," said the sergeant. "Unlike the others, we received some results."

This was what Miss Withers had been waiting for. "Whose were they?"

Sergeant Secker smiled again. "Yours!" he said.

"Mine? Impossible! Besides, how do you know?"

"We have a set of everybody in the case," he explained. "An old dodge—we give them their statements to read over, and presto—they're printed on the specially prepared paper. It always——"

He stopped, for Miss Withers wasn't listening. She knew that the case was solved. She had the last link in her chain—a chain which surprisingly seemed to bind her own hands.

"Of course," went on the sergeant, "it's a dodge on the part of Rosemary. Her last act must have been to get hold of an envelope you'd handled and sent it down to the woman she wanted to frighten."

Miss Withers shivered a little. "You're staying at the Queen's, I suppose. Well, go back there, and I'll ring you up there after I've prepared the others for your interview. We'd better make it tomorrow. . . ."

The sergeant was disappointed, but she managed to overrule him. "In the meantime I'll be thinking about the holes in your case," she said.

"But you agree, don't you?"

"Almost entirely," said Miss Withers, with a bland stare. "You've certainly taken the wind out of my sails."

She left him there, and as the tide had risen over the causeway she was forced to hire the boatmen to transport her across. She was thinking very long thoughts of her own.

Dinner that night at Dinsul was cheerful enough, in spite of Miss Withers' preoccupation. She made no announcement of the sergeant's impending visit, for she desperately needed time to think. As she rose from the table, Treves announced that a gentleman was calling on the telephone. "A Mr. Gunga Din, ma'am," said Treves after swallowing with some difficulty.

Miss Withers took the instrument. "Young man," she said reprovingly, "I said I'd call you. Getting impatient?"

"Impatient!" echoed the sergeant. "Listen—I just got a message from Cannon back in London. You said you agreed with the case as I outlined it to you tonight. Well, we were both wrong."

"Wrong? You mean—the body wasn't Rosemary's?"

"Oh, it was she, all right enough. And dead, too. In fact, much too dead. Sir Leonard reports that death was due to a blow on the head—and that it happened at least fifteen days ago!"

"Oh," said Miss Withers blankly.

"So you see, Rosemary Fraser didn't kill anybody, and I'm right back where I started." The young sergeant forgot to be a policeman, and was simply a woebegone youngster.

"I wouldn't be too sure of that," said Miss Withers gently. "May I make a suggestion?"

"For God's sake, do!"

"Wire London for a complete report on the body—every minor detail. And then go to bed and sleep on it."

"Thanks," said Sergeant Secker.

Miss Withers had an hour or so with the Honorable Emily in the large and draughty sitting room of Dinsul and then climbed the stairs toward her own bedroom. Halfway up she saw the window open and heard voices outside.

Leslie and Candida Noring seemed to be having a party of their own, hung between sea and sky. She paused to eavesdrop and soon saw that they had not sprouted wings like the gulls.

Lighted only by the moon, the young couple were edging their way out on the narrow pathway cut in the rock, toward the Saint's Chair.

Leslie was ahead. "Go back, you silly," he was saying. "It's too risky."

But Candida, with a low laugh, suddenly brushed past him, leaning for one terrible moment over the brink of the cliff, and then clutching with strong sure fingers at the rock again.

"Beat you!" she cried. "*I'm* going to wear the trousers."

But Leslie Reverson, startled by what had happened, slipped to his knees. Miss Withers tried to scream, tried to jump through the window and catch him, but she found herself paralyzed, like a person in a nightmare.

Reverson scrabbled and clawed at the granite, but he was off the path. The rock sloped away steeply. . . . Candida, almost mounted to the Chair, looked back. She did not scream nor faint. For a long moment she stared, her face white and frightened in the moonlight, and then she rushed to his aid.

Flinging herself on her face on the rock, she caught Leslie's wrist and drew him back over the edge.

Neither of them spoke, but Candida was holding him in her arms, tenderly. It was a scene beautiful and terrible, and Miss Withers knew that she had no right to watch. She softly withdrew from the window and went to her room, still seeing clearly outlined before her weary old eyes the picture of the boy and the girl clinging together.

It was a picture that Miss Withers was to remember for a long time.

CHAPTER XIII

*

In at the Kill

What with one thing and another, it was not a good night for Hildegarde Withers. After much difficulty in falling asleep she awakened with a start to see something white and ghastly slip across her room and disappear into the wall.

"Angels and ministers of grace, defend us!" she said aloud. "Don't tell me it's a ghost!"

The apparition obligingly repeated itself, and she realized that what she had taken for a specter was simply the white glare of a pair of high-powered automobile headlights rounding a turn in the road on the mainland.

All the same, she found herself very wide awake. Outside, white moonlight was shining. Feeling for her slippers, the school teacher rose and went to the window. There was moon enough so that she could see the face of her watch—it was barely one o'clock—and here and there in a fisherman's cottage window a light still glowed.

She threw the window high and leaned out to enjoy the cool perfection of the night. But it was marred by what she knew must be the truth of this unreal, impossible problem—and by the decision which she must make.

After considerable self-communion, Miss Withers returned to her bed and lay sleepless until the soft light of early morning began to slant through her window shades.

Then she slept brokenly, moaning a little as she lay. For all her weariness, her curtains were snapped back, with a noisy jingling of rings, at exactly eight o'clock.

"Good-morning, madam. Not a very fine morning, but it may clear. Shall I draw your bath?"

Miss Withers opened her bright blue eyes with a jerk to see Treves approaching her with a steaming cup of tea.

She was not accustomed to having men—even butlers with families at home—in her bedroom. But Treves was equal to anything. "How do you like your eggs, madam?"

"Er—boiled," mumbled Miss Withers. "Very boiled."

"Thank you, madam. I shall bring your tray here in fifteen minutes."

Miss Withers remembered that she had work to do. "Never mind bringing a tray," she ordered. "I'll go down and breakfast with the others."

Treves paused near the door and cleared his throat. "Your pardon, ma'am. But her ladyship usually warns house guests here at Dinsul that on three days of the week the castle is rather—a public place, so to speak. Today is a Monday, and at any moment a party of tourists is likely to visit the castle. They are not permitted above stairs, and so her ladyship usually spends most of the day in her rooms, and luncheon and dinner are served in her sitting room, very cosy-like. I suggest that you would prefer to breakfast here."

"Of course," agreed Miss Withers. "When in Rome, burn Roman candles. If that's what the others are doing . . ."

"Master Leslie and the young lady have breakfasted in their beds, and are preparing to go golfing this morning," he informed her. "I have ordered the car for them."

"And your mistress?"

"Her ladyship has also had her breakfast tray, and she is, I believe, in her bath." Treves showed no surprise at her insistence upon checking up on the members of the household. She wondered if he guessed at her mission here.

"When you bring my tray, I'd like the morning papers," she requested.

"They don't arrive until ten o'clock, madam," he said, "coming from London." Treves departed, and Miss Withers drank her tea. Then she slipped into a bathrobe and went out into the hall.

The bathroom was between her room and Candida's. She opened the door and saw the young woman dropping bath salts into a full tub.

"I'm sorry," said Miss Withers, as the other hurriedly pulled her negligee around her.

"It doesn't matter," smiled Candida. "Thought I turned the key in the door. But I'll be through in a jiffy—Leslie is waiting for me to go and play golf."

"Sometimes it's good for a young man to be kept waiting," Miss Withers advised. She went back to her room, breathing a plague upon houses in which the one guest bath was always occupied.

Breakfast awaited her—a singularly tasteless meal of tea and cold toast, eggs very hard boiled indeed, and a limp slab of bacon, or so it seemed.

She finished, and then, hoping that Candida really meant what she said about being through in a jiffy, she went out and tried the bathroom door. But this time the key had been turned in the lock, and from within came the faint gurgle of running water. Miss Withers went back to her room, and in a moment Treves knocked to take away the tray.

He balanced it on the palm of one hand and was halfway to the stairs when there came a most tremendous crash from the direction of the wing occupied by the Honorable Emily. Treves dropped the breakfast tray, neatly caught it again in midair, and placed it on a hall table. Then he hurried down to the Honorable Emily's sitting room.

He was back in a moment, and noticed Miss Withers in her doorway. Over his arm hung Tobermory, a limp gray fur piece.

"Won't the mistress make a proper row about *that!*" he observed. "It's her bird, ma'am. The red-breasted American bird that she brought back with her."

"Well, what about it?"

"The cat has knocked down the cage, ma'am. It's smashed on the floor. And he's ate up the bird, claws, beak, and all."

Miss Withers shook her head at this announcement of a sad domestic tragedy. "Didn't you tell your mistress?"

"She's in her bath, ma'am. I thought it best not to disturb her, ma'am. It seemed wiser to take Toby down to the kitchen for a while."

Miss Withers didn't understand. "As a punishment?"

"No, ma'am. You see, if the mistress sees only the cage smashed on the floor, she may think it fell naturally and that the bird flew out of the open window. Otherwise she'd give the cat a good drubbing with a folded newspaper, and it's bad luck."

"What?"

"Yes, ma'am. Bad luck for a household, we believe here in this part of the country, to punish a cat. Dogs are the better for it, but not cats. Cats have powerful friends, ma'am." His face bore a wild, almost fanatical look. "The piskies and bus-keys, ma'am . . . *Themselves*, as we say."

Touched by this disclosure of Cornish folklore, Miss Withers resolved to become a party to the protection of Tobermory from his just fate. "Leave him in my room," she said. "I'll swear that he's been there all morning."

She was left alone with the cat, who made a leisurely survey of her room, sniffed at her belongings, and then took his place on her bed, where he stared at her. The school teacher made advances to him, stroking his silvery fur and whisking away the soft feather or two which clung to his whiskers. Finally he purred. . . .

But Miss Withers did not intend to spend the day in a dressing gown. She tried the bathroom door again, rather roughly this time. It was unlocked, and the tremendous iron key fell inwards on the floor as she opened it. She locked herself in and heard the swift footsteps of someone passing by—no doubt Candida hurrying to her golf game.

She bathed, after carefully hanging up the wet towel and washcloth which Candida had draped on the side of the tub. Not for her was any such soaking in hot water as the Honorable Emily delighted in. She soon climbed out upon a delightfully soft and dry bath mat and dried her long and angular body with swift and decisive strokes of the towel.

Back in her own room she dressed swiftly and efficiently, while Tobermory watched. Then suddenly the cat arose, stretched himself, and leaped down to the floor. He went over to the door, and cried "Meowr," loudly.

"Hush," said Miss Withers.

"Meowrrr," cried Tobermory. But he did not want to go out, because when she opened the door he still stood on the inside, waiting.

After about five minutes Treves knocked. He was bearing a saucer of milk.

"Toby always has his breakfast at this time," he explained. "And beasts are always thirsty after meat."

"Meowr," said Toby, and drank his milk with noisy gusto. It did not seem to Miss Withers that he could have had a meal for some time.

"There wasn't anything but a couple of feathers left of the robin," Treves informed her. He bore away the empty saucer, and Tobermory leaped up to the bed again and resumed his purring.

Miss Withers had no time to pat him. It was nearly nine o'clock, and she had things to do. Already the first group of tourists were straggling through the lower hall when she went down to the telephone. They stopped short, and stared after her in unison.

Miss Withers barely noticed them. She was beginning to feel a thousand tiny flickering doubts—but one large and important question for the moment overshadowed them. Fifteen days ago Rosemary Fraser was in mid-Atlantic. If she died then, how could her body get to the Thames yesterday?

Ocean currents did strange and wonderful things, she knew. But no ocean current could pick up a dead body, carry it eight or nine hundred miles, and set it down at the exact point at which all the hue and cry was being made—just at the river doorstep of Scotland Yard. That was a little too thick, even in the history of criminology, which, as she knew, bristles with sterling-true coincidences.

Yet Rosemary Fraser could not have died in London fifteen days ago, either. That was equally impossible.

Losing sight of everything else in the face of this problem, Miss Withers was temporarily deaf to the countless hints and impressions which her super-acute mind was usually attuned to receive. Somewhere in the back of that mind a little red warning light was flashing on and off, but she did not heed it.

She called the number of the Queen's Hotel in Penzance, and finally heard the voice of the sergeant. "I've got information for you," said that young man, "or at least, information that you may be better able to use than I. Shall I come to the castle?"

Miss Withers was about to say yes, when the door of the little room in which she sat was rudely opened. "And here you see an excellently preserved specimen of a bygone era," the guide was reciting. His arm pointed at a fireplace beside her, but the sightseers all stared at Miss Withers, and some of them snickered.

She frowned. "I'll come to your hotel," she told the young policeman. "This place has all the privacy of a Strand show window."

She bustled out of the place. Half an hour later, having been forced to phone for the skiff and use the local sixpenny bus service for the rest of the trip, she sat in the hotel lounge, beneath the inevitable potted palms, and listened to young Secker.

"Here we are," he was saying. "Complete description of the body in the Thames. Female, age about twenty, dark hair, small bones, delicate hands, wearing white evening shoe on one foot, white silk stockings, French underwear of a fine quality, scraps of a white silk gown, and a torn midnight blue scarf around the neck. Scarf badly torn, and had evidently come into contact with a ship's propeller, because it bore marks of rust and paint. Deep wounds on face and body, some before and some after death. Death caused by one of several severe head injuries, inflicted by edged instrument."

"Stop," commanded Miss Withers. "That's enough to keep me thinking for days." She was still uneasy. "I must run along home now," she said. "Must have a talk with my hostess." The young man protested loudly.

"I know that you've got wind of something," said Secker. "Mind letting me in on it?"

"I know—nothing," lied Hildegarde Withers. She felt suddenly stifled and hemmed in. "I really must go," she said. "I'll telephone you later."

"Wait," protested the sergeant. "Can't you tell me anything? Old Cannon never was convinced of my theory of the murders being committed by Rosemary herself, and I've got to give him something. Won't you——"

She shook her head and stalked away, and the young man stared after her in a very queer manner indeed.

Miss Withers stood for a few moments on the Esplanade, but no sixpenny bus appeared. Finally she set out to walk. A few minutes brought her to Newlyn, and as she came up the single winding main street she saw a sign: "Sailors' Refuge—reading room, rest, and recreation. . . . All mariners welcome."

She was no mariner—or at least she sailed strange and hidden seas—but she turned on an impulse and entered that cosy little reading room with a firm and defiant step. Red-faced and weatherbeaten old gentlemen glared at her, a dog snarled from the hearth, but she crossed resolutely to the bookcase and from the meager list chose the most hopeful title—*Standard Seamanship*, by one Captain Felix Riesenberg.

Without sitting down, and entirely oblivious of the distrustful and resentful stares of the habitués of the place, she thumbed through the thick volume, peering at diagram after diagram. At length she found what she was searching for, and put back the volume. She stared at the fireplace. So that was it!

On the mantel were several models of sailing ships, and one steamer cut in soft pine. She studied the latter for a time and nodded. Then she hurried back to the street, and the Sailors' Refuge relaxed into its immemorial peace.

Still there was no sign of the bus that could take her along the shore to the village and Dinsul. She began walking, and before she had reached the curve in the road she was overtaken by the limousine.

"Get in!" shouted Leslie Reverson.

Miss Withers hesitated—for what was almost an impolite lapse of time. Then she stepped into the car and was whisked away so swiftly that she plumped down between the two youngsters. She found a place for her feet between the golf bags.

"How did the match go?" she inquired.

"Great," said Leslie. "I beat Candy 88 to 94."

"I was a little off my game," said Candida. "How can anybody play golf when you insist on—well, you know."

"It's no secret," said Leslie. He was bubbling, buoyant and youthful. "I want her to set the day, you know. Aunt'll come around—I know she'd forgive us if we ran off to a registrar's office and got it over with. But Candy won't say no and she won't say yes." He laughed. "I'm afraid I don't know the proper way to propose. I'm thinking of calling in some help." He turned to Miss Withers, gayly. "*You* ask her why," he said.

"I don't need to ask Candida why she won't set the day," said Miss Withers. "Because I happen to know."

"What? Why?" Leslie leaned forward wonderingly.

Miss Withers smiled rather oddly. She turned to Candida. "Shall I tell him?"

"I suppose——" Candida stopped short and stared.

"Shall I tell him the real reason?" repeated Hildegarde Withers calmly.

Candida said nothing. The car was approaching the causeway, now black as the receding tide splashed against it. Then the girl shook her head slowly.

She felt in the pocket of her overcoat. "Good heavens," she said. "Stop the car!"

They paused on the slope. "Leslie," she said, "I've left my jeweled vanity on the golf course. I used it when we stopped at that bench near the seventh green, you remember. Where you—I mean, where we rested. Would you mind terribly——"

"Of course not!" Reverson was all politeness. "I'll drop you at the castle, and then run back for it."

"Never mind, I'd enjoy the walk across the causeway," said Candida.

The young man was driven away in the ancient Buick, and Miss Withers and Candida set out, on the narrow black lane above the water, toward Dinsul. For a while they walked in silence.

"How long have you known?" asked Candida finally.

"Since I came down from London," Miss Withers told her. "But what are we going to do about it?"

Candida didn't know.

"We'd better have a good talk," Miss Withers decided. "Meeting of the ways and means committee, you know. It's not a simple problem."

"Simple!" cried Candida.

Treves admitted them to the castle. "I hope there are no tourists about," Miss Withers observed.

"No, madam. The last party just left. But there was a certain unpleasantness, madam. I'm afraid the mistress will be very upset about it when she finds out. One of the visitors, you see, made an attempt to visit the top floor of the castle, which is strictly against the rules. When stopped, he was very unpleasant about it." Treves rubbed his jaw, which Miss Withers noticed was a trifle swollen. "He was—er—persuaded to leave quietly. You know these Yankees, ma'am."

"He was a tall young man with a mustache, wasn't he?" inquired Miss Withers.

"Oh," said Treves, "you must have met him on the causeway."

But Miss Withers and Candida were already mounting the stairs. As they approached her room, Miss Withers thought how lucky they were not to run into the Honorable Emily. She would be no help at the interview which was ahead of them.

Miss Withers locked her door, while Candida sank upon the bed. The school teacher took a chair, while Tobermory rubbed against her ankles affectionately.

"The meeting stands open for suggestions," said Miss Withers. But there were no suggestions. Candida could but wouldn't, and Tobermory would but couldn't.

Finally the school teacher said what was in her mind. The two women talked for a long, long time.

At one o'clock Treves knocked on the door. "Luncheon will be served in twenty minutes in the mistress's sitting room."

"We'll be there," Miss Withers told him. "Oh, Treves! Will you telephone for the limousine and have it waiting in time to catch the four-thirty train for London."

"Right away, ma'am. Shall I help you pack?"

"The car is for me," said Candida Noring. "No, thank you, I can manage." Treves departed in the direction of the telephone.

"Don't worry," said Miss Withers to Candida. "I won't use what you have given me unless it is a matter of life or death for someone. Now, run along and freshen up for dinner. It will all come straight in the end."

Candida stopped in the doorway. "But the police! Suppose they suspect me?"

Miss Withers smiled a faint smile. "They won't. Police are all alike. They can't see the forest for the trees."

The school teacher washed her hands and face in the bathroom. In spite of the excellent hot-water system of Dinsul, about which the Honorable Emily had bragged so much, the water was barely warm.

Miss Withers then headed for the wing of the castle which was sacred to its mistress. Treves hailed her in the hall, announcing that a gentleman was calling downstairs.

She hurried down and found Sergeant John Secker, very strained and official, in the drawing room. "Sorry to burst in on you," he said.

"Well?"

He took a slip of paper from his pocket. "You're in at the death," he advised her. "It's all over—and I've missed the target clean. I just got this from Chief Inspector Cannon at the Yard. It was sent last night, though some fool of a boy at the hotel shoved it under my door and also under my rug, so I just found it."

The message was brief enough. It read:

KEEP NORING UNDER OBSERVATION UNTIL I ARRIVE WITH WARRANT IF SHE TRIES TO ESCAPE ARREST HER FOR THE MURDERS OF PETER NOEL AND ANDREW TODD.

"For heaven's sake," said Miss Withers. She stared at the young man. "But—this is impossible!"

He shrugged.

"How could Candida get Noel to swallow poison? How could she force Todd to jump down a lift shaft? Even if you believe that she would be capable of exposing herself to the danger of dying with a cyanide cigarette in her mouth, will you answer me this one question—if Candida came down here with the Honorable Emily, as we know that she did, how could she have a black-bordered letter mailed from London two days later?"

"Search me," said the sergeant. "I think Cannon is crazy myself. But I'm just a cog in the wheel, you know. Mine not to do or die, mine but to reason why, or something. . . ."

"Police!" said Hildegarde Withers. "Ugh!"

"I've got my job to do," said the sergeant. "We don't have to wait for a warrant, but we like to, in cases where there's likely to be a trial with a defense attorney accusing us of all sorts of sharp practice. In the meantime, I've got to keep this Miss Noring in sight."

Miss Withers nodded slowly. "You'd better think up some excuse for hanging around the castle. Come on—we'll call on the Honorable Emily."

Leslie Reverson threw two golf bags near the door and was introduced to the detective. "What a time," he told Miss Withers. "Went over the whole course, and couldn't find Candy's vanity. Guess I'll have to get her another." He was more worried about the lost vanity case than about the advent of the young detective.

Treves was in the upper hall, looking rather uneasy. Miss Withers asked him if luncheon was ready.

"Yes, madam," he said. "I've laid luncheon in the mistress's sitting room. But——" He shook his head. "I don't know what to make of it, I don't. She never did it so long before."

"Who did what?" Miss Withers demanded.

"The mistress, ma'am. She loves to read and doze in her bath, but she's never stayed there all morning before. The water is still running, but she doesn't answer a knock." He shook his head doubtfully. "The doors to the bath are locked. . . ."

"Come on!" ordered Miss Withers. They came.

Four times Secker flung his weight against the door of the room in which John of Pomeroy had let his lifeblood ebb forth so many years ago. But the door held fast. Miss Withers pushed him away and bent over the keyhole.

"Bolted on the inside," she decided. She led the way into the hall and around to the other entrance.

"That door is always kept locked," said Treves.

But Miss Withers was doing things with a bent hairpin. After a moment she straightened up and turned the knob. The door swung inward, and they looked at the woman in the bathtub.

Water still ran from the "hot" faucet—water that was cool. The Honorable Emily lay in the soapy water of the big old-fashioned tub, with her knees arched and her head beneath the surface.

The sergeant knelt beside her. "She's still warm," he cried. "There's a chance . . ."

Throwing a near-by bathrobe over the figure, he carried the woman in through the door which Miss Withers unlatched, into the bedroom. Putting her down on the bed, he began frantically to apply artificial respiration.

Miss Winters watched, her face an expressionless mask. But all the blue seemed to have drained from her eyes, leaving them murky gray pools.

The sergeant stopped at last, out of breath. "It's no go," he said, apologetically.

Miss Withers stared at him. "You're sure she's quite dead?"

"Certain positive. But it hasn't been for long, I'd say. Of course, the police surgeon will be better able to tell than I. Where's the telephone? I'll turn in the alarm—no, you'd better do it. Rules are that the officer stands guard over the body."

She nodded but she did not move. "You think it's foul play, then—as they say on the stage?"

Sergeant Secker shrugged. "No odor of bitter almonds on her mouth, if that's what you mean. And not a mark on the body. But it's not for us to say."

Miss Withers stared down at the singularly calm and self-satisfied expression of the dead woman. In the last few weeks she had come to have a great liking and respect for the brisk and good-natured person who now lay so warm and yet so still, victim of life's last practical joke.

"We shall see," she promised. "We shall very soon see!"

CHAPTER XIV

*

The Reticence of Tobermory

Miss Withers met Leslie Reverson on the top landing of the stairs. "I say, what's the row about? Good old Treves just rushed past me with his face a nasty green color."

She told him what the row was about. He blanched.

"No," insisted Leslie Reverson. "That couldn't happen to Aunt——"

"It happened," Miss Withers snapped. "I'm sending for the proper authorities. Where's Candida?"

"Candy? She's in her room. Said something about packing, and that's something I wanted to ask you about. Why——" He stammered wildly.

"Not now, at any rate," Miss Withers told him. "Get Candida and take her down to the drawing room. There will be questions asked."

"But I don't understand——"

Miss Withers did not think it necessary that he should. She was going down the stairs two steps at a time.

The telephoning took almost no time at all, but when she came into the high-ceilinged drawing room of Dinsul she found Candida on a davenport and Leslie beside her making vague and nervous gestures toward cheering her up. Almost immediately there came a thundering upon the main door of the castle.

"The police!" gurgled Leslie. "I'll go——"

Miss Withers waved him autocratically back to his seat. "If it is the police, I want to talk to them," she said. "But unless the country authorities are practically instantaneous, I don't see——"

Treves, still an unhealthy green in color, was already at the door. Here was no detachment of police. Into the hall, pushing wrathfully past poor Treves, came Loulu Hammond. She had bought a new and very becoming hat in Paris, but she was wearing a very unbecoming expression. Loulu Hammond was, as she would have put it, boiling mad.

"You!" she cried, as soon as she caught sight of Miss Withers. "Of all the colossal crust!"

She plunged on into the drawing room and stopped short as she saw that Miss Withers was not alone.

"Good-afternoon," said the school teacher calmly. "I believe we all know each other?"

"Bother that!" Loulu blurted out. She snapped open her pocketbook and produced a cablegram. "I want an explanation of this!"

Miss Withers took the bit of paper, though she knew very well what message it contained. "Signed with my name," she observed. She read aloud:

"GERALD INJURED SERIOUSLY COME AT ONCE."

She smiled. "Of course, the injury was only to his sensibilities. But my intentions were of the very best."

"Intentions?" Loulu gasped. "Do you know that I dropped everything I was doing in Paris and flew across the Channel at the ungodly hour of six this morning—and then found that the only quick way to get down here was to take another plane to St. Ives? It cost me a small fortune, and I found Gerald in a disgustingly healthy condition. The man at the school hinted that I might find you over here. What is this, a practical joke? Didn't we have enough of that on board ship?"

Loulu stopped for breath, and just then four men, two in blue uniforms, marched into the hall past the butler.

"Where's the body?" demanded the foremost, a gruff person in a worn raglan overcoat.

Sergeant John Secker came to the head of the stairs and beckoned. "Up here, sir." The squadron tramped upward noisily.

"Body!" whispered Loulu Hammond. "Did he say *body*?"

Miss Withers gave a brief explanation. "Believe me, I did not plan to bring you here under such circumstances," she said. "But there was something I had to say to you, and I could not mention it in a cable."

Loulu's eyes were very wide. "Never mind that. What happened to the Honorable Emily? Was it another——?"

"That," said Miss Withers, "is what we are waiting to find out."

Loulu turned to Leslie Reverson. "This is your place, isn't it? Well, will you forgive me for bursting in at a time like this?" Leslie murmured something vague about being delighted, he was sure. But Loulu went on. "I'll be at the Queen's in Penzance until tomorrow," she advised Miss Withers. "In case you care to give me an explanation of this—this stupid trick. I suppose Tom got round you somehow. But it's no use your playing Miss Fixit, and you can tell him so for me!"

"Your husband had nothing to do with it," Miss Withers began. But Loulu was heading for the door, evidently anxious to get out of the place before something more happened. Instead of Treves, a six-foot young constable with rosy cheeks stood against the door, his arms folded.

"Sorry, miss," he said, "but you'll have to wait."

"But I just came here!" protested Loulu. "I don't live here!"

"Then you shouldn't mind waiting," said the red-cheeked constable without offense. "It's the show place of all Cornwall, and well worth a bit of study."

"Ugh!" was the only bit of repartee Loulu could think of at the time. She came back into the drawing room and plumped herself in her chair. There was an interminable silence, for even Candida and Leslie had nothing to say to each other now.

"If somebody doesn't say something before the clock strikes again, I shall scream and roll on the floor," Candida promised herself through her teeth.

She was saved by the barest fraction of a minute, as the great-grandfather clock in the corner under the stairs began to whir inwardly in preparation for the striking of half-past two.

There were heavy footsteps descending the stair. It was one of the policemen. He nodded toward Leslie Reverson. "The chief constable would like a word with you, sir."

It was apparent from his tone that the policeman realized that he was addressing the new lord of the manor, and that Dinsul with all its parapets, blackened oak, tapestries, portcullis, gulls, and tourists was the property of this frightened young man.

With a last despairing look toward Candida, Leslie Reverson stalked out of the room and up the stairs in the wake of the constable. He was back in ten minutes, looking as if a tremendous weight had been lifted from his sloping shoulders.

Candida was called, and likewise returned looking considerably more care-free.

"You next, ma'am," said the constable. Miss Withers almost trod on his heels as she went up the stairs.

She prepared herself to face again that poor clay upon the bed, but she was shown into the sitting room of the Honorable Emily's suite. The man in the raglan coat was seated at the writing desk, with an open notebook before him. Sergeant Secker stood beside him. "This is the lady I told you about," he said. "Miss Withers—Chief Constable Polfran of the Duchy Police."

She was bursting with questions, but her attempt at securing information was nipped in the bud. Short, sharp queries came from the lips of the man at the desk, queries that dealt purely with the events in the Dinsul household that morning. As she finished her story of the locked doors and the discovery of the body in the bath, the bedroom door opened, and a man emerged who could be nobody but a provincial doctor. He carried a glistening top-hat, and looked very grave.

"Well, Doctor?"

"I knew this would happen some day," said the medico. "As you know, besides being police surgeon, I've had a private practice here on the Cape for twenty years, and most of that time I've been Miss Pendavid's medical man. She had a leaky valve in her heart, and a few months ago I gave her some smelling salts. She complained of seizures of giddiness and worse—they were nothing in themselves to endanger her, at least, not for some years yet—but I warned her not to attempt driving a car or swimming or anything where an attack might do real harm. She must have had a seizure while soaking in a full bathtub and drowned. All evidences of death by drowning."

The chief constable leaned forward. "Careful, doctor. This woman may have been subject to seizures, as you call them.

But she was also afraid for her life. A short time ago, I am informed, she received a warning letter, and Sergeant Secker of the C.I.D. is here making an investigation. It is of the utmost importance that we make sure that there could be nothing off-color about this death."

The doctor looked annoyed. "Of course I was careful. I know drowning when I see it. Besides, wasn't she locked and bolted in the bathroom?"

Polfran nodded. He turned to Sergeant Secker, and Miss Withers, who was trying to make herself inconspicuous in the offing, sensed a barely concealed rivalry between the representatives of the urban and rural forces. "Well, sergeant, are you convinced that this has nothing to do with the case that brought you down into country society?"

The sergeant was not convinced. "I could answer you better if I knew the exact time of death," he admitted.

"That's easy enough," cut in the doctor. "Less than three hours ago, certainly." Miss Withers breathed again.

"You are sure of that?" demanded Secker.

"Positive. A cadaver cools off at approximately the rate of two degrees an hour, and we can set the time of death by that fact. The body registered just over 93 degrees when I got here, setting the time of death at—" the doctor consulted an ancient golden watch—"between eleven-fifteen and eleven-thirty."

"Good enough," said the chief constable. "You heard young Reverson testify that he and the young lady house guest left to play golf at nine and returned a little before one? The girl says the same. And this lady—" he motioned toward Miss Withers—"bears them out in her statement. So does the butler, who was in the hall all morning. Reverson was the only person who could profit by his aunt's death, and little enough when you consider that he would have inherited everything in a few years anyhow. Of course, we'll check with the golf course people, but I don't see how there could be anything to it."

Nor did the sergeant. "Only it's damned awkward just at this time," he admitted.

"Perhaps Miss Pendavid herself would rather have postponed this event," said the doctor pointedly. Nobody laughed.

"Very well, then," said the chief constable. "There'll be an inquest, of course. But I shan't order an autopsy unless young Reverson, as the next of kin, demands it."

"He won't," prophesied Miss Withers softly.

She went down the stairs with a tremendous feeling of relief coursing through her veins. It was a coincidence—but they happened everywhere in life. For a time she had feared that her juggling with dangerous matters had resulted in a horrible mistake, but it was turning out all right. The end justified the means. There was still Chief Inspector Cannon to contend with, but she could point out certain facts to him of which he seemed to be unaware. She went to her room for her handbag, made sure of its contents, and then hurried down.

If there had been a state of tension in the drawing room when Miss Withers mounted the stairs, it was there a thousandfold when she came down, for two new arrivals had appeared on the scene.

Chief Inspector Cannon of the C.I.D. brushed past her, headed for the stair. She would have stopped him, but he gave her a blunt "good-afternoon" and went up three steps at a time. He was wearing a very streaked motor duster and cap, and his feet left little puddles of water on the stair.

"Good heavens," said Miss Withers to herself. "Is the Yard equipped with airplanes?" She had not expected him until after the five o'clock train pulled in. "Anyway," she thought, "it won't be long now."

She came into the drawing room and saw Tom Hammond standing stiffly by the portières. He, too, made unpleasant little puddles on the floor.

"That frozen-faced schoolmaster said you'd set out in this direction," he was saying to his wife. The reunion did not seem to be a warm one. Loulu turned her shoulder to him and gave Miss Withers a baleful glance.

"And you said Tom had nothing to do with arranging this!" she accused.

Miss Withers shrugged her shoulders. "I should think you'd blame Mr. Cannon," she suggested. "He seems to have escorted your husband to Dinsul."

"We met on the pier or whatever you call it that leads to this movie set of a place," retorted Tom Hammond. "Of all the impossible houses to get to——" He snorted. "This

190

morning I came here and they threw me out. This afternoon I can't get out for love nor money!"

Miss Withers nodded to herself. Then it had been Hammond—the young man who had an argument with Treves that morning. She could think of only one reason why he might have come. But there were worse worries on her mind.

Miss Withers did not have her heart and soul in the somewhat unpleasant gathering in the drawing room. She highly valued her excellent eye teeth, but she would cheerfully have had both of them pulled in order to know what was going on in that room upstairs.

Leslie Reverson pulled himself together and remembered that he was host. "I say," he said brightly, "it's getting on. We might have some tea." He pulled at the bell rope. But there was no answer. The faithful Treves seemed to have made himself invisible.

Nobody wanted tea anyway. There was a long silence in which nothing was heard except the remorseless striking of the grandfather clock in the hall. It struck three mellow notes and was silent again.

"We could tell riddles," suggested Loulu Hammond. "Anybody know any good parlor games?"

"I suggest Truth and Consequences," said Miss Withers wickedly. And it was at that moment that the police constable reappeared.

"Miss Noring," he said. "The chief inspector would like a word with you."

"It's come!" Miss Withers breathed. She rose—and then sat down again. Candida went somewhat nervously out of the room and up the stairs. She did not reappear.

"Excuse me," gasped Miss Withers, who could remain an onlooker no longer. The three who waited in that drawing room excused her—in fact, not one of them but felt easier when she went. Tom Hammond dripped on the carpet and stared at his wife. Loulu Hammond pretended to read a book which she picked up from the table. It was *Pre-Roman Remains in Cornwall*, but as she held it upside down that did not matter. Leslie Reverson wished that they would all go away—all except Candida.

Miss Withers met Sergeant Secker in the upper hall. "Where are they?" she demanded. "Cannon and the girl. Did he arrest her?"

"He did not," said the sergeant. "You see——"

At that moment Chief Inspector Cannon came out into the hall. As a matter of fact, he stepped from the door of the room that was Candida Noring's.

Miss Withers seized upon him. "Before you place that girl under arrest," she began, "listen to me. Don't you understand——"

Cannon smiled wearily. "You here again? Well, you may as well know. I spent yesterday afternoon trying to get a warrant for the Noring girl's arrest out of the D.P.P.——Department of Public Prosecutions, you know. In an international case of this kind I have to have their backing. And this morning they turned me down flat. Insufficient evidence, they decided, the bloody idiots. And I had a marvelous case against her, too."

"Case! Don't you ever try to achieve justice?"

"That is for the courts," said Cannon stiffly.

"But if you didn't come here to arrest her . . . ?"

"I drove down here," said Cannon, "to put an end to this whole business. The D.P.P. spiked my guns by refusing a warrant on the evidence at hand. But we've got other weapons. I came to warn Candida Noring that the Yard knew all about her and that in five days our Special Branch, which deals with aliens, would see that her passport visa was cancelled. She's got to get out of England." His manner implied that he wished Miss Withers were in the same predicament.

"That," said the school teacher, "will probably break her heart."

"More likely break mine," said the chief inspector humorously. "But what can I do? My hands are bound. . . ."

"Muscle-bound," Miss Withers told him.

Cannon stared at her. "You don't think that she had anything to do with the death of Miss Emily Pendavid, do you? I've naturally paid a considerable bit of attention to that possibility."

"Not unless she managed to be in two places at the same time," Miss Withers admitted. "It's easy enough for you to check up at the golf course and make sure that Reverson and Candida are telling the truth."

"I already have done so," said Sergeant Secker quietly. "They arrived before nine, and were seen on the course until after twelve."

Cannon nodded. "I'm satisfied," he said. "You can't fool a police surgeon. And that man swears that the Honorable Emily died between eleven-fifteen and the half hour . . . in a locked bathroom." He began to put on his faded dust coat. "Well, I bid you good-afternoon, ma'am. The sergeant and I will soon be getting back to our day's work in London."

"Are you taking Candida with you?" asked Miss Withers. He shook his head. "She's not in custody. And I only have a two-seater. But the girl is packing her things. Says that she intended going away this afternoon anyhow. We'll make certain, of course, that she takes the next boat for the States."

"And thus ends the mystery of the stolen cyanide," Miss Withers murmured. "Well, you have your cases solved, even if you cannot get a conviction. I suppose that Candida Noring admitted the crimes, after she knew that you were not going to arrest her?" The school teacher gave him an odd look.

"She's not a fool," said Cannon. "I only wish she had, that's all! She'd cook her goose then, right enough. But she just listened meekly and promised to leave the country."

"I don't blame her," said the school teacher. She shook hands with the detectives. "It has been a real pleasure seeing Scotland Yard in action. Until we meet again——"

Chief Inspector Cannon almost said "God forbid!" but stopped himself just in time.

"A pleasure, ma'am," he assured her. "But, of course, we won't push off until we make sure that the girl gets aboard the train for London. No more mysterious 'suicides' in this case if we can help it, eh, sergeant?"

Sergeant John Secker seemed to have something on his mind, but he nodded amiably. "Bon voyage," he told Miss Withers.

"But I'm not going anywhere!"

"When you do!" he said.

She left them there, at the head of the stairs. Everything seemed to be over, and yet that little red signal was still flashing in the back of her mind. It vaguely annoyed her intense feeling of self-satisfaction.

She went into her own room and began to pack. There was nothing to remain for, now. Certainly Leslie Reverson did not need her, and his aunt was beyond all human help.

Tobermory arose from her pillow and stretched himself. It had been a very long and boring afternoon for the big silver-gray cat. He blinked his great amber eyes and miaowed hungrily.

"Insatiable stupid monster," Miss Withers accused him. "And you claim to be hungry after your grisly feast of this morning!"

Tobermory was hungry, in spite of the feathers which she had brushed from his mouth. He miaowed once more.

Then the cat sat up straight, as regal as any of his ancestors—the ancient felines who were sacred in Persia and worshiped as gods in Egypt. Tobermory set about washing his face with a supreme indifference to Miss Withers and to everything in life except his own proud self.

The school teacher stroked the fur of his silver back. "If you could talk——" she said. Suddenly she stopped short, and her hand pressed so heavily upon Tobermory's back that he twisted away, spat, and then leaped down to the floor, where he stalked up and down angrily.

The world whirled, and readjusted itself. The little red signal in the back of Miss Withers' mind flared like a beacon.

"And I called *you* stupid!" she cried aloud to the impassive beast. "That's funny—so funny! I called you stupid—and you were the only one to know!"

Tobermory stared through wise amber eyes.

Chief Inspector Cannon of the C.I.D. was leisurely descending the stairs in company with Chief Constable Polfran, two constables, and Sergeant Secker, the doctor having long since departed. Their friendly, if somewhat guarded, conversation was rudely interrupted by the advent of a middle-aged school teacher, who darted past them like a frightened greyhound.

"Candida! She isn't in her room!" wailed the apparition, and then disappeared down the stair.

The officers looked at each other. Polfran made a circle with his forefinger, around his large red Cornish ear. "Quite completely batty," he said.

But Miss Withers was not batty. Never before in her forty-odd years had she been in as complete control of her faculties. She saw the apple-cheeked constable at the door and turned toward the drawing room.

There was Candida, two black traveling bags beside her. She was saying good-bye to a bewildered Leslie Reverson. Tom Hammond and his unfriendly young wife watched from opposite ends of the room, waiting until they would be permitted to depart upon their separate journeys.

"I must, I *really* must," Candida was saying. "It's been wonderful, but I must go."

"No, you mustn't!" cried a stern New England voice. "Wait! Stop her, somebody!"

The people in the drawing room froze into a dreadful immobility. But Miss Hildegarde Withers did not realize how insane she appeared and sounded. "She killed your aunt!" cried the school teacher. Leslie Reverson blinked foolishly. "Don't let her go!"

Candida smiled and shook her head. Tom Hammond put his hand on Miss Withers' arm. "You're overwrought," he suggested. "This has been too much for you. Why——" She shook him off.

They all looked at Miss Withers as if she had been particularly vulgar. "You fools!" she cried. "Don't you see? Look at her! Look at her eyes!"

Candida's eyes were rather strange—smoky yellow pools that belied the polite marble of her face.

"She drowned Miss Pendavid in her bath—she's mad! Oh, don't let her go!"

"Steady," said Tom Hammond. "You can't——"

His voice trailed away as he looked at Candida. Her mouth betrayed her, twisting like a nest of worms, so that her teeth gleamed. It was quite horrible for a moment.

Then the girl moved. She bent down and snatched at the bags at her feet. One of them came hurtling through the air, knocking Miss Withers and Tom Hammond into an entangled heap. She ran past them.

"What's all this?" cried Cannon from the stair. "I say——"

Whatever he may have meant to say was forever lost as a smart suitcase struck him in the face.

Candida ran for the door. The constable, caught off his guard, blinked stupidly. "Here!" he said.

He said nothing more, for the desperate girl snatched a mashie-niblick from the golf bag which stood in the hall and hit him just beneath the ear. He went down with a thud which shook the stone flagging.

The way lay clear for the girl who stood in the open doorway, but she waited. With desperate, sure fingers she reached for the rusty chain of the portcullis, putting all her weight upon it. There was a creaking of ancient bolts——

Then the massive barrier fell—iron spikes dropping with a terrible, remorseless swiftness—but Candida plunged forward.

"It's got her!" cried Cannon, struggling to his feet. But the descending spears had missed their mark. Candida was free, running down the interminable stone steps. Her pursuers beat against the heavy iron grille which blocked the doorway. It was immovable as fate.

"Stop her!" screamed Miss Withers. But nobody could stop her. There was not a gun in the pocket of any policeman. "Stop her! The limousine is waiting—she'll get away!"

Candida ran on, down and down and down. Then she stopped short. The limousine waited, as it had been ordered to do. But it waited at the pier on the mainland. For almost a quarter of a mile between, the green rolling sea stretched over the causeway. Since noon the tide had been coming in—the tide which had wet the feet of Cannon and Tom Hammond—and now it made an unbroken, unbreakable circle around the ancient castle-fortress of Dinsul.

It was the end for Candida Noring. She crouched there, cursing the smooth, implacable ocean, until men poured under the painfully raised portcullis and took her away.

CHAPTER XV

*

The Happy Ending

"I suggest that you have a good bit of explaining to do," said Chief Inspector Cannon mildly, as he faced Miss Withers across the table in the magnificent old dining hall of Dinsul.

She nodded, and smiled wryly. "You know more than I hoped you did," she admitted. "I'm afraid that years of reading Sherlock Holmes stories gave me a false impression of Scotland Yard. You're not exactly a Lestrade, you know."

"Thank you," said the chief inspector. "Well?"

She went on. "When I heard that you were coming down here to arrest Candida Noring, I felt terribly sick. By the way—just how did you come to suspect?"

Cannon grunted. "Official secrets and all that. As a matter of fact, I got the idea that this whole case involved a woman. Poison and trickery and so forth, you see. Black-bordered letters and the rest of the frippery. As soon as I found that Rosemary Fraser had died more than two weeks ago, I eliminated her. Mrs. Hammond left the country and eliminated herself—for she couldn't have mailed any warning letters in London while she was in Paris. That left Candida and Miss Pendavid, and I wasn't inclined to the opinion that the Honorable Emily would be at the bottom of all this. Besides, when I came to check over the statement that Candida Noring made to me on board ship, just before the death of Noel, I discovered a contradiction or two. She swore that Noel must be responsible for the death of her friend Rosemary, who was supposed to have confessed to her all about what happened in the blanket locker, etc. But only a short time before, when the disappearance was first discovered, Candida was crying 'suicide' to the captain. It occurred to me that she must have learned something in the meantime to make her change her mind."

"The diary," interrupted Miss Withers. "But go on."

"There isn't much more," said Cannon. "Except that I had a pretty good idea that Candida was the mysterious 'Mrs. Charles' who slipped from cheap hotel to cheaper boarding house here and there in London. She was seen smoking a 'cigar,' you remember. The sergeant saw through that—it was one of the Porto Rican brown-paper cigarettes that both girls smoked on board ship. Secker was sure it meant that Rosemary Fraser was alive. When we got the report from the autopsy and knew that she couldn't have been, I jumped at the conclusion that the cigar-smoker was Candida. It wasn't much to go on, and no wonder the D. P. P. refused me a warrant." The chief inspector leaned forward. "But to come back to you. Why were you so worried when you heard that I was planning to come down here to arrest the girl?"

"Because I thought it wouldn't be justice," Miss Withers told him. "Not knowing how much you knew, I still hoped to present the facts of the case to you in such a light that you wouldn't be able to go ahead with the arrest."

"What? But *why*, in the name of——"

"Oh, I was wrong, terribly wrong," Miss Withers assured him. "But I thought that I had a chance to play judge and jury. You see, I came over on this trip to forget a case out in California where I was the instrument in bringing a young man and a girl to the gallows. Theirs was a brutal crime, murder for money, but all the same I had a rather bad night of it when I knew that they were to step off into thin air when daybreak came to dreary San Quentin prison."

Cannon knew that feeling. "But I never let any murderer get away because I couldn't stomach his being hung."

"Wait," said Miss Withers quickly. "I knew that Candida killed Peter Noel and Andrew Todd—both of them persons that the world could do well without. She had a twisted sort of justification, I thought, for killing them. I didn't think at the time that she meant to go any farther. I was sure that the warning letters were simply to throw a scare into the hearts of those whose laughter had driven Rosemary Fraser to suicide."

"Suicide?" cut in Cannon. "I'm not convinced of that. Seems to me that Candida Noring started all this in order to make sure of getting the person who murdered her room mate—a personal 'vengeance is mine' affair."

"Please!" said Miss Withers. "Let me tell it my own way. I still have work to do tonight, unless you decide to arrest me as an accessory after the fact.

"I'll begin at the beginning," she said. "On board the *American Diplomat*. Candida and Rosemary Fraser, a younger girl who had been her charge since both were children, started on a trip which was to be a world cruise. Rosemary was a peculiar girl, emotional, easily swayed, and likely to lose her head. She snubbed Andy Todd in the bar of the ship, when his only fault was in being too loud and too friendly. She refused his drink because she didn't like his voice or his accent or something. He was not the type to forget that, you see. And when that detestable Hammond child informed him that she was friendlier with other men, and that she was having an assignation with the handsome bar steward, Todd planned a cruel and vicious revenge. He nearly missed—for he found the blanket locker empty when he led the others to it. But he saw, from the hairs of a fur coat caught in the lid, that Rosemary had been there. And he waited—a nasty person, Todd. Not typical at all of the Rhodes scholars that America sends to Oxford, or of his own university.

"Rosemary was filled with shame at the thought of what she had done—or what she appeared to have done. That is why she hid herself in her stateroom until the night of the captain's dinner—a real event on board, when the sea was as calm as a mill pond and her absence would, as Candida must have assured her, be taken as a sure sign of guilt. She came down to dinner, and Todd, still smarting from her refusal to dance or drink with him, was prepared for her. He had bribed the table steward to make a change in the gift parcel which was placed at her side, and he made certain that a key marked 'key to the blanket locker' was waiting there. It assured the poor girl that her sin—if it was a sin— was known to someone. Up to then she may have been hoping that she had gotten by with it.

"She read the message aloud, hysterically. That was something that even the fiendish Todd had not hoped she would do. And everyone at the table laughed except Candida, who knew her friend's suffering, and except myself, who was ignorant of the scandal. The laughter drove Rosemary to her stateroom.

"She turned to her diary and poured forth in its pages everything that she could not say. She wrote horrible, hateful things, and said much of death—for it was in her mind. The outpourings did not quiet her, and she could not cry. She was too young to know how little the scandals of shipboard matter when port is reached, and she feared that Colonel Wright, the business acquaintance of her father's, would see that her family heard about it. Throwing aside the diary, she eluded Candida's well-meant comfort and went up on deck. Probably she did not see me there, or thought me asleep as I lay in my deck chair. Anyway, she jumped overboard."

"You're mad," put in Cannon. "I follow you so far. But she didn't jump into mid-Atlantic and come up in the Thames two weeks later."

Miss Withers nodded. "It's quite impossible. But she did it all the same. And that's what threw this whole case off balance. It was a queer trick of fate. She leaped into the sea—but having spent every summer at the seashore, she knew how to dive. She struck the water as a diver does, making almost no splash at all. She went deep beneath the surface. . . ."

"No matter how deep she dived, she couldn't come up in the Thames," objected Cannon. "It won't wash."

"Wait," commanded Miss Withers. "I'll convince you. It seemed impossible to me—until I remembered the trailing blue scarf she wore. She went deep beneath the surface, and like most things flung into the water, she was sucked in by the powerful screws of the ship. That was what killed her—not drowning. I spent some time this morning—it seems years ago—in reading up on the mechanism of a ship. The propellers cause a tremendous flurry of water, you see. Enough to wind the loose silken scarf tightly around the rudder-post. And there Rosemary Fraser must have dangled, towed deep under water by the ship, until the *American Diplomat* docked in the Thames or after!

"Then the scarf must have rotted or torn. The body remained under water until natural decomposition set it free and brought it to the surface." Miss Withers saw that Cannon was frowning.

"All right—then *you* tell me how she got there!"

The chief inspector rubbed his chin. "There were marks of paint and rust on the fragments of the scarf," he admitted. "But still——"

"They would hardly have been there if the scarf had not been caught firmly on some part of a ship," Miss Withers reminded him. "I found that there have been other cases of such things—in the Mediterranean a few years ago a French sailor fell overboard and was found next day hooked hard and fast to the rudder—because the ship refused to answer her helm. If the *American Diplomat* had not been worked by an automatic steering device I'll wager that a helmsman would bear witness to the difficulty in steering on the remainder of the voyage."

"Ingenious," admitted Cannon. "Very likely you're right. But——"

"But me no buts," Miss Withers snapped. "But to go back to the ship. Suicides almost always leave some message behind—and Rosemary left her diary. Candida Noring found it that same night and knew the whole story. She tore the telltale sheets out of the diary——"

"She didn't get them ashore," the Yard man interrupted. "Because we searched her baggage with a fine-tooth comb."

"Well, you didn't search the mails with a fine tooth comb," Miss Withers told him. "Nor the bottom of her powder box—though that comes later. As a matter of fact, there was a letter-drop in the writing room of the ship. Candida simply tore out the sheets of the diary, put them into an envelope or several envelopes addressed to herself care the hotel or the American Express in London, and found them there soon after the ship landed. It was as simple as A B C.

"Anyway, the morning after the disappearance of Rosemary, I saw Noel disposing of some scraps of paper. He said they were an old deck of cards, but I found one scrap and saw that it bore the letters 'osem.' That was part of Rosemary's signature. She wouldn't sign an entry in her diary, but she might very well have written him a note on one page. Perhaps she really loved the man, infatuated with his tales of adventure. 'She loved him for the dangers he had met' or whatever it is. At least she wrote to him.

"All this time Candida was boiling. She felt that her friend had been murdered—forced into suicide. The next day I myself advised her, when she came out of the bath, to seek out the ship's doctor and get a sleeping draught. Evidently she arrived at his office when the doctor was out—he spent most of his time chatting to the lady passengers—and the sight of the unlocked medicine cabinet gave her a black inspiration. She would kill Peter Noel in such a way that no one would ever know—and yet Rosemary would be avenged upon her seducer. Candida had had enough college chemistry to tell her what the symbols meant, and she stole a whole bottle of cyanide of potassium."

"I don't suppose you know where she hid it?" Cannon asked.

"Of course! Remember the japanned powder box that was a favor at the captain's dinner? I wondered, when I saw it on her dressing table in the hotel, just why she had kept such an unpleasant reminder of that night. The cyanide was dumped in the bottom and perhaps covered over with powder."

Cannon leaped to his feet. "Then we've got our case. If we can find that——"

"Sit down," Miss Withers told him. "You won't find it. I've been through her room. Either she destroyed it in London, or else she used the last of it to pack the cigarettes with. But she was versatile, you see, and quick-witted. I searched her cabin on board while she was at the bath, but she had already got rid of the diary pages—all but one sheet, which she must have carried around with her.

"She had a use for that. As soon as she knew that there would be an investigation into Rosemary's death, she worked out a devilishly ingenious plot. Noel had already given her the idea—Mrs. Hammond told me about his yarn of a card-game in Alaska in which he swallowed an extra card and won the pot.

"She gave information to you of such a nature that you were sure to place Noel under arrest. Yet only a few moments before she had slipped a piece of paper in his pocket—a note in Rosemary's writing. No doubt it was the girl's last accusation of the man. At any rate, he had no chance to get rid of it in front of all the assembled passengers. And, until he found himself under arrest, no need

202

to do so. But if that came to light, he stood a good chance to lose his berth on the ship, and possibly the rich widow for whom he was angling out in Minneapolis.

"It was a long shot, but if it failed, Candida lost nothing. It succeeded—Noel remembered his own story of the card and swiftly swallowed the incriminating message as you arrested him. Then he dropped—for the paper had been soaked in a solution of Candida's stolen cyanide. Clever, eh?"

"Damnably! But what was her motive? A girl doesn't usually kill in order to avenge a friend—not even an old friend." The chief inspector hesitated. "Unless of course there was——"

"No need to get Freudian," Miss Withers cut him off. "Murderers are always neurotic, but in this case I think we can ignore the possibility of anything abnormal. My own opinion is that Candida felt toward Rosemary a tremendously protective and fierce motherliness. That tendency in her character came out later, when she adopted poor helpless Leslie Reverson.

"When Candida got to the hotel she found, in her mail, the letter she had sent to herself containing the diary pages. She set to work preparing warning notes, using sentences here and there from the diary and combining them to intensify their meaning, and pasted them upon black paper to confuse the fact.

"I entered her room and almost surprised her. But she had one letter ready for herself, as writers of poison-pen letters always do. That was a clue, however, for if the letters were from Rosemary, as they appeared to be, Candida herself was the one person who should *not* have received one.

"She sent a letter immediately to Andy Todd, perhaps by placing it under his door. She thought it dramatic justice to send each person the message that poor Rosemary had penned in the last hour of her life. She addressed the envelopes in a copy of Rosemary's writing—there wasn't enough written on any of them to give handwriting experts much to work from.

"Then that night both Andy Todd, who felt guilty about what he had done, and Leslie Reverson, who sensed the new and vivid personality that Candida had put on with her new mission, argued over who should take her out. She

203

went with Leslie, but I saw her whisper something to Todd which I later came to believe must have been a promise to meet him after she returned. I wondered why he looked so appeased. Anyway, he came up to her room on the fifth floor that night, probably rather drunk. Perhaps he became amorous—he was the type, if admitted to a girl's room late at night. That may have made it easier for Candida. Anyway, she killed him."

"Killed him how?" protested Cannon. "She's only a girl——"

"A strong, athletic girl, borne up by a terrific purpose," Miss Withers reminded him. "And Todd was easy pickings that night. He had three bottles of whisky in his room when I called on him, and only one empty was ever found. He must have taken the others up to Candida's room, and she encouraged him to drink himself into a stupor. It was not as difficult as it all sounds now—she told him some cock-and-bull story about hearing moans at the bottom of the elevator shaft. They went out together to look, and after she had put her hand through and opened the catch, she gave him a sudden push through the open door. His hand was too large to have done it, you see. Then she dropped the bottles after him and shut the door."

"From the fifth floor, eh? Then that's why the body was so crushed—much more than the surgeon would have thought likely from a fall from the third," Cannon said. Then his eyes narrowed. "You're not guessing now," he told her. "How did you happen to deduce that bit about moans at the bottom of the shaft?"

Miss Withers realized that she had said too much.

"I wasn't guessing," she admitted. "Candida told me. And she went on to say that, when there was no outcry or alarm at the fall of Todd, she went down and opened the elevator door on the third floor, wearing gloves, so that it would seem he fell from his own hallway. The hotel was quiet as a tomb, she said, at that hour."

"She *told* you?" Cannon was on his feet. "That's a bit——"

"Never mind that now," she said wearily. "I'll tell you everything. But let me tell it my own way. The next step for Candida was the attack on herself. She was afraid that the police, or perhaps myself, might suspect her. So she bought the cigarettes in the character of the mysterious Mrs. arles——"

"Wait," demanded Cannon. "What about the fur coat? She didn't have any fur coat."

"She could have bought one," Miss Withers told him. "Of course, she was lying when she said that Rosemary went to her death with their joint funds. Suicides don't need carfare. Candida had the money, and she got a fur coat somehow. She was trying to make the police believe that Rosemary was alive, or else play-acting that she *was* Rosemary and carrying out the dead girl's revenge. . . ." Miss Withers frowned. "If only Rosemary's belongings hadn't been sent back to the States——"

"Blimey!" said the chief inspector. "They weren't! I just remembered. The personal effects of Rosemary Fraser were turned over, at the cabled instructions of her parents, to her friend Candida Noring. She was supposed to take care of sending them back!"

"It's a great pity," Miss Withers remarked, "that you didn't tell me that. It makes everything simple. She built up her identity in Rosemary's clothes as 'Mrs. Charles'— prepared her later letters in those cheap rooms, and no doubt left the things in one of them or in a check room somewhere when she decided to come down here.

"Anyway, I mustn't get ahead of myself. Candida brought the gift cigarettes to the hotel, found the flowers which Leslie Reverson had sent her, and put his card into the ebony box. It was meant only as a herring across the trail, although she may not have felt toward him then as she did later. She offered me one of the poisoned cigarettes, perhaps hoping that I would take it and be put out of the way. I refused, and soon after I left the room she sat down before the fire with a doped cigarette, hoping to be found there. . . ."

"Here's a bad flaw," pointed out Cannon. "How'd she know you would return?"

"She couldn't have known, of course. I hurried back because I remembered that Leslie had touched his aunt for only ten shillings in the tea room, and the cigarettes cost much more. His flowers had probably been put into the plumbing. Candida didn't count on my return—she wouldn't have tried to fool me with a fake faint. Perhaps she really did pass out from the fumes of the cigarette burning beside her—you can rest assured that she did not puff on it—but she only planned on fooling the maid, who was due any moment with a hot-water bottle to turn the bed back for the night.

"She was flushed with success of her plotting," Miss Withers went on. "She was sure that she was getting by with it and that no one suspected her. As a matter of fact, at that time I didn't. But you did—because you adjourned the inquest."

Cannon nodded. "But go on—you've been a lot closer to this case than I."

"It was then," said Miss Withers, "that Candida sent a message to the Hammonds, which I wasted a good deal of time in appropriating. But they were out of her reach, and I read very little from the letter. It confused me, in fact. Then the Hammonds separated, or rather I discovered that they had separated. . . ."

Cannon held up his hand. "What about that couple?" he demanded. "Tom Hammond worked for a New York chemical firm, and for a while I wondered . . ."

"So did his wife," Miss Withers told him. "But Hammond's connection with chemicals is only through his being advertising manager for a commercial fire extinguisher company. His only sin in this affair was to run wild after his wife walked out on him. But I'll come to them later. It was at about this point in the development of the case that Candida Noring took Leslie, who was at least five years her junior, under her wing. On the trip down to Cornwall she slipped a warning letter into his coat, but that must have been as far as she could go. She weakened in her sworn purpose, as you shall see.

"Up in London I was wasting my time in suspecting Loulu Hammond, and in shadowing her husband in hopes that I might catch her trying to attack him. That ended in a fiasco, as you know."

"And as Sergeant Secker knows, to his sorrow," put in Cannon.

"All in the game," said Miss Withers sternly. "Anyway, the message from Cornwall asking me to come down caught me just in time. I had made up my mind that nothing would happen in London. I'd been thinking about that message which the Honorable Emily received. It pointed to some-

206

one in London—and I decided to be contrary and do what I thought the murderer expected me not to do.

"I came down here yesterday. The sergeant followed close behind, with a clever explanation of the murders which I did not entirely agree with, although I kept my own counsel. You see, he brought word of the fact that my fingerprints were found on the warning letter which the Honorable Emily had sent up to the Yard after it had put a good scare into her. That told me everything. I saw to the bottom of the mystery, or thought I did. The sergeant was sure that Rosemary Fraser had lived to exact vengeance upon the two men she hated, and then had jumped in the Thames. I knew that couldn't be true—for Rosemary would never have sent poisoned cigarettes to her one friend, Candida. Nor could Rosemary have managed to get my fingerprints upon a letter she sent to the Honorable Emily.

"No, the sergeant was wrong, and the person who had sent that last warning message had sent it, not from London, but from Dinsul Castle itself! For it was simply the post-marked envelope from my letter to the Honorable Emily, which arrived one morning—with the original address washed out by ink-remover from the town stationery store! The address was re-written, the black border was added, and the message put inside. Of course, the envelope was open, but the Honorable Emily never realized the significance of that. Nor did Candida know that my prints were on the letter—she simply saw to it that she used gloves.

"Why didn't I suspect the Honorable Emily or Leslie? Simple enough. The former had neither motive nor was she the type to concoct such a fantastic plot. She would hardly have sent for me to come down here, either, if she had been trying to get by with anything. Leslie—well, if you can picture that young man having the devilish cleverness to see that a London postmark would give the murderer a wonderful alibi, and take that means of getting it on a black-bordered letter, you have a better imagination than I.

"The fact that Rosemary's body had been found I simply set aside as something beyond explanation for the moment. At dinner I dropped a hint saying that I knew Rosemary had not been murdered, because at that time I was convinced that Candida had been killing off the persons she suspected of murdering Rosemary—a sort of Lone Avenger idea. I hoped that the case would be closed, with dead Rosemary as the culprit. When the sergeant phoned that the body had been dead for more than two weeks, I was not surprised. I let him stew, for all my energies were given up to the problem—what would be the highest justice in a case of this kind? For I knew that Candida had a very real motive for killing the two men whose acts had forced Rosemary into suicide. I did not think that she meant to go on with it, I was sure that the warning messages were simply designed to worry the persons whose laughter had hurt Rosemary at that dinner table. But I was not sure. . . ."

"You made a fine mess of it," said Cannon. "You rush in where courts would deliberate for hours——"

"And so I did!" declared Miss Withers. "All that night. You see, on my way up to bed I saw Candida and Leslie Reverson out on the rock path which leads from the hall window to the Saint's Chair. I saw him slip and nearly fall to his death. Candida saved him when she could have let him fall—and then I knew that she was not bent on more murders. She had saved a life—a life more valuable than the two she had taken. And so I made my decision. Sometime in the forenoon I would have it out with her.

"But I could not bear to think of handing her over to the police. You see, I was still haunted by the thought of the young couple whom I had sent to the gallows out in the Catalina Pepper-Tree affair."

Cannon saw the light. "I read the papers sometimes," he cut in. "So that was you!" His voice had a new note in it. "Then you're not just a bloody meddler."

"I'm afraid I am," said Miss Withers. "But let's get on to the end of this. This morning there was no opportunity for me to have it out with Candida. She left the place early to play golf. But while she was bathing—as I thought—the butler and I heard a crash in the Honorable Emily's room. Tobermory the cat had knocked down the robin's cage—he had had his eye on the bird for weeks. Considered it his by right of capture, I suppose.

"That meant nothing to me at the time, nor did the fact that when I finally got a chance at the bathroom I found the towels and washcloth wet but the mat dry. I spent the morning interviewing the sergeant and in explaining to my own satisfaction the manner in which the body of Rosemary could possibly have appeared in the Thames. On my way back to Dinsul for lunch I was picked up by young Reverson and Candida in the limousine, and I learned to my horror that the young man wanted to marry her. That wouldn't do at all. I was convinced that she had had a change of heart, but I wasn't prepared to let her settle down calmly in that way. And so I dropped a hint which made her understand that I knew something, and she sent him away on a wild-goose chase. We came to my room, Candida and I, and I told her frankly that I knew why she killed Noel and Todd—that I understood the powerful forces which made her go off the track. She convinced me that she had completely recovered from her fantasy. The warning letters to the others, she maintained, were simply to frighten them. Remembering how she had saved Leslie's life when she herself had marked him for death, I believed her, like a sentimental old fool."

Inspector Cannon did not disagree with the phrase. "Go on," he said.

"I made her promise that she would leave Dinsul this afternoon, giving Leslie any excuse which she could think of, and giving me a surety that no innocent person would ever suffer for her crimes. Oh, I know what you think. But I decided that her conscience would punish her enough. She had suffered terribly already, you see.

"Then Sergeant Secker arrived with word that you were on your way to arrest Candida. I was stupefied, for that was the first intimation I had had that you were not blinded by the idea that Rosemary had lived to commit the murders. I racked my brains for a way to convince you, using the information which I had, that Candida could not have committed the murders. I hoped to argue you out of your purpose when you arrived. Then we found the body of the Honorable Emily—where Candida had killed her that morning!"

"Whoa!" cried Cannon. "Not so fast. What about the locked and bolted doors and the time of death?"

"One door was bolted on the inside—the one leading into the bedroom," said Miss Withers. "The other was simply locked, with a lock which I picked in five minutes with a hairpin. Furthermore, I have an idea that the key of the other bathroom—the one in which Candida left the water running and wet the towels in order to establish an alibi—will fit that door, too." Miss Withers shrugged.

"I was fooled, utterly. I did not have sense enough to read the message of the bath mat and the attack on the bird. She must have gone down the hall, opened the Honorable Emily's bathroom door, and drowned her in the brimming tub before she could cry out."

Cannon smote the table. "Brides in the Bath! That's it—too easy if you know how. One of our big cases some years back. Fellow named Smith married two or three women and killed them off presto chango—by simply coming into their bathrooms, putting one hand under their knees and the other at their throats, and it's done. Up with the knees as the head goes under water, and the victim gives a great gasp and goes out like a light. I was a sergeant then, and witnessed an experiment that the chief inspector in charge made. He got a friend, young lady in a bathing dress, to play the part of the victim, in a big tub. It was just an experiment, but she gasped and went under. It took twenty minutes to bring her back to life."

Miss Withers nodded. "Candida may have read of it. Anyway, she came out of the room, locked the hall door behind her, and went calmly out to play golf. Perhaps by accident she left the hot water running over the body, and it kept on all morning, with the overflow drain taking care of it as it came in.

"The Honorable Emily was in the habit of soaking herself, you see, and nobody thought anything of her long absence. It was also her habit to keep to her rooms on the days when tourists were permitted to visit Dinsul. Candida did not know it, perhaps, but the hot water would keep up the temperature of the corpse and so give her a perfect alibi. The hot water ran out shortly before noon, so that the body was found in cold water. That fooled the doctor, though an autopsy will probably change his mind."

Cannon nodded. "But what made you change your mind? One moment you were quiet about all this, and then you break loose——"

Miss Withers was shamefaced. "Of course, I suspected that Candida, as a reaction from saving Leslie, whom she liked very much, might have struck down his aunt. But I trusted the verdict of the surgeon and the local police—and made up my mind that it was an unfortunate coincidence that the Honorable Emily had died of her old heart trouble just at this time. Until I knew of the witness——"

"Witness to the murder? Don't be——"

"I'm not!" cried Miss Withers testily. "There was a witness. A witness who knew, through solid walls, that the Honorable Emily was dead. A witness who later proved his eerie powers by signaling anticipation when the butler started up from the kitchen with his milk, five minutes before the man arrived. I'm speaking of the first witness for the prosecution—Tobermory!"

"The cat? But how on earth could he know?"

"You don't know cats, then. Tobermory had waited weeks for his chance at the bird. While his mistress was alive, he knew he was due for a spanking with a newspaper if he harmed it. As soon as his super-senses told him that authority was removed, he sprang for the bird cage. That proved to me that his mistress died no later than nine o'clock this morning—died before Candida had left for the golf course!

"It's clear enough, for those who have the wit to see. It would be too great a coincidence to believe that when he had waited so long he should choose just that moment by accident. I only saw through it when I went to my room. By then I knew that Candida, with your permission, was leaving Dinsul. She must have been in deadly fear of me. If she had reached London, or even Penzance, perhaps, she would have managed to disappear.

"Then I acted—for instead of my optimistic hope that she had killed only two rather guilty persons, I realized that she was a true killer—knew that she had struck down a friendly, innocent woman who did no one any harm, and whom I had come down here to try to protect. I failed in that—and I was determined not to fail in apprehending her murderer."

"Well," said the inspector after a moment, "you succeeded, with the help of the tide. It's all clear to me now—you've filled in the gaps splendidly—but I still don't see that I have any better chance of getting a warrant out of the D.P.P. than I did before. This is all circumstantial—and I can't bring this what's-his-name of a cat into court."

"I suppose that this wouldn't be any help to you?" Miss Withers asked hesitantly. From her handbag she took a single sheet of notepaper covered with fine writing and signed with Candida Noring's name. "I forced her to write it, for fear some innocent person might later be charged with the crimes. It was the price of my silence."

The chief inspector, wonder growing on his face, read a terse and brutal confession of the murders of Peter Noel and Andy Todd. "Good Lord," he cried. "Why, this will hang her!"

Miss Withers winced a little at that. "I thought that confessions were no use in court."

Cannon carefully put the paper into his notecase. "Not in American courts," he said. "Over here, where people have confidence in their bobbies, the juries know that we never use third-degree methods to extract confessions. This is all that we need.

"Well, then!" Miss Withers rose wearily to her feet.

"But the Hammonds——" began Cannon.

"Them? Why, that was simple. Their child saw an opportunity to get back at his father for punishing him over some trivial misdeed. He told his mother that Tom Hammond was the man with Rosemary in the blanket locker. It was a barefaced lie, but the foolish young woman believed it, as people always believe unpleasant things they hear. She walked out—first throwing away her engagement ring. When I heard that the child was playing with it, I knew what must have separated the Hammonds, that it was something very personal and delicate. But she didn't suspect him of the murders, or she would never have stood by him until the inquest for appearance's sake.

"She never gave Tom Hammond a chance to explain, and the child was too much afraid of punishment to admit his lie. Things in that household, I gather, hadn't been running too smoothly for some time. It must have been largely due to the child, who seems to have a propensity for doing harm. He nearly caused a complete break between his father and mother."

"Nearly?" said Cannon.

Miss Withers nodded. "There's still a chance," she said. "I must try to play goddess from the machine again and see what I can do." She stopped short. "I hope you won't blame the sergeant for any of this," she said. "He did take me into his confidence, which was, I suppose, against the rules. But he is very young. . . ."

"Secker? Why, his opening up to you was the smartest thing he ever did. I know now that I could have talked to you without any harm being done. But as for the sergeant, don't forget that he's solved his first case nobly. He was assigned to the disappearance of Rosemary Fraser, you know. It was fine work on his part to identify the mangled body in the Thames. We don't expect miracles in the Yard, and I shall see that a crown is sewed above his chevrons as soon as he comes up to London. And I'll recommend him for the inspectorship exams in March."

"When he comes up to London?"

"Yes. Of course, I'm leaving him here at the castle for a few days—as soon as he gets back from depositing Candida in the Penzance station house. Just to keep an eye on things."

Miss Withers was relieved to think that Leslie Reverson need not be alone immediately. This was hardest on him. She rose and held out her hand. "We said good-bye some hours ago," she pointed out.

"Hands across the sea," quoted the chief inspector almost gaily, as they shook. "And if ever you feel like a job in London, remember that we have recently admitted several ladies to the C.I.D."

Miss Withers shook her head. "I know," she said "Policewoman giving good advice to erring girls. Not for me, thank you. And I still have a job to do right here, if the Hammonds haven't gone."

The Hammonds had not gone. Perhaps it was because the tide still covered the causeway and they did not know how to signal for the skiff. At any rate, the school teacher gave Loulu Hammond what is usually known as a piece of her mind.

The young woman took it like a lamb. "The little beast!" she cried. Then she turned to her husband. "Oh, Tom! How could I have believed it for a moment?" She stood with her arms outstretched, like somebody in a Victorian novel. "Tom, can you ever forgive me?"

"No, damn you," said Tom Hammond. "You gave me a spell of hell on earth. I have no intentions of forgiving you. But I'll take you back, and I promise you that you'll pay through the nose for this. If you had the brains that God is supposed to have given geese . . ."

"Tom!" cried Loulu, her voice trembling.

He took her in his arms. "Oh, for heaven's sake! All right, baby, all right!"

There was a long silence, during which Miss Withers beamed proudly. Then: "I suppose that you two will take your little boy and go back home where you belong?"

"I suppose so," said Loulu slowly.

"You're crazy if you do," Miss Withers snapped. "Leave him where he is. You've done a bad enough job of it, what with farming him out to indulgent grandmothers. Who can tell? A few years in a strict school may do wonders. As for you two—" her voice softened—"why not try it again? You might have a human one this time. Try using common sense instead of the newfangled books on child personality and developing the ego." She bustled toward the doorway. "Understand?"

Tom and Loulu Hammond understood. But they were speedily forgetting her existence again.

Miss Withers took her bag and umbrella and prepared to depart. Leslie Reverson, wearing new lines in his young and vacant face, met her in the hall. Tobermory was gayly rubbing against his new master's ankles.

"This is hardest on you," said the school teacher to Leslie. "But it had to come. Just think, you can leave Dinsul and live in London or wherever you want, now."

Leslie smiled, and the school teacher saw that from beneath his smooth exterior something rugged was coming to the surface—something with breeding and backbone.

"Thank you," he said. "It has been a bit filthy. But of course I'll stay on here. To you from failing hands we throw the torch, and all that sort of rot. Aunt wanted me to, you know. Dinsul muddles on. . . ."

She wished him good luck. "Cheerio!" he called after her.

Miss Withers passed under the jaws of the portcullis and went down the interminable steps. At the landing a skiff waited, and the last rays of the afternoon sun flickered on the water. "Thank God it's over," she breathed.

But it was not quite over. In the fading light of the autumn day, just outside the open windows of the Honorable Emily's sitting room, a fat and pessimistic robin clung to the rock. He was minus most of his tail feathers, but otherwise quite unharmed. The crash of the cage had opened its door, and Tobermory had missed his spring.

The red-breasted bird ventured a hop or two. For the first time since his captivity he managed a feeble song. "Chirrup-eether!" he warbled.

From the twisted trees at the edge of the cliff came an answering call, familiar yet strange. "Chirrup-eyether, chirrup-eyether," sang the sober English robins—his kinfolk, though a bit redder of the breast and duller of the coat.

Dicon, the American robin, felt somehow abashed. He fluttered along the rock, and by a miracle discovered a worm moving on a bit of muddy turf. It was a good fat worm, as good as any worm the robin had ever tasted on the other side of the Atlantic. It gave him a different point of view.

Dicon fluttered toward the twisted trees. "Chirrup-eyether," he practised softly. Like most of his countrymen abroad for the first time, he had set about acquiring an English accent.

From a narrow window in the ancient castle of Dinsul, a silver-gray cat watched with implacable amber eyes. Not yesterday, not today, but some day he would get more than feathers from that fat robin.

Tobermory knew.

Special Offer
Buy a Bantam Book
for only 50¢.